Zero MINUS Ten

Also by Raymond Benson

The James Bond Bedside Companion

ZERO
MINUS
TEN

Raymond Benson

G. P. Putnam's Sons
New York

G. P. Putnam's Sons
Publishers Since 1838
200 Madison Avenue
New York, NY 10016

Library of Congress Cataloging-in-Publication Data

Benson, Raymond, date.
Zero minus ten / Raymond Benson.
p.   cm.
ISBN 0-399-14257-6 (alk. paper)
I. Title.
PS3552.E547666Z47   1997   96-45284 CIP
813'.54—dc21

Printed in the United States of America
1   3   5   7   9   10   8   6   4   2

This book is printed on acid-free paper. ∞

Book design by Amanda Dewey

ACKNOWLEDGMENTS

The author wishes to thank the following individuals and organizations for their assistance:

In the United States and Canada—Kevin Chin, Paul F. Dantuono, Sandra Groark, Alexandra Harris, Dan Harvey, Daisy Koh, Joseph Lau, Hen Chen Lee, Charles Plante, Doug Redenius, David A. Reinhardt, Moana Re Robertson, Kathy Tootelian (for the *mah-jong* illustrations), Mike VanBlaricum, Amanda Wu, Kenneth Yung, and Everyone at Viacom New Media.

In the United Kingdom—Peter Janson-Smith, Carolyn Caughey, Man Wei Tam, Corinne B. Turner, the Staff of Glidrose Publications Ltd., and the heirs of the late Ian Lancaster Fleming.

In Hong Kong and Australia—Sarah Cairns and Henry Ho of the Mandarin Oriental; Terry Foo of the Hongkong and Shanghai Bank; Eric Lockeyear, Mark Bowles, and Peter IP Pau-juk of the Royal Hong Kong Police; Marg Mason of the Kalgoorlie-Boulder

Acknowledgments

Tourist Centre; Jacqueline L. S. Ng; James Pickard; and Jeanie Wong and Stephen Wong of the Hong Kong Tourist Association. Special acknowledgment is made to the Royal Hong Kong Police for permission to use material from the Government Press book *Triad Societies in Hong Kong* by W. P. Morgan, Crown Copyright Reserved, 1960.

Author's Note: The architecture and layout of the Hongkong and Shanghai Bank is as described in Chapter 11. The events and action contained therein, however, are totally imaginative, as the corporation's highly effective security system would realistically prevent such a scenario. Furthermore, the company EurAsia Enterprises Ltd. is entirely fictional and is not intended to represent any existing trading and shipping firm. Lastly, the actual location for the handover ceremony has not been decided upon at the time of writing. (In fact, China has not yet even agreed to a joint ceremony!) My choice of Statue Square as the site is based on its historical significance and geographical importance to the city, as well as speculation by Hong Kong associates.

This novel is dedicated to Randi and Max,
and to the people of Hong Kong

CONTENTS

Contents

1

Shamelady

Someone long ago had called it the "Undertaker's Wind," but hardly anyone in Jamaica referred to it by that name anymore. The Undertaker's Wind was supposed to blow the bad air out of the island at night. In the morning, the "Doctor's Wind" would come and blow the sweet air in from the sea. The Undertaker's Wind was certainly at work that night, whipping the long red strands of the English woman's hair around her head like the flames of a torch.

The woman was dressed in a skintight black diving suit and stood on the cliff above the grotto, looking out to sea. Forty stone steps cut into the cliff led down to the grotto, in front of which was a small, sandy beach. It was very dark in the grotto, for the cliffs blocked the moonlight. Up above it was just bright enough for every tree, plant, and stone to emit an eerie glow.

The woman glanced at her watch and tapped the button to illuminate the time. He would not be late. He never was.

The grotto and its private beach faced the Caribbean, not far from Port Maria, on the north shore of the island. The small community of Oracabessa was just along the coast to the west, and Cuba was a hundred miles to the north. The area was considered Jamaica's most lovely coastal country. The woman had never been here prior to this evening, but she knew the layout of the place inside out. It was her job to know. The land was private property and a modest, three-bedroom house had been built above the grotto near the top of the stone steps. If her plans were successful, the house would later be the location for an evening of unbridled passion and pleasure. The man with whom she hoped to share the pleasure had a reputation that preceded him. Other women who had known him had indiscreetly prepared her for the man's intense sexual allure.

Although accomplishing the Primary Objective was her main goal tonight, one of her motives for participating in the evening's escapade was a rather selfish Secondary Objective—the physical rewards she would give and receive after the job was done. She couldn't help it. Danger stimulated her sexually. It was why she had sought a career as a mercenary, a contemporary Boadicea. It was why she liked to play with fire.

"I'm here," a male voice behind her whispered.

"You're on time," she said.

"Of course I am," the blond man said in a thick Cockney accent, moving closer to stand beside her, looking out to sea. He, too, was dressed in a black diving suit. "You know what to do?" He gazed at her, taking in the shapely body.

The woman knew she was beautiful and that men found her attractive. She enjoyed being able to manipulate them. As she looked at the man, she wondered again if the night would end as she desired.

He had blond curly hair, a muscular build, and classical Roman features. Most women, she thought, would gladly follow him anywhere.

"When he arrives, I get him to come up to the house. You'll 'surprise' us and kill him."

The man smiled. "Too right."

2

Shamelady

They were both in their mid-twenties and had trained for weeks to get this far, but already possessed the skill and expertise required by any assassin to perform a simple execution. The job at hand tonight was anything but simple, as their target was a formidable one.

"Leave the first part to me, Mr. Michaels," she said, smiling and rubbing her hand across the man's chin. "Give us a little time, and I'll have him thoroughly distracted."

"Well, don't get carried away. I don't want to have to take you out with him."

"You sound pretty sure of yourself. Remember who he is."

"He's history."

As if on cue, a Royal Navy jet suddenly appeared, passing about half a mile from them, heading north out to sea at about two hundred knots. They could just see the figure of a man jumping from it.

"There he is," the blond man said. "Right on time." They clasped hands, and he kissed her roughly on the mouth. "See you later, love . . . when we're done." And then he was off as she began to walk down the steps into the darkness of the grotto.

The man who made the low-altitude jump from the plane had opened his SAS Modified XL Cloud Type Special Forces rectangular parachute before exiting the aircraft, and the jump master threw it out of the plane behind him. It served as not much more than a brake in the short fall, an extremely dangerous maneuver over water; but the jumper was a pro who knew what he was doing. He was one of the Double-Os.

The woman reached the bottom of the steps and peered out to sea. The man hit the water hard, and for a few moments only his dark parachute could be seen floating on the surface. Then he emerged and divested himself of the parachute. She walked to the edge of the water so that he could see her. The tall, well-built man swam steadily until he was able to stand and walk toward her. He tore off the face mask and snorkel and tossed them aside, and then he stepped out of his fins.

3

Like the blond man, he had a sexual presence that was so overpowering that she had to catch her breath before she spoke.

"The bad air is blowing out tonight," she said.

"But the sweet air will surely come in the morning," he replied as agreed.

"Right on time, Double-O Seven. I'm 05, but you can call me Stephanie. You okay?" She pronounced the number "oh-five."

"I'm fine, thanks, and my name's Bond. James Bond."

"It's pretty dangerous, isn't it, jumping at such a low altitude?" she asked, taking his outstretched hand.

"As long as the parachute is already open when you leave the plane, it's okay. Did you bring the transmitter?"

In the dim light, his features looked harsher than Stephanie had remembered them. The first time she had seen him was two weeks ago, at the funeral, when she had been struck by his casual self-confidence. Dark and handsome, he had piercing blue-gray eyes. His short black hair had just a hint of gray at the temples, was parted on the left, and was carelessly brushed so that a thick black comma fell down over the right eyebrow. There was a faint three-inch scar on his right cheek. The longish straight nose ran down to a short upper lip, below which was a wide and finely drawn but cruel mouth.

"It's up in the house, Mr. Bond. Come, I'll show you." She took his hand and gently pulled him toward the stone steps, then dropped it and walked on ahead. Bond followed her, eyes and ears alert.

She had been told to observe him at the funeral, at which he had remained stubbornly stoical. Commander Bond, like the other pallbearers, was dressed in Royal Navy uniform with three rows of ribbons. Everyone who was anyone had been there, including Sir Miles Messervy, the recently retired M, head of SIS; the new M, a woman only just beginning to take command of the Secret Service; Sir Miles's faithful secretary, Moneypenny; Major Boothroyd, the Armourer; and even the Prime Minister. When a country loses someone of the stature of Admiral Derek Plasket, all the important people are sure to be there to pay their respects.

Admiral Plasket was something of a legend. A war hero, he had organized a commando assault team that specialized in raiding Nazi bunkers to collect intelligence to be passed on to the Allied forces. After the war he had been Special Adviser to the Secret Service, and had been a personal friend of the old M.

As she had been instructed, Stephanie Lane had kept her eye on Bond throughout the ceremony. He had performed his duty with military precision, standing at attention and displaying no emotion whatsoever. Only afterward, when she saw him embrace Moneypenny, did she detect some semblance of warmth.

Stephanie had continued her surveillance of 007 for two more weeks, taking note of his daily habits. She had followed him to his flat off the King's Road in Chelsea, where he lived alone. She tailed him to Blades, that exclusive gentleman's club that had only recently begun to admit women. She observed him enter the gaudy building, across the Thames from the Tate Gallery, that was the SIS headquarters. Finally, after fifteen days, the operation had been arranged and the time had now come. Stephanie had a lot riding on the outcome of this mission, for James Bond was the target in tonight's Objective and she and her blond partner must be able to anticipate his every move.

When the attack came, it surprised her. She had thought Michaels would wait until she and Bond were in the house, but he appeared at the top of the stone steps from out of darkness. With a perfectly executed maneuver, the man spun and jump-kicked Bond full in the face. The assault surprised Bond as well, for he fell backward down the steps. Stephanie stood aside while the blond assassin, who was armed with an ASP 9mm semiautomatic handgun, ran down the steps after him.

Bond had rolled halfway down the steps and then stopped. He didn't move. He lay on his back at a grotesque angle, his head lower than his legs, his shoulders twisted unnaturally.

Michaels raised his gun and pointed it at the still body. "Wait," Stephanie whispered. "I think he has broken his neck!"

Cautiously, the man moved down to Bond's body and crouched to examine him more closely.

It was then that Bond made his move. He jackknifed out of his frozen position, thrusting both forearms into the blond man's face. In a split second, he formed a spear-hand and slammed it down on the man's right wrist, knocking the ASP onto the steps.

Recovering quickly, Michaels butted Bond in the stomach. Both figures tumbled down to the bottom of the steps and rolled out onto the sand, ending up with the younger man on top with his hands around Bond's throat.

This boy's strong, Bond thought.

Stephanie ran down the steps and stood waiting, feeling the adrenaline surge through her body as the two men fought. It gave her a thrill to imagine that they were fighting over her. Her breathing became shallow and she felt weak at the knees.

With a superhuman effort, Bond thrust his arms between the other man's elbows and delivered dual lightning sword-hand chops, which made Michaels loosen his grip. Then, with split-second timing, Bond jerked his head forward against the man's nose, breaking it and causing him to cry out in pain.

Then they were both on their feet, each waiting for the other to make the next move.

Bond's Walther PPK was in a waterproof holster attached to the belt around his diving suit. Unfortunately, that was tightly buttoned and it would take more than two seconds to retrieve the weapon. Bond knew he didn't have two seconds. The young man was good—a bit inexperienced, perhaps, but not someone to underestimate. Bond was ready to concede that the other man was the stronger since, although he was in excellent physical shape, Bond was no youngster anymore.

The blond man made a move. With a shout, he leapt in the air and delivered a *Yobi-geri* kick to Bond's chest, knocking him back. The blow was meant to cause serious damage, but it landed too far to the left of the sternal vital point target. Michaels was momentarily surprised that Bond didn't fall, but he immediately drove his fist into Bond's abdomen. That was the assassin's first mistake — mixing his fighting styles. He was using a mixture of karate, kung fu, and traditional Western boxing. Bond believed in using whatever worked, but he practiced hand-to-hand combat in the same way that he gambled. He picked a system and stuck with it.

By lunging at Bond's stomach, the man had left himself wide open, enabling Bond to backhand him to the ground. Giving him no time to think, Bond sprang on top of him and punched him hard in the face, but Michaels used his strength to roll Bond over onto his back, and, thrusting his forearm into Bond's neck, exerted tremendous pressure on 007's larynx once again. With his other hand, the young man fumbled with Bond's waterproof holster, attempting to get at the gun. Bond managed to elbow his assailant in the ribs, but this only served to increase his aggression. Bond got his hands around the man's neck, but it was too late; Michaels deftly retrieved the Walther PPK 7.65mm from the holster and jumped to his feet.

"All right, freeze!" he shouted at Bond, standing over him, the gun aimed at his forehead. "I hit you in a vital point earlier, but you didn't go down," he said with incredulity, looking at Bond as if he were a ghost.

007 caught his breath and said, "That was your first mistake. You were a half-inch too far to the left."

The man straightened his arm, ready to shoot.

"And now you're making your second mistake," Bond said.

"Oh, yeah?" Michaels whispered. "Not from where I'm standing."

Bond snapped his legs up and kicked him hard in the groin. Michaels screamed, doubled over, dropped the gun, and fell to the ground.

"You were exposing a vital point, my friend," Bond said, getting to his feet and retrieving his Walther PPK. "And I do mean vital."

1

He leaned over the writhing man. "Who are you?" The man only groaned. "Are you going to talk?" Then he remembered the girl.

Stephanie stood behind them, by the steps. She was uncertain whether to run or drop to her knees.

"Come here," Bond commanded. She stepped forward, looking at the man groaning on the ground. "Do you know him?" Bond snapped.

She shook her head convincingly. "No."

Bond handed her the Walther. "Then retire him."

She looked surprised.

"He's an assassin. He came here to kill me," Bond said. "He knows I live here. I don't care who he is, just get rid of him."

She took the pistol and aimed it at her partner. The blond man's eyes grew wide. Bond watched her closely. She hesitated, staring at the man on the ground intently.

"05, I gave you an order," Bond said firmly.

The wind howled as the woman stood there frozen.

After ten tense seconds, Bond said, "All right. Relax."

Stephanie dropped her arm and looked dismayed.

"I couldn't do it," she said. "I just couldn't pull the trigger."

Bond walked over to her and took the gun. "If it's a matter of not blowing one's cover, a good agent may have to kill an ally or a friend. Don't ever forget that. You gave yourself away, 05. In the old days, if I had been KGB, or worse, I would have immediately perceived that you not only recognized 03 here but knew him well."

"Yes." She sighed. "You're right. You really get the unexpected thrown at you in these training missions. I'm sorry. I didn't think you'd win the fight—it confused me."

"Double-Os must expect nothing *but* the unexpected," Bond said. He crouched down to the man he now called 03.

"How are you, 03? You put up a bloody good fight, lad. You almost had me at one point," Bond said with good humor. "You blew the mission, Michaels, but you'll get good marks, don't worry."

The man groaned and then vomited.

"Yes, well, sorry about that, 03," Bond said. "You'll feel all right in a few hours. Sometimes Double-Os have to learn their lessons the hard way. Remember what you learned about vital point targets. God knows I did. Better luck next time."

Bond stood, turned, and walked up the stone steps, and Stephanie ran after him.

"So did you *know* he was going to be here?" she asked.

Bond shook his head. "No, but I suspected something, especially when you didn't try to help me. These Double-O training sessions you two are taking are also exercises for me. I'm unaware of your objectives and you are unaware of mine. Someone in London orchestrated the entire scenario. Apparently my challenge was dealing with someone who has penetrated the privacy of my home. And I take it you two had a mission to assassinate me?"

She laughed. "Yes, real kamikaze stuff, isn't it? A Single-O–level agent assassinating a Double-O . . . !" Bond smiled too.

"Is Agent Michaels going to be okay? Not that he was one of my favorite people. He was always chatting me up."

"He'll be fine. I don't fight dirty unless I have to, but he left me no choice. Besides, he was careless. I didn't hurt him badly—he'll be up and on his way back to Kingston in no time. In any other situation he would have been killed. My kick was nothing compared to a carpet beater."

"A what?" she asked.

"Never mind," he said as he led her onto the top of the cliff. In contrast to the darkness below, up here the moon was very bright, flooding the grounds of the estate in a chalky white light.

Bond had purchased the property a year ago. Even though the heyday of a British Jamaica was long gone, Bond had always loved the island. For years, the memories and dreams he had of Jamaica haunted him. He had a compelling desire to be there. When a well-known British journalist and author died, the property became available, and Bond bought it. Thus, in addition to his flat in London, he now owned a secluded holiday home on his favorite island. Since buying it, Bond had spent all of his available time between missions at the sparsely furnished house. He called it "Shamelady," after a plant that grows wild along Jamaica's north shore, a sensitive plant that curls up if touched.

Stephanie Lane followed Bond inside. He immediately began removing his wet suit, stripping down to briefs. He seemed oblivious to the fact that a beautiful woman was watching him undress. "You know, you should be dead too," Bond said. "If you can't hide convincingly behind a cover, then the cover's no good."

"I'll remember that," she promised. She watched him with increasing interest as she fingered the Walther PPK that he had placed on a coffee table. "Isn't this gun a little old-fashioned?" she asked. "It's not standard issue, is it?"

"No. It was once, though," Bond said. "I was using an ASP for a few years, and I just recently got an urge to use the old one again. I don't know, it feels very . . . familiar, and I've decided to use the Walther again from now on. Old habits die hard."

Stephanie picked up the gun and pointed it at him.

"So if I shoot you now, I will achieve my Primary Objective after all," she said with no trace of humor.

Bond squinted at her. There was silence. His cold stare dared her to fire.

She pulled the trigger. It clicked empty. Her mouth dropped open.

Bond held out the clip in his hand. "You don't think I'd put a loaded pistol down with a stranger in the room, do you? Sorry, 05. You flunked this one." Bond walked into the bedroom. "I'm going to take a shower. Make yourself comfortable. But before you get too relaxed, turn on the transmitter and see if there's anything from London."

Did Stephanie detect a hint of flirtation in his voice? She smiled. When she heard the shower running, Stephanie opened an attaché case she had left in the house earlier. Inside was a small black device that looked like an ordinary beeper. She flicked a switch and the code "33" appeared on an illuminated display. Bond would want to know this.

She stepped into the bedroom and called to him. "It says thirty-three!"

Bond shouted back from the shower, "Damn! That means I have to go back to London as soon as possible. Some kind of emergency. . . ."

Stephanie was disappointed. Well, she thought, she had to take what she could get. Stephanie unzipped her wet suit, peeled it off, and stepped into the bathroom.

She had failed in accomplishing her Primary Objective that evening . . . but if she acted now she would have a little time. It was a shame that the night of pleasure she had anticipated earlier would not last until dawn. If she was lucky, though, she still had an hour or two.

At least she had got the right man. Secondary Objective accomplished! Naked, she pushed back the shower curtain and got in with him.

2

Three Events

Approximately seventy-two hours earlier, a large cargo vessel called the *Melbourne* sailed into the bay between the Isle of Wight and West Sussex, facing Portsmouth. She had traveled thousands of miles in the last few weeks. From Hong Kong, her point of departure, she went to Perth in Western Australia, unloaded cargo, picked up containers, and refueled. From there she sailed west through the Indian Ocean and around the southern tip of Africa into the Atlantic and on to New York. She stayed in New York Harbor for three days, then finally began the last leg of the voyage to the United Kingdom.

When word of the *Melbourne*'s arrival reached the desk of the Hampshire Constabulary Tactical Firearms Unit, Sergeant David Marsh picked up the telephone and called his detective chief inspector. The TFUs, along with Firearms Support Teams, are tactical special weapons groups within U.K. police forces, available twenty-four hours a day. Many of the members of these elite police units are ex–British Forces personnel.

"She's here, sir," Marsh said when the DCI answered. Marsh

listened closely to the instructions and nodded. "Consider it done, sir." He rang off and dialed a new number. If the tip they had received was correct, there could be some trouble.

A lighter had already begun to deliver cargo from the *Melbourne* to shore. A group of four Chinese men unloaded the large wooden crates from the lighter as soon as it docked and used a forklift to transfer them onto a waiting lorry.

The two token Hampshire Police officers on duty that night, Charles Thorn and Gary Mitchell, walked along the dock area, noting that the weather was unusually pleasant for a June night. Unfortunately, due to a breakdown in communications, they were not apprised of the message that was received by TFU police sergeant David Marsh. Even more calamitous was the fact that neither of them was armed.

Thorn stopped his stroll suddenly and asked his partner, "Do you hear anything?" In the distance was the whir of a hydraulic crane used to unload cargo.

Mitchell nodded. "Sounds like someone's unloading. I wasn't aware of a scheduled docking tonight, were you?"

Thorn shook his head. "Customs and Excise didn't tell me about it. Let's have a look, shall we?"

The two men hurried around a corner past a warehouse where they could get a full view of the harbor. Sure enough, four men were loading crates onto a lorry.

"Where are Customs and Excise? They should be supervising the unloading, shouldn't they?" Mitchell asked.

"Unless this is an unscheduled unloading," Thorn said. He quickly radioed his office to request additional officers. The Communication Centre Dispatcher informed them that the Hampshire Constabulary TFU was on the way and to stay put.

The Chinese were finished with the lighter and it was already pulling away. The lorry was nearly full—only two crates remained on the ground. They would be gone in minutes.

"We have to stop them," Thorn said. "Come on."

The two men stepped into view of the Chinese men. "Good

evening," Thorn called out to them. "May we inquire what you're doing?"

One of the Chinese stepped out of the truck and produced some papers. Thorn glanced at them. "You know this is highly irregular, sir. Customs and Excise are supposed to clear your unloading. What have you got in those crates?" The Chinese man, who apparently spoke little English, pointed to the papers.

"Right," said Sergeant Thorn, looking closely at the shipping numbers and comparing them to the crates. One crate was still on the ground; another was on the forklift. "That one has half a ton of tea, and the other one is what?"

The Chinese man smiled. "Toys. Made in Hong Kong."

Mitchell whispered to Thorn, "Imports from the Far East generally come into Southampton."

Thorn nodded and said aloud, "Let's open 'em up, now, all right?"

Mitchell took a crowbar from the side of the hydraulic crane and prized the lid off the wooden crate. It was filled with straw, Styrofoam, and large bags labeled with Chinese characters. Mitchell opened one of the bags and found dozens of smaller bags marked with similar characters. He tossed one of the small bags to Thorn, who promptly used a pocketknife to open it. It was full of tea.

"Fine," Thorn said. "Let's open the other one."

As the forklift was pulled in front of the officers, a fully marked TFU jeep containing four men, including Sergeant David Marsh, sped quickly into the cargo area of the dock and stopped.

"Sergeant Marsh," Thorn said. "Good to see you. It seems these chaps aren't aware of Customs and Excise standard operating procedures."

"A word with you, Sergeant?" Marsh said, gesturing toward the jeep. Mitchell watched Marsh whisper to Thorn, then glanced over to the four Chinese men who had gathered near the forklift. They were all young, probably in their late teens or early twenties.

The conference was over. Marsh took the crowbar from Thorn

and slammed it into the side of the crate containing the tea, cracking one of the side panels. He then worked the panel off, exposing a mess of straw packing. Marsh dug into the packing with the crowbar, pulling it out.

"We have reason to believe you've got something hidden in here," Marsh said to one of the Chinese. The sharp end of the crowbar struck a large canvas bag, bursting it. A white, crystalline powder oozed out of the tear. Having just completed a two-year tour of duty in the Hampshire Constabulary's Drug Squad, Marsh hadn't shaken the habit of carrying a drug test kit with him. He quickly retrieved a plastic vial from the kit, opened it, and scooped a bit of the white powder into the vial with his finger. He replaced the cap and shook the vial vigorously, mixing the white powder with a reagent. The clear liquid changed color.

Marsh turned to the Chinese men. "I have reason to believe that is heroin. Now I'm going to have to place you under—"

Fully automatic machine-gun blasts interrupted him. Taken by surprise, Mitchell and Thorn were the first to fall. Fortunately for Marsh, his team had come prepared.

Marsh hit the ground and quickly rolled behind the crate, shielding himself from the barrage of bullets. The three other officers also deftly leapt for cover. Using MP5 Standard Operating Rifles, the TFU returned fire on the Chinese. Even though the weapons were single shot only, the TFU were sharpshooters. One Chinese went down.

Marsh was armed with a Smith & Wesson 15 Mag Self-Loading pistol. He peered around the container and got off a couple of shots before a thunderstorm of bullets tore into the side of the crate, forcing him back.

The Chinese were formidable opponents who knew how to use their guns, which to Marsh looked like MACH 10s. He knew that they were really COBRAYs, a 9mm machine gun modeled after the MACHs. Even though they were not well-made, criminal gangs favored COBRAYs because they were sold and traded in pieces and were therefore easily concealed.

Three Events

After a minute it was almost over. All but one of the Chinese were dead. There were no casualties on Marsh's team. The lone Chinese gunman realized the predicament he was in and attempted a kamikaze stunt. He yelled something in Cantonese and ran toward Marsh, his gun blasting wildly. Marsh threw caution to the wind. He stood up, used both hands to steady his pistol, aimed at the running man, and squeezed the trigger. The running man jerked back and fell to the pavement.

Marsh breathed a sigh of relief, then ran to where Thorn and Mitchell lay. The TFU member everyone called "Doc" was attending to the two constables, but he turned to Marsh and shook his head.

Marsh frowned, then barked an order to one of his men. "Get Doc some help with these officers and get in touch with the DCI. Tell him the tip was good. Tell him the villains would have got away had they not been detained by two heroic Hampshire Police officers."

June 18, 1997, 8:00 P.M., Hong Kong

Of Hong Kong's many attractions, elegant restaurants on boats provide visitors not only with a superb dinner, but with one of the best tourist attractions of Aberdeen's Shum Wan Harbour on the south shore of the island. Most of them were linked together by walkways, and their ornate gilded and painted facades were particularly glorious lit up at night. One such "floating restaurant," the *Emerald Palace*, had been reserved for a special event on June 18 and was closed to the public.

EurAsia Enterprises, a long-standing shipping and trading corporation owned privately by a British family since the mid nineteenth century, was throwing a dinner party for its chairman, who was retiring after thirty years of service. A swing band, made up entirely of Chinese musicians, was playing surprisingly faithful renditions of Glenn Miller and Benny Goodman hits as the dance floor filled with formally dressed British men and women.

Guy Thackeray, the corporation's forty-eight-year-old CEO, had lived in Hong Kong all his life. His great-great-grandfather had founded EurAsia Enterprises in 1850, not long after Hong Kong was ceded to Britain. The family had steadfastly refused to allow the corporation to go public, and Guy Thackeray presently found himself the sole owner of 59 percent of the company's stock. The remaining stock was held by other members of the board of directors, including John Desmond, the retiring chairman. All of them were present, sitting with their spouses at one table.

Guy Thackeray felt out of place at his own company's events. The past month had been hell. As the July 1 deadline approached, Guy Thackeray was becoming more desperate and anxious. The secret burden he held on his shoulders regarding EurAsia Enterprises' future was taking its toll. He knew that very soon he would have to make public a fateful bit of knowledge, but it would not be tonight.

Thackeray surveyed the dance floor, catching the eye of a friendly face here and there and nodding his head in acknowledgment. He glanced at his watch. It was almost time for his speech. He took a last swig of his gin and tonic and approached the podium.

Back in the kitchen, the sixty-one-year-old Chinese cook Chan Wo grumbled to himself. He enjoyed cooking and considered himself one of the best chefs in Hong Kong. In fact, the *Emerald Palace*'s reputation had been built on Chan's abilities to create magnificent concoctions of Szechuan, Cantonese, and Mandarin styles of Chinese cuisine.

Glancing at the new order brought to him by a waiter, he shrugged and walked over to the large metal refrigerator to fetch more previously prepared uncooked dumplings. Much to his dismay, they weren't inside. Had he used them all already? Chan Wo silently cursed his assistant. Bobby Ling must have forgotten to make more that afternoon.

"Bobby!" he called. The kid was probably in the storeroom.

"Bobby!" he shouted again. Chan slammed the refrigerator shut and left the kitchen.

The storeroom was adjacent to the kitchen, conveniently soundproofed from the noise in the dining areas. Chan thought he wouldn't mind hiding in the storeroom for a while, too; he couldn't blame Bobby for taking a break. Chan entered the container-filled room. It was dark, which was odd. He could have sworn Bobby was here. Chan flicked on the light switch. There was nothing but boxes piled on other boxes, cans, and containers. "Bobby, where the hell are you?" Chan Wo asked in Cantonese. Then he saw the tennis shoes.

Bobby Ling was out cold, lying between two stacks of cardboard boxes. Chan bent down to examine the motionless body. "Bobby?"

Chan never knew what hit him. All he felt was a lightning bolt in the back of his neck, and then there was blackness.

The instrument that broke Chan Wo's neck was a heavily callused hand belonging to a man whose appearance was undoubtedly unusual, even in a massively populated area like Hong Kong. He was Chinese, but his hair was white as snow, his skin very pale—almost pink—and behind the dark sunglasses were pinkish-blue eyes. He was about thirty years old, and he had the build of a weight lifter.

The albino Chinese grunted at the two dead figures on the floor, then moved to the only porthole in the room. He opened it, leaned out, and looked down at the water, where a rowboat containing two other men was rocking steadily next to the larger floating restaurant. The albino loosened a coil of rope he had over his shoulder and threw one end out the window. Next, he braced himself by placing one foot on the wall beneath the window, and clutched the rope tightly. One of the men from the rowboat took hold of the rope and swiftly climbed up to the window. The albino was strong enough to hold the rope and the other man's weight.

The other figure appeared in the porthole and snaked through, dropping to the floor. He also had a full head of white hair, pinkish skin, and sunglasses, and was about thirty years old. While the first albino secured the rope to a post, the second albino opened a backpack, removed some instruments, and set to work.

Meanwhile, in the dining room, Guy Thackeray stopped the music and began his speech.

"My friends," he said. "I'm afraid I don't always give credit when credit is due. On such a special occasion as tonight, I must apologize for that oversight. Everyone who works for me and for EurAsia Enterprises is always deserving of praise. I want you to know that I am very proud of each and every one of you. It is because of you that EurAsia Enterprises is one of the leading shipping and trading establishments in the Far East. But it also took someone with superior management skills, leadership, and fortitude to guide this great ship of ours through sometimes troubled waters. For thirty years he has been an inspiration and mentor to us all." He looked straight at John Desmond and said, "And you've been something of an uncle, or perhaps a second father, to me personally, John."

Desmond smiled and shifted in his seat, embarrassed. Desmond was nearly eighteen years older than Thackeray. Unlike the CEO, Desmond had been born and raised in Britain, having moved to Hong Kong in the early fifties.

Thackeray continued, "If ever there was a person deserving of a distinguished service award, it would be Mr. John Desmond. I, for one, shall miss him. He will be leaving us as of the thirtieth of June. What's the matter, John, afraid the Communists will take away your health benefits come the first of July?"

There was laughter and applause.

"Anyway," Thackeray continued. "Without further ado, allow me to present you with this plaque, which reads 'To John Desmond, for Thirty Years Distinguished Service at EurAsia Enterprises.'"

There was more applause as Desmond left his seat and approached the podium. The two men shook hands. Desmond then turned to the room and spoke into the microphone.

"Thank you, everyone. It's been a wonderful thirty years," he began. "EurAsia Enterprises has been good to me. Hong Kong has been good to me. I don't know what the future will bring after July first. But I'm sure . . ." Desmond hesitated. He seemed to be searching for the appropriate words. ". . . it will be business as usual."

Everyone in the room knew that on July 1 Britain would no longer be in possession of Hong Kong. The entire colony would be handed over to the People's Republic of China at 12:01 A.M. Despite China's assurances that Hong Kong would remain a capitalist and free-enterprise zone for at least fifty years, no one could be sure.

"I wish you all the best of luck," Desmond continued. "Thank you again. And to my good friend Guy Thackeray, the man who really guides EurAsia Enterprises, a very special thanks."

Over the applause, the two men shook hands again. Thackeray signaled the bandleader and the room filled with the swinging rhythm of Glenn Miller's "Pennsylvania Six-Five-Thousand."

Thackeray accompanied Desmond back to the table. "John, I have to get back to Central," he said. "I suppose I'll see you at the office tomorrow?"

"Leaving so soon, Guy?" Desmond asked. "Whatever for?"

"I left some unfinished business at the office which must be taken care of. Listen . . . enjoy your party. I'll speak to you soon."

"Guy, wait," Desmond said. "We need to talk about this thing. You know we do."

"Not now, John. We'll go over it tomorrow at the office, all right?"

Guy walked away without another word. With concern, John Desmond watched his friend leave the room. He knew that the roof was going to cave in when the rest of the board discovered what he had learned only two days ago. He wondered how Guy Thackeray was going to emerge unscathed.

Guy Thackeray stepped out of the dining room, onto the deck, and into a small shuttle motorboat. The boat whisked him to shore, where his personal limousine was waiting. In a flash it was off to the north part of the island and the panorama of buildings and lights.

By then, the two strange albino Chinese had finished their work. The first man slithered through the storeroom porthole, slid down the rope, and dropped into the waiting rowboat. His brother followed suit, and moments later the boat was heading east toward a yacht waiting some two hundred meters away. The third man, the one rowing, also had a full head of white hair, pinkish skin, and sunglasses. Not only were the albino brothers the most bizarre trio in the Far East, they were also the most dangerous.

Exactly fifteen minutes later, the *Emerald Palace* exploded into flames. The brunt of the detonation enveloped the dining room, and the dance floor caved inward. It didn't happen fast enough for the terrified people caught inside the death trap. Those not burned alive were drowned trying to escape. In twelve minutes, the structure had completely submerged. Everyone was killed, including John Desmond and the entire board of directors of EurAsia Enterprises.

June 21, 1997, 11:55 A.M., Western Australia

At approximately the same moment that James Bond fell asleep on a red-eye flight from Kingston, Jamaica, to London, the sun was beating down on the Australian outback desert. A young Aboriginal boy who frequented the area for its availability of kurrajong, an edible plant, was still frightened of the white men he had seen earlier. The men had driven to this isolated location in four-wheel-drives, which the boy knew only as "cars."

The boy's family lived at a campsite about a mile away and had done so for as long as he could remember. He knew that farther south, more than a day's walking distance, were towns populated by the white men. To the east, closer to Uluru, the mystical rock-like formation in the desert that the white men called "Ayers Rock," there were even more encroachments on the Aboriginal home territory.

The white men had arrived early that morning in two "cars." They had spent an hour at the site, digging in the ground and burying something. Then they left, heading south toward the white man's civilization. They had been gone three hours before the boy decided to inspect the ground.

The dig occupied an area about six feet in diameter. The dirt was fresh but had already begun to bake and harden in the sun. The boy was curious. He wanted to know what the white men had hidden there, but he was afraid. He knew that he might get into trouble if he was seen by the white men, but now there was no one else around. He thought he should go and find a lizard for that evening's meal, but his desire to inspect the burial mound was too great.

If he had been wearing a watch, it would have read exactly 12:00 noon when the sun exploded in his face.

The nuclear explosion that occurred that day two hundred miles north of Leonora in Western Australia sent shock waves throughout the world. It was later determined that the device had roughly three-quarters the power of the weapon that destroyed Hiroshima: approximately the equivalent of three hundred tons of TNT. The blast covered an area of three square miles. It was deadly indeed, but crude by today's standards. Nevertheless, had there been a city where the bomb was buried, there would surely have been nothing left of it.

Within hours, an emergency session at the United Nations degenerated into nothing but a shouting match between the superpowers. No one knew what had happened. Australian officials were completely baffled. Inspectors at the site came up with nothing aside from the fact that a "homemade" nuclear device had been detonated. Everyone was grateful that it had been in the middle of the outback, where they assumed there had been no casualties.

What was truly frightening, though, was the implication of the location. It was, in all probability, a test. Someone—a terrorist group or a foreign power operating in Australia— was in possession of rudimentary nuclear weapons.

As Australia, the United States, Russia, and Britain combined forces to investigate the explosion and search for answers, they also waited for the imminent claim of responsibility and possible blackmail. It never came. When James Bond arrived in London in the early hours of the same day, London time, the nuclear explosion was still a total mystery.

3

Call to Duty

James Bond never had trouble sleeping on a plane, and the flight from Jamaica to England was no exception. He felt refreshed and alert when the office car pulled into the high-security SIS parking garage by the Thames. Things were so open now: Bond was one of the few veterans still around who could remember a time when SIS hid behind the front of Universal Export Ltd.

The British Secret Service had a relatively new leader. Her name was no longer a secret, but Bond would never dare address her by name, just as he had never addressed his irascible former chief, Sir Miles Messervy, by name. Since his retirement, Sir Miles had mellowed considerably. He often invited Bond to Quarterdeck, his home on the edge of Windsor Great Park, for a dinner party or a game of bridge. They still met from time to time at Blades. Once they were strictly a superior officer and a civil servant with mutual respect for each other; but now, after all the years, they were close friends. Even so, Bond had consciously to refrain from addressing the man as "sir."

Bond couldn't say he was friends with the new M. He wasn't

even sure he liked her, but he respected her. In her short tenure, she had already shown she was capable of being an effective leader. She wasn't afraid of proactive operations, which was something Bond had feared might be discontinued. If some dirty work needed to be performed, she had no problem with ordering Bond, or one of the other Double-Os, to carry it out. She wasn't squeamish, and she wasn't gullible. Bond felt he could say whatever he wanted to her and he would receive an honest response. He also knew what the woman thought of him personally. Bond was a chauvinist and, in her words, "a coldhearted bastard." She had said it one evening over a working dinner. Bond understood why the woman had called him that, and he didn't hold it against her because, for one thing, she was right.

Bond stopped by his private office on the fourth floor before going up to see M. His personal assistant (Bond couldn't help still thinking of her as a "secretary"), Ms. (not Miss) Helena Marksbury, was busy holding the fort. Helena worked for all of the Double-Os, having been with SIS for about a year. Since the days of Loelia Ponsonby and Mary Goodnight, there had been a steady succession of lissome blondes, brunettes, and redheads occupying the front desk. As for Helena Marksbury, she was a brunette with large green eyes. She was bright, quick-witted, and damnably attractive. Bond thought that had she not been his personal assistant, the lovely Helena would have made an enjoyable dinner date . . . with an option for breakfast the next morning.

"Good morning, James," Helena said. She had a lilting Welsh accent, something Bond found extremely attractive.

"How are things, Helena?"

"I was called in the middle of the night. Again," she said with a sigh.

Bond had been briefed about the Australian incident. By now every department was digging into the matter.

"It happens to the best of us," Bond replied.

"I imagine you have no problem rising in the middle of the night," Helena said with a twinkle in her eye.

Bond smiled and said, "Don't believe everything you hear, Ms. Marksbury."

"Well, if you ever find that you *are* up and can't sleep, Mr. Bond, I have a very nice herbal tea that is very relaxing."

"I avoid tea at all costs," Bond said. "You should know that by now."

"As a matter of fact, I have noticed. You don't drink tea at all, James? How un-English of you!"

"I'd as soon drink a cup of mud." He shrugged. "And besides, I'm half Scots, half Swiss." He smiled warmly at her, then stepped into his office.

Bond had never been keen on office decoration. The one piece of artwork on display was an obscure artist's watercolor of the clubhouse at the Royal St. George's Golf Course. The one framed photograph on the desk featured Bond and his closest American friend, former CIA agent Felix Leiter, sitting in a bar in New York City. It was an old photo, and the two men looked surprised and slightly drunk. It never failed to make Bond smile.

He had no urgent messages, so he picked up the phone and dialed Miss Moneypenny's line (one of the few women at SIS who still didn't mind being called "Miss"). She answered after the first ring.

"Hello, James, welcome back."

"Penny, you have a wonderful phone voice, did you know that?" he said. "You could start a second career entertaining lonely men with sweet nothings."

"Hmm, and I daresay you'd be a regular client. But I'd have to go the Chinese route and entertain you with sweet and *sour* nothings."

"Now, that's an appetizing idea for a takeaway, Penny," he said, chuckling.

She laughed too. "Listen, you'd better get up here right away. She asked for you just five minutes ago."

"I'm on my way. Bill there?"

"He's here too."

"Right." Bond hung up, left the sanctity of the one quiet place in the building, and took the elevator to the eighth floor.

Miss Moneypenny's manner was no-nonsense, but her blue eyes betrayed how pleased she was to see Bond. Throughout the years, their relationship had been a mutually flirtatious one, and it had settled into a comfortable friendship. Like most of Sir Miles's staff, she had been reticent about working for someone new after such a long time, but for her the new M was a pleasure. They got along splendidly, and Miss Moneypenny had decided not to transfer out but to stay on. It was a good thing, for many believed that SIS wouldn't function properly without Miss Moneypenny's vast knowledge of the entire organization and its history.

Bill Tanner, the chief of staff, was a Service veteran who had been around even longer than Bond. He remained 007's closest friend inside SIS and one of the few with whom Bond regularly socialized. They enjoyed the occasional game of golf, but the chief of staff's forte was tennis. Tanner had originally resigned when Sir Miles retired, but he was asked by the new M to stay on during what was called the "transition period" of six months. Those six months became a full year, and now Tanner had no intention of leaving.

"Hello, James, welcome back," Bill said.

"Bill . . . Penny . . ." Bond nodded with a smile.

"Sorry you couldn't spend more time in Jamaica, James," Moneypenny said. "I received a report on the exercise. It went well, I heard."

"I have no complaints," Bond said, vividly recalling the sight of Stephanie Lane stepping into his shower. "This is about Australia, I suppose?"

"Isn't that appalling," Tanner exclaimed, shaking his head. "No one knows what the bloody hell is going on. Unfortunately, it's not officially in our laps yet. Australia wants it handled her way for the moment, and the P.M. has agreed to stay away for the time being. God knows America and Russia are sticking *their* noses into it. Anyway, that isn't what she called you in for."

Call to Duty

Bond was surprised. The atomic blast, even in the few hours since it had happened, had become international news.

Moneypenny picked up the phone and buzzed M. "007's here, ma'am." The green light above the door flashed, indicating that Bond should go in. Some things never changed.

On the other hand, M's office had changed drastically with the new regime. Sir Miles's domain had been the "captain's quarters" of a naval vessel, while the new look was more akin to a posh psychiatrist's office. Sparse, ultramodern furnishings filled the place with a stark black-and-white scheme that was surprisingly pleasing to the eye. There was a lot of shiny metal, glass, and black leather, as well as an array of artwork of all types, including an original Kandinsky on the wall behind the desk.

M sat at her glass-top desk, looking down at an open folder. Bond stood in the doorway until she motioned to the black leather chair in front of the desk. Her eyes never left the page until Bond was sitting and facing her. Then she looked up at him. M's striking blue eyes were much like Bond's—very cool, with thin streaks of white in the irises. She was in her late fifties, had short grayish hair and a rather severe face. Not a slender woman or a tall one, M nevertheless possessed a charisma that commanded one's attention, due mostly to the obvious intelligence within her ice-cold blue eyes. Their shape hinted at some distant Asian blood, but that was only speculation on Bond's part.

"Good morning, ma'am," Bond said.

"Hello, 007, how was your flight?" Her voice was calm, even, and soft.

"Fine, thank you."

"I understand the training exercise went well."

Bond nodded.

"Your report can wait," M said. "I'm sure 03 will fill us in. Or do you think 05 will have a more favorable view of events?"

M looked hard at Bond. He shifted uncomfortably. Sir Miles had never approved of Bond's womanizing, and it was one of the bones of contention between the new M and 007. Bond swallowed and managed to say, "I'm sure either agent will give you an accurate reconstruction of the exercise."

M frowned but nodded briskly.

Bond quickly changed the subject. "What do we know about this explosion in Australia?"

"Never mind about that, 007," M said. "We've been told to stay out of it for the moment. Regardless of those orders, I have Section A doing reconnaisance. There's hardly any information at the moment. Until we hear from the party or parties responsible, I've got something else for you to look into."

"Yes, ma'am."

"Bond, do you know what's happening to Hong Kong on the first of July?" M asked.

"Well, yes, ma'am," Bond said. Didn't everyone? "It reverts back to the People's Republic of China after a century and a half of British rule."

"That's less than two weeks away, 007."

Bond nodded, his brow creased. What was this all about? He vaguely remembered a report he had read before leaving for Jamaica. Could it involve that solicitor who was killed in a bomb blast earlier in the month?

"Do you know what's happened there in the past few days?" M asked.

"There was a car bomb in the business district, what, a week ago?"

"On the eleventh of June, just over a week, yes. What else do you know about it?"

"It was a solicitor visiting from England, wasn't it? Someone in a large firm here."

"Gregory Donaldson, of Fitch, Donaldson, and Patrick. A partner in one of our most prestigious law practices."

"Do we know who was behind the bombing, and why he was targeted?" Bond asked.

"An anonymous caller phoned Government House and

claimed that the People's Republic was behind it. Why Donaldson was targeted is still a mystery."

"Why was Donaldson in Hong Kong?"

"I'll get to that in a moment. You know about the two Red Chinese officials who were assassinated?" she asked.

Bond remembered. "Oh, yes. That was a few days later, wasn't it?"

"The thirteenth."

"Yes, ma'am, two officials from Beijing were killed in a shopping mall by a man dressed in a military uniform."

"A British army uniform, to be exact. The two men were working with the local government on last-minute preparations for the changeover. They had taken some time off and were buying souvenirs or something to take back to China. Some loose cannon in uniform calmly walked up to the men, pulled out an automatic pistol, and shot them dead. Witnesses said the 'officer' ran out of the store and disappeared into the crowd. All we know is that the man was certainly Caucasian."

"There's been a lot of tension over the past year. People have been waking up to what's happening to them," Bond said. "It had to come to a head eventually."

" 'Waking up' is only the half of it," M said. "People are starting to panic. Something else happened in Hong Kong two nights ago that has escalated the problem."

"What's that?"

"A bomb exploded on a floating restaurant off of Aberdeen, killing thirty-three people. All of them were important members of the British business community in Hong Kong."

This was news to Bond.

"The report is probably on your desk. The first incident was disturbing, the second one was bewildering, but this third one has caused the P.M. to sit up and take notice. Something's going on, 007, and it isn't pretty. Fingers are pointing. There was another anonymous call to Government House the morning after the bombing."

"China."

"Right."

"That's it? Just 'the People's Republic of China'? Nothing more specific?"

"There were allusions to some general in Guangzhou, north of the Hong Kong colony. His name is Wong. It was enough to get the rumor mill churning. The press got hold of it, and needless to say there is a lot of tension in the air. Anti-Communist groups are making themselves heard, and the democracy foes are just as loud. The P.M. has been talking with Beijing . . ."

"But the official party line denies all knowledge of the actions."

"Correct, 007. And they are just as quick to accuse us of killing their two officials in the shopping mall."

"Sounds like someone is stirring up trouble just before the takeover."

"Well, there's going to *be* trouble. Chinese troops are massing along the border, just above the New Territories. The Hong Kong people are afraid that they're going to invade and do away with the idea of a peaceful transition. It didn't help when a group of Hong Kong teenagers threw rocks at the soldiers. There was gunfire, but no one was hurt. There was also some kind of panic-induced incident in one of the tourist areas in Kowloon just yesterday. The memory of Tiananmen Square is still very vivid."

"Isn't this a job for the politicians?"

"Normally it would be," M said. "But something else has come up that interests me."

She waited until Bond asked, "And what is that, ma'am?" The new M tended to have a flair for the dramatic.

"The three incidents—the car bomb that killed Donaldson, the assassination of the two Chinese men, and the bombing of the floating restaurant—are all connected to a multibillion-dollar international shipping and trade corporation that is privately owned and operated by a long-established British family in Hong Kong."

4

A British Legacy

M pressed some buttons on a control panel to her right. The room darkened slightly and the Kandinsky painting slid up into the ceiling. A television monitor built into the wall flashed on, revealing a logo: that of EurAsia Enterprises Ltd.

"EurAsia Enterprises is one of the biggest shipping corporations operating out of Hong Kong," M said. "You'll find all the background you need in this file." She gestured to a manila folder on the edge of her desk. "Briefly, I'll give you some of the details."

Bond took the folder but didn't open it. He gave his full attention to M.

"The company was founded in 1850, just a few years after Hong Kong was ceded to Britain at the close of the so-called First Opium War. How much do you remember about British colonial history, 007?"

Bond cleared his throat. "In a nutshell, the war resulted from China's refusal to open ports to the west. I believe the catalyst was an incident in which the Chinese government in Canton seized a tremendous amount of opium from British traders and destroyed it."

"Twenty thousand pounds, to be precise," M added. "At the time, it was worth three million sterling. Opium trading was a ghastly business; but in the early nineteenth century, opium was the world's most valuable commodity. Be that as it may, the crux of the problem was as you said—China didn't want to trade with the West. They had reluctantly allowed Canton—they call it Guangzhou now, you know—and Macau to become the only ports open to the West. Our East India Company had a monopoly in Guangzhou until the 1830s, but the demand for Chinese tea, as well as silk and porcelain, was overwhelming."

"It wasn't easy for the traders," Bond said. "I seem to remember that they were restricted to the fringes of the city, not allowed inside."

"That's right," M said. "And all business had to go through the Co-hong, a guild of Chinese merchants. Corruption flourished, and these constraints encouraged dreams of a base on the southeast coast of China where traders could operate freely. There was a trade imbalance, and it greatly favored China. The balance of trade in tea alone ran six to one in China's favor. They didn't particularly care for anything we had to offer, except silver, perhaps. China was under the impression that she didn't need us."

"And that's where the opium trade came in."

"Precisely. The traders discovered that there was a certain faction in China that desired Indian opium, and we were in the dubious position of being able to offer it. It was how several of our largest companies came into existence over there. In retrospect, I suppose, it was a nasty business; but it suited the mercantile ethic of the time. Opium traders shrugged off these scruples and maintained that trade, and the missionaries that followed, would ultimately benefit China. Well, the Chinese government became increasingly concerned about opium. Justifiably, it was an extravagant habit that ruined minds and morals—and it caused the trade imbalance to tip to our favor. Finally, in 1839, the emperor ordered the governor of Hunan Province to go to Guangzhou and end the opium trade. The British Chief Superintendent of Trade, a man named Charles Elliot, was ordered to surrender all of the merchants' opium."

"And he did."

"That's right, and the traders watched helplessly as the Chinese destroyed the opium that was the basis of their livelihood. One thing led to another, and skirmishes began. By 1840, an expeditionary fleet had arrived in Hong Kong with a mission to obtain compensation and an apology from China for the destroyed opium, and to secure a British foothold on the China coast."

"It was rather a one-sided war, wasn't it?" Bond asked rhetorically.

"Yes, China was ill-prepared to deal with Britain's warships. It all came to a temprorary end in 1841 with a treaty that was never signed. The treaty promised compensation for the confiscated opium, permission for British merchants to return to Guangzhou, and the cession of Hong Kong Island to Britain. Neither side was happy with this outcome and the war continued into 1842, when the Treaty of Nanjing was finally signed and reluctantly accepted by China. The result was a hefty compensation in millions of pounds, as well as the opening of several ports to British trade."

"And Hong Kong was officially ceded to Britain."

" 'In perpetuity' the treaty said," M added. "Hong Kong became a British Crown Colony in 1843, and trade resumed. We don't have to cover all of the history, but I suppose you know how we acquired Kowloon and the New Territories?"

"That was a result of the *Second* Opium War," Bond replied, feeling like a schoolboy.

"Well, we prefer to call it the Second Anglo-Chinese War now," M said with a shrug. "It was a result of a ridiculous mistake in 1856 made by Chinese officials. They boarded one of our ships, the *Arrow*, believing it to be a pirate vessel. A battle ensued, and another war broke out. It finally ended in 1860 with the treaty signed at the Convention of Peking. We got Kowloon with that one."

"In perpetuity once again," Bond chimed in.

"Of course. Opium was officially legalized in China from then on until the start of the Second World War. China ended up making a tidy profit from the filthy substance, using it as an excuse for levying taxes. The big blunder on our part came some forty years later, when the Second Convention of Peking was held and a new treaty was signed. A larger chunk of land north of Kowloon, along with 233 surrounding islands, was leased to Britain for a ninety-nine-year term. As you know, this area became known as the New Territories."

"Why was it not ceded in perpetuity?" asked Bond.

"Carelessness on the part of the British foreign secretary. He had hoped for an open-ended lease to be terminated by mutual agreement, but he ultimately agreed to the ninety-nine-year lease. I suppose that seemed like forever in 1898, when the treaty was signed."

"And now that time has run out," Bond mused. He recalled the historic agreement made between Great Britain and China in 1984. "Why did we agree to hand over Hong Kong and Kowloon in 1997? Why didn't we just give up the New Territories and keep what was still legally ours?"

"Because Hong Kong and Kowloon depend on the natural resources that are derived from the New Territories. Without the New Territories' abundance of freshwater and other utilities, Hong Kong Island would be extremely difficult to support. And, I think, there was a certain amount of guilt involved as well. Looking back, both sides felt that Hong Kong rightfully belonged to China. It was ceded under circumstances which weren't entirely ethical. It's a shame that everyone had to wait a hundred years to come to terms with that realization. The poor people of Hong Kong are now feeling the brunt of that mistake. After over a century of Western and democratic rule, they are now faced with the prospect of life controlled by the People's Republic of China. But enough of the history lesson; let's get back to the topic at hand."

M pushed a button on her desk and the picture on the monitor changed. The image of a Caucasian man appeared. He had black hair with streaks of gray, dark brown eyes, and looked to be in his late forties. His face was severe and cold.

"EurAsia Enterprises was one of the trading corporations that flourished in Southeast Asia after the First Opium War. It was founded by an Englishman named James Thackeray. This is Thackeray's great-great-grandson, the current CEO of EurAsia Enterprises. His name is Guy Thackeray."

Bond knew very little about EurAsia Enterprises. "The company has branches all over the world?"

"Yes," said M. "Toronto, London, New York, Tokyo, Sydney— they have a significant gold-mining operation in Western Australia—but they're based in Hong Kong. That's where Thackeray has lived all his life."

"Funny," said Bond. "I've never heard of him."

"Thackeray's not a very public person," M said. "You can count on one hand the number of times he's been to England. He rarely leaves Hong Kong, and if he does he goes only as far as Australia. There's really nothing particularly sinister about the man. By all accounts he's a perfectly respectable businessman. He's forty-eight, never married, and lives quietly and comfortably on Victoria Peak. He was the only child and sole heir of his great-great-grandfather's legacy, which was passed down from James Thackeray to his son, then to his grandson, and so on. Guy Thackeray became CEO of the company when he was twenty-eight."

"What did he do before that?" Bond asked.

M chuckled. "He was a magician."

"What?"

"He had an act that he started when he was a child," M said. "A magic act. He performed it on floating restaurants, in nightclubs, wherever. He even had a short-lived television show in Hong Kong in the early sixties. Sleight-of-hand stuff, optical illusions, sawing women in half, you know what I mean. He gave it up once he reached his twenties and entered the family business in pursuit of a 'real' career. Although he was independently wealthy, I suppose he felt he must live up to the family name and all that. So he learned the business and was very good at it. After his father died, he became CEO. Never bothered with show business again. And up until now, the only black mark we had against the man is that he apparently enjoys playing high-stakes *mahjong* in illegal betting parlours."

"So why are we interested in him?"

"Gregory Donaldson, the lawyer who was killed in the car-bomb blast, was Guy Thackeray's solicitor," M said with raised eyebrows.

Bond nodded thoughtfully. The slide changed, revealing a photo of Guy Thackeray with Gregory Donaldson.

"On June tenth, Donaldson arrived in Hong Kong on an urgent mission to meet Guy Thackeray. Donaldson's partners here in London were not privy to what it was about, only that it had something to do with the privately owned EurAsia stock. Thackeray owns fifty-nine percent of the stock, and the rest is owned by the other members on the board. On June eleventh, Donaldson was killed."

"Interesting," Bond said.

"That's not all," M continued. "The two visiting Chinese officials from Beijing who were shot by the alleged British army officer were shopping at a mall owned by EurAsia Enterprises. In fact, the mall is part of the huge complex that houses the company on Hong Kong Island."

"So they were killed at EurAsia's corporate headquarters?"

"That's right," M said.

"And the floating-restaurant business . . ."

"That bomb killed the entire board of directors, the chairman, and all the other executive officers of EurAsia Enterprises; everyone but Guy Thackeray. It was a company party of some kind. The chairman, a fellow named Desmond, was retiring. Guy Thackeray was there, made a speech, presented Desmond with one of those distinguished-service awards, then disappeared. At first, everyone thought he had been killed in the blast as well, but he was found at EurAsia headquarters working in his office two hours later, completely oblivious to what had happened. He's been cooperating with the local authorities in their investigation into the blast, but it's still very early. No one has any reason to suspect that he might be involved. From what I can gather, most people believe the bomb might very well have been meant for him, and to hell with the other people who were killed."

M paused a moment, then continued. "There's one more piece of the puzzle you haven't heard about. Three nights ago, the Hampshire Constabulary Tactical Firearms Unit busted a drug-smuggling operation in Portsmouth. Some Chinese were caught unloading a ton of heroin off of a cargo ship. That ship just happened to be owned by none other than EurAsia Enterprises."

Bond nodded. "The Chinese were Triad, I would wager."

"You're absolutely correct, 007," M said. "They were all killed in the raid, but a quick investigation revealed they were part of a Triad known as the Dragon Wing Society. It's an offshoot of the San Yee On Triad."

Bond frowned. The San Yee On was one of the largest Triads in the world. Triads had existed in China for centuries and were the most misunderstood, most complex, and most dangerous criminal organizations to infect the modern world. Chinese Triads made the Sicilian Mafia look amateurish. They usually originated in Hong Kong, but their tentacles reached into nearly every Chinese community in the world. More formidable than the Tongs, the Triads had in the last fifty years become responsible for most of the worldwide drug trade. They also had their hands in illegal arms distribution, prostitution, gambling, illegal immigration, and other activities associated with organized crime. A Triad's oath of loyalty was absolute, and a member would rather die than reveal any of his organization's secrets.

"So you think that EurAsia Enterprises is involved with this Triad?" Bond asked.

"That's what I want you to find out," M said. "A lot of British subjects were killed the other night. At first I thought it could all very well be coincidence that the events in Hong Kong were connected with this otherwise very respectable company. But when the raid in Portsmouth occurred and we learned that the company's ship was smuggling heroin to Triad members, that's when we became alarmed.

"If you can, 007, I want you to find out who is behind these terrorist acts and stop them. All Britain needs is a war with China on the eve of giving back Hong Kong! And that's what we're going to get if the pattern keeps up. You're to fly to Hong Kong this afternoon—there's a flight leaving at two-thirty and it arrives tomorrow morning. They're eight hours ahead of us, you know. Our man in Station H will meet you at the airport, a fellow by the name of Woo. I understand he's been with the service for years."

"I know of him, ma'am," said Bond. "Never met him, though."

"He'll be your guide and contact. How's your Chinese?"

"I speak Cantonese pretty well, ma'am, but I'm not so fluent in Mandarin."

"Well, I hope you won't need it. Although I daresay that we'll be hearing more Mandarin in Hong Kong next year."

"Will Guy Thackeray be accessible?"

"I have no idea," M said. "You'll have to find a way to meet him. Size him up. You are to determine if we have any reason to be suspicious of the man. I trust you won't fail. You have got ten days. The countdown to July the first is already in progress."

"Zero minus ten . . ." Bond said. "Plenty of time. No pressure at all."

She ignored his flippancy. "That's all, 007. Be sure to stop by Q Branch on your way out. I believe the Armourer has something for you."

Bond stood as M shut off the monitor and returned the lighting to normal. He cleared his throat and said, "Ma'am, I'm very concerned about the Australian thing."

"We all are, 007. I'll keep you informed, but for the moment it's not our brief. You've got your assignment, and that's where I want your concentration."

With that, M looked down at the document she had been reading when Bond first entered. It was a signal that the meeting was over.

"Very well, ma'am," Bond said, and started out of the room.

"James."

Bond stopped, surprised that she had called him by his Christian name.

"Yes, ma'am?"

"Those Triads can be vicious. They'll cut off your hand with a butcher's knife as soon as look at you. Be careful."

Bond nodded. "Yes, ma'am. Thank you," he said, and walked out of the inner sanctum.

Seven minutes later, Bond punched in the keypad code and entered the unmarked gray metal doorway in the basement. He was immediately assaulted by the smell of chemicals and the noise of machinery. Q Branch was a virtual Santa's Workshop for grownups, and not very nice grown-ups at that.

In one corner, behind a wall of glass, technicians were spray-painting a BMW. Against a far wall was a line of cardboard human cutouts with bull's-eyes painted on various portions of the figures' anatomies. Two technicians stood twenty-five feet away from the wall and fired propellants at the targets from what appeared to be crude prototypes of 35mm cameras.

"Oh, please, can I get just one shot of you, 007?"

Bond turned to see a tall, thin man with gray hair. He was holding one of the cameras.

"Major," said Bond, "I wouldn't have taken you for a paparazzo."

Major Boothroyd, the Armourer and head of Q Branch, replied, "It's for the wife and kids, actually. Come on, say 'cheese.' *Please.*"

"Major, I never photograph well," Bond said, chuckling. "I'm a bit camera-shy."

Boothroyd placed the camera on a table. "I shutter to think what this camera would do for you!"

Bond winced at the pun.

"Follow me, 007. What size shoe do you wear?"

He followed Boothroyd into a room containing a bench and a shoe salesman's stool with an inclined side. On a rack against the wall were a number of pairs of leather shoes in brown and black. Boothroyd gestured to the bench and sat on the stool. Bond sat, shaking his head. "Major, why do I feel like I'm in Harrod's? I wear a nine and a half."

Boothroyd turned to the shoes on the wall. "Nine and a half . . . nine and a half . . . Do you prefer black or brown?"

"Black, please. Is this a joke?"

Boothroyd placed a pair of black shoes in front of Bond. "You know better than to ask that. Well, take off your shoes and try them on!"

Feeling ridiculous, Bond did as he was told. "Now I suppose you want me to walk around the room and see if they feel all right?"

"I want to make sure they're comfortable, 007," said Boothroyd. "There's nothing worse than sore feet."

Bond walked back and forth twice. "They're fine. Now, what's the point?"

"Take a look at the bottom of the tongue on the left shoe. You'll find a small prying tool. Remove it."

Bond did so. "Right," the Armourer continued. "Now use the tool to pry open the heel." The heel snapped off, revealing several items fitted neatly within. "As you've probably guessed by now, these are upgrades of our standard-issue field shoes, model F, which all Double-O operatives are required to wear when on assignment."

"Then you've made quite an improvement. I never could get the old ones open."

Boothroyd ignored him. "As usual, they contain a variety of helpful items. In the left heel you'll find not only the plastic, X-ray-proof wire cutter and file, but also our new plastic dagger. It's very sharp, so be careful."

Bond picked out a round object with a lens on either side.

"Ah, that's a microfilm reader. Press the little button on top to activate the light. Look through it as you would a child's kaleidoscope. There's a small compartment there in the heel to store strips of microfilm maps. We have an extensive library of microfilm maps detailing every square mile on the face of the planet. Before you go abroad, simply put in a request for microfilm covering the areas you may be visiting. With that handy contraption, you'll never get lost, 007."

"Thank God for that," Bond quipped.

"Right. Now pay attention, 007. These shoes could save your life."

"Major, I do believe you've found your second calling."

Boothroyd went on. "The shoelaces are now easily inflammable, generating enough heat to melt a half-inch iron bar. There's a spare shoelace in the heel."

"Good thing, too," Bond said. "Shoelaces break at the damnedest times."

"There are pieces of flint and steel in there as well to start fires. Now take a look at the other shoe. You'll find the same prying tool under the tongue. Open up the heel on that one, if you would."

Bond did as he was told and found yet another cache of objects.

"As you know, this one's geared more for first aid. In the heel you'll find some vital medicines and supplies. There's a bottle of antiseptic, a pair of tweezers, acetaminophen tablets, generic amoxicyllin, and some bandages that are folded neatly in the sole of the shoe. We've added small tubes of sunblock and petroleum jelly."

"That's great," said Bond. "I can dispense with my sponge bag altogether and travel light for a change. What about an electric razor and toothbrush?"

"Why is it you never appreciate the things I do for you, 007? I work my fingers to the bone, put in extra hours at weekends, and what do I get for it? You think my salary is anything to write home about? Why can't you ever say 'thank you' for once?"

Bond stood and patted Boothroyd on the shoulder. "Thank you, Major, but you're beginning to sound like my dear old aunt Charmian did back when I was in my teens."

"Hmph. I imagine you were just as disrespectful to her."

"Never. She had a temper worthy of SMERSH."

Boothroyd stood. "Do you have any questions about the shoes, 007?"

"Only one," Bond said.

"What's that?"

"Do you have any socks to go with them?"

5

The Pearl in the Crown

Zero Minus Nine: June 22, 1997, 10:30 A.M., Hong Kong

There was once a pilot who adequately described the flight to Hong Kong as "hours of ennui, followed by a few minutes of sheer terror!" Kai Tak, or Hong Kong International Airport, consisted of a single runway; yet there was an average of 360 movements a day, scheduled at two-minute intervals in peak periods. Pilots considered it among the more challenging landings on the globe; for passengers, it's one of the most nerve-wracking.

Certainly no stranger to daredevil aerial maneuvers, James Bond nevertheless felt a surge of excitement as he looked out the window of the British Airways 747 on its approach to the fabled city. Down below was a harbor littered with boats and surrounded by layered levels of skyscrapers. It seemed that the plane would fly straight into the buildings; but it quickly lowered to make a steep, forty-seven-degree turn and touched down on the narrow strip of land on the Kowloon peninsula.

If India was once known as the "Jewel in the Crown," then Hong Kong was perhaps the "Pearl in the Crown." Its mere existence was one of the wonders of the modern world. It began as a barren island with very little population, and now it ranked among the world's fifteen largest trading entities and was Asia's busiest tourist destination. The mix of British management and Chinese entrepreneurial enthusiasm made Hong Kong a cosmopolitan harmony of East and West. It was a commercial, manufacturing, and financial dynamo; and it was the communication and transportation intersection for all Asia.

In nine days, Hong Kong would no longer be Britain's Pearl in the Crown. People had speculated for years on what would happen when the colony was handed back to China. One school of thought was that Hong Kong was finally being returned to the China it had economically and culturally always belonged to. Britain had only "borrowed" it long enough to encourage it to blossom in a British structure. Bond had heard people ask, "What will China do to Hong Kong?" He thought the more intriguing question might be "What will Hong Kong do to China?"

The airport terminal was noisy, crowded, and chaotic. Bond moved with the crowd into the Buffer Hall. The office had provided him with plenty of Hong Kong currency, so he didn't have to bother with foreign-exchange queues. Immigration went smoothly and quickly. Bond's cover was that of a *Daily Gleaner* journalist covering the Hong Kong handover to China.

Bond took the third exit out of Buffer Hall into the greeting area, which was packed with the families and friends of incoming passengers. He spotted the yellow baseball cap, and beneath it, the friendly smile of a Chinese man.

"No charge for ride to hotel," the man said to Bond.

"But I have the correct change," Bond replied.

"No problem," the man said, turning his *r*s into *l*s the way Chinese often do. "I even take you on scenic route, uh huh?" His English was slightly broken, but his vocabulary was very good.

"That would be lovely, then," Bond said, and smiled. These code exchanges, though necessary, were sometimes ridiculous.

The man held out his hand. "T. Y. Woo at your service. How was flight?"

"Too long." Bond shook his hand. "I'm Bond. Call me James."

"You call me T.Y. You are hungry, uh huh?" He had an endearing habit of adding "uh huh?" to his sentences.

"Famished."

"Your hotel has excellent restaurant. I take you, okay?" Woo reached for Bond's carry-on bag, which Bond gladly allowed him to take. Bond held on to the attaché case, which contained documentation of his cover identity and other assorted personal items. His Walther PPK was stored in an X-ray-proof compartment in the case.

When the men reached the street, a red Toyota Crown Motors taxicab with a silver roof screeched to a halt on the double yellow line edging the road.

"Quick, get in," Woo said. He opened the back door and gestured for Bond to jump inside.

A policeman on the street blew his whistle and shouted something in Chinese at the driver. The driver, a young teenage boy, shouted something back in Chinese. By then, both men were inside and the cab sped away.

"That was restricted zone. Cabs not supposed to stop," Woo explained, smiling.

Bond noticed the meter wasn't running. "Is this a company car?"

"Yes, James," Woo said. Bond noticed that his new friend rarely relaxed his broad smile. "Meet my son Woo Chen, you call him Chen Chen, uh huh?" The boy grinned at Bond in the rear-view mirror. Bond nodded at him and smiled.

"Relax, we go for ride!" Chen Chen exclaimed enthusiastically.

The cab pulled in front of a Rolls-Royce, making room for itself in the congested traffic. Although the flow moved slowly, Chen Chen managed to swerve in and around vehicles to maintain a significantly faster speed. Bond held his breath a couple of times during the first few minutes of the journey until he assured himself that the boy knew what he was doing.

"Chen Chen too young to drive," Woo said, still grinning. "I pull strings to get him license!"

Bond cleared his throat and said, "He drives very well. How old are you, Chen Chen?"

"Fifteen," the boy said, grinning just like his father. "Sixteen next month!"

The cab moved along through the traffic and finally entered the Cross-Harbour Tunnel. It was a two-lane, congested thorough-fare two kilometers long.

"Your hotel on Hong Kong side. Airport is on Kowloon side," Woo explained. Bond knew that, but he nodded as if he was learning something. "Very nice hotel," Woo continued. "Expensive. They have good restaurant at top. Private. We can talk, uh huh?"

The cab pushed its way through the tunnel and emerged into the light of Hong Kong Island. Throngs of people cluttered the sidewalks. At intersections, there were queues eight people deep waiting to cross the street. Bond had studied the latest intelligence and census reports on the city-state during the flight. Between five and six million people now resided in the relatively small area that comprised the territory. It was essentially a Cantonese city, most of the population being ethnic Chinese. The other small percentage were known as "expats," or foreigners who had taken residence in the colony. These expats were of many nationalities—Filipinos, Americans, Canadians, British, Thai, Japanese, and Indians being the most prominent. Bond thought it was a cultural melting pot like no other.

"If you get tired of hotel, you come to safe house," Woo said. "Near Hollywood Road, east end of Western District."

The cab zigzagged through Connaught Road in the Central District of the island and screeched to a halt beside a white block building over twenty stories tall. The Mandarin Oriental's unimpressive exterior apparently did a fine job of hiding one of the world's most sophisticated hotels. While most English businessmen might have stayed at the more Colonial-style Peninsula Hotel in Kowloon, Bond always preferred the Mandarin Oriental whenever he was in Hong Kong. Hotel rooms were hard to come by this week, as many had been booked as much as a year in advance of the July 1 transition. Luckily, SIS had made a reservation long ago in anticipation of sending someone just to be present on the fateful night.

Woo said, "You check in. I meet you in Chinnery Bar at noon, uh huh?"

"Fine," Bond said, taking his bag and opening the door. "Thank you, Chen Chen."

"No problem," said the grinning youth.

The hotel lobby was discreetly elegant and surprisingly subdued. Bond checked in and was ushered to his room on the twenty-first floor by a cheerful bellhop. It was the "Lotus Suite," consisting of two large rooms and a terrace overlooking the harbor. The hotel even provided a pair of binoculars for sight-seeing. The sitting room included a writing desk, bar, television/stereo system, and a bathroom for guests. The bedroom contained a king-size bed and a large private bathroom. Once he was alone, Bond immediately opened the refrigerator and pulled out a bottle of vodka. He put two ice cubes into a glass and poured a large measure. It was early, but the flight had been long and he needed to unwind.

Bond stood and watched a small section of the harbor as *kaidos*, sampans, junks, and *walla-wallas* scurried back and forth. There were people in Hong Kong who lived and worked on their little boats and rarely set foot on land. As Westernized as it was, Hong Kong was still a very different world.

Bond changed from his business suit into a light blue cotton short-sleeve polo shirt and navy blue cotton twill trousers. He put on a light, gray silk basketweave jacket, under which he kept his Walther PPK in a chamois shoulder holster.

At noon, he went down to The Chinnery, a bar decorated much like an English gentlemen's club with masculine brown and red deep leather-upholstered armchairs; in fact, Bond remembered that it used to be exclusively all-male. It was only in 1990 that the bar began to admit women. It was adorned with original paintings by British artist George Chinnery, whose drawings and paintings of the landscapes and people of Macau, Canton, and Hong Kong made him the undisputed doyen of foreign artists of the China coast in the mid-1800s. The room was already filling with smoke from businessmen's pipes, cigars, and cigarettes. Bond noted that the collection of seemingly countless bottles of Scotch whisky was still behind the bar.

T. Y. Woo was already there, and Bond joined him.

"Welcome to Hong Kong, Ling Ling Chat," Woo said. Bond knew that Ling Ling Chat was "007" in Cantonese. "Let us drink. Then we will go upstairs and have lunch, uh huh?"

Bond ordered a vodka martini, but he had to explain twice to the waiter that he wanted the drink shaken and not stirred. Woo shrugged and had the same. "We drink mostly cognac here," he said.

"Hmm," Bond said. "That's more of a nightcap for me."

Over their cocktails the two men began to get to know each other. T. Y. Woo had been with the Secret Service for twenty-five years. His family had come from southern China several decades ago and had made a fortune in the antique and curio business. Woo and his brother ran a shop on Upper Lascar Row, and this provided a perfect front for the Hong Kong headquarters of the British Secret Service. SIS, then called MI6, had recruited him in the sixties. A British agent on self-imposed R and R had wandered into Woo's shop during the Vietnam War. He was an elite Double-O operative who had been assigned to assist American GIs deep in the jungle. Impressed with Woo's cheerful disposition and willingness to "do something exciting," the agent brought Woo to London. After several months of training, he could get by with what he had learned of the English language and could make succinct intelligence reports. Woo's double life as a shopkeeper and an intelligence officer took its toll on his wife, who left him ten years ago. He had raised Chen Chen on his own.

At 12:30, the men took the lift to the twenty-fifth floor and entered the Man Wah Restaurant, one of the finest in the colony. A lovely Chinese woman wearing a slinky *cheongsam*, a traditional tight-fitting dress with a seductive slit revealing a bit of leg, led them to a table. Unlike most restaurants in Hong Kong, which were usually noisy and full of cheerful clamor, this one was an intimate, quiet place. The blue carpet, wood-framed maroon paneling, and Oriental paintings all contributed to a luxurious ambience. A bonsai tree covered with tiny white blooms sat on their table, which was next to a large picture window overlooking the harbor.

The menu specialized in Cantonese-style cooking, the distinctive cuisine of Guangdong Province. It was considered the most varied and interesting in all China. This was due partly to south China's subtropical climate, which produced a huge range of fruits and vegetables and all kinds of seafood. The style of cooking used steaming and quick stir-frying to enhance the qualities of food. An experienced cook knew when a dish was done by the sizzling sound that emanated from the wok. It was the lightest and least oily of all the regional cooking styles, seasoned by a wide variety of sauces rather than spices. Vegetables, seafood, pork, and chicken were the main ingredients.

"Mr. Bond! Welcome to Hong Kong!"

He knew the voice at once. It belonged to Henry Ho, the general manager of the Man Wah, a fellow Bond had known for years. Ho was a most pleasant gentleman, and an expert in the culinary delights. The soft-spoken man had dark hair and smiling eyes. Never hesitating to join a party at their table, Ho always had a story to tell about the food he served. Today was no exception.

"Hello, Henry," Bond said, shaking his hand. "It's good to see you again."

"Yes, yes, it is very good to see you, too," Ho said. "Mr. Woo called yesterday to say an important guest was coming. He didn't say it was you! I have prepared some special dishes!"

The meal began with an appetizer of cucumber and what Ho

called "black fungus"—ginger covered in a dark red crust. The first course was Chili Prawns, a Szechuan-style dish. Bond liked Szechuan cuisine, which was infinitely spicier than Cantonese. It was said that China's leader, Deng Xiaoping, preferred Szechuan food. Ho explained that the food from Szechuan Province was hotter because of the humid climate—the people ate spicy food to help release moisture from their bodies. The large prawns were cooked in garlic, chili, and sesame oil, and were simply delicious.

A rich plum wine called "yellow wine," served warm, was brought to the table between courses. Bond thought it tasted like sake.

The second course was an elaborate serving of sautéed filet of sole with green vegetables in a black bean sauce. The presentation was spectacular—several large carrots had been carved to resemble a dragon boat, the kind used in the famous Dragon Boat Festival that occurs every summer, and the food was placed inside the boat. The sole was quite tender and flavorful, because in Hong Kong the sole can swim in both fresh and salt water.

The main course was called Beggar's Chicken, which was Chef Lao's creation of baked chicken in clay with black mushrooms, barbecued pork, ginger, and Chinese spices. This dish must be ordered at least a day in advance, as it is cooked many hours before serving. The chicken is cleaned and stuffed with the various ingredients, then wrapped in lotus leaves. Then the package is packed in clay and baked until the clay is hard.

When the dish was brought to Bond and Woo, all the waiters and staff stood around and applauded as the diners took turns whacking and breaking the clay with a mallet. A waiter then picked out the large bones from the extremely tender chicken, mixed in a special sauce, and served it in shreds on small plates. Bond thought it was one of the tastiest meals he had ever had in his life.

Ho brought them tea after Bond and Woo had stuffed themselves and, joining at the table, said, "There is a region in southeast China called Fook Tien Province, and there the largest variety of tea is produced. There is one leaf that is very intriguing. Its name is Monkey-Pick-Tea.

"According to legend," Ho continued, "the tea leaves are collected by monkeys because they are positioned on high cliff-tops. But the monkeys were not very obedient, and they needed to be disciplined. Whenever a monkey disobeyed, a part of his tail was cut off—a half-inch or so! This would continue until the monkey learned to do as he was instructed. Monkey-Pick-Tea is very highly regarded because it is difficult to come by, and also for the reason that it is rich in both aroma and taste. Therefore, its qualities are compared to those of a fine wine. We drink it after a meal, not only because it is enjoyable but because it also helps one to digest."

After the meal, Bond and Woo were left alone to discuss business.

"So, T.Y., what's going on? What do you know?" Bond asked.

"The solicitor who was killed—that bomb was not act of China, uh huh?" Woo said.

"That's what M thinks, too," Bond replied. "Who do you think is behind it?"

"There is a general in Guangzhou. His name is Wong. Very militant. He is violently opposed to any kind of democratic rule in Hong Kong after takeover. He has been in favor of taking over colony by force for years. He is biting his nails on other side of border, just waiting for chance to move in his troops and take control. Beijing keeps him on short leash. Someone trying to put blame on him. Not sure he is responsible."

"Why do you say that?" Bond asked.

"It is stupid! Why would he do such a thing weeks before Hong Kong goes back to China? What would he gain by starting war between China and Britain? On second thought, he just might be that stupid. Not a rational man, uh huh?"

"Those are his troops lining the border?"

"Yes. Mostly his. He would march into New Territories tomorrow if Beijing gave him okay." Woo shrugged. "It is possible that he is trying to provoke confrontation between Britain and China. He wants excuse to move in. And from looks of things, he is succeeding."

"But surely he wouldn't dare bring his troops across the border before the first of July. The whole world is watching."

"General Wong does not care. He is madman. He considers himself national hero in China. He is hard, cruel man. I tell you something else about him. Wong spent most of 1980s in Beijing. He was one of high commanders responsible for Tiananmen Square tragedy. He enjoyed giving orders to shoot those people. After that, he was promoted and moved back to Guangzhou, where he was from."

"All right, he's a suspect. Who else is on your short list?"

"My personal opinion? I think it is someone local. Could be Triad. On other hand, it is not their method. Not many criminals have guns or bombs in Hong Kong. You would be surprised— Hong Kong is quite gun-free."

"What about the two Chinese officials who were killed by a British officer?"

"That is big mystery," Woo said. "Again, I do not think it was real British officer. Whole thing was staged. He was impostor."

"I was thinking the same thing."

"Again—why would this officer want to cause trouble? Unless he has a personal grudge. And who is he to take on the government of China?"

"And the floating-restaurant bomb?" Bond asked.

"Same thing. It was not China. It was not General Wong in Guangzhou, although that is rumor."

"What do you know about EurAsia Enterprises?"

"Big company. Very respectable. The *taipan*, he is well-liked but very private man, uh huh?"

"Thackeray."

"Yes. I have met him. I see him sometimes at casino in Macau. One of my few vices, I admit. I have played *mahjong* with him once or twice. Always lost a lot of money to him. EurAsia not as big as other major companies, like Jardine Matheson. But it does okay. Involved in shipping and trading. Their docks are at Kwai Chung."

"Do you know what happened in England a few nights ago?"

"Yes, I got briefing. Heroin. That surprised me. I have no records that EurAsia is involved in anything illegal. My contacts with police have assured me that nothing out of ordinary is on record."

"Yet that heroin came from one of their ships."

"I think Triad is involved. They have their fingers in everything. It is quite possible that someone in EurAsia is being squeezed by Triad and Thackeray does not know anything about it."

Bond ordered a brandy. "Are you familiar with the Dragon Wing Society?"

"Yes, I am. They are splinter group of San Yee On. Very powerful. Dragon Wing Society has interests in many nightclubs in Hong Kong. Most of their known activities involve prostitution and gambling. The police believe they are involved in heroin trade but have not acquired evidence. They put squeeze on entertainment industry, too. Movie sets are prime targets, uh huh?"

"Do you know anyone in the Triad?"

"A Triad leader is called the Cho Kun, or Dragon Head. Cho Kun of Dragon Wing is Li Xu Nan. Very powerful businessman. Owns several nightclubs and girlie bars. The identity of Cho Kun is supposed to be secret—no one outside of Triad knows." Woo grinned. "But I know."

"All Triads work that way?"

"Usually, yes. Only top men in Triad know. Their Lodge is secret, too."

"Lodge?"

"That is Triad's headquarters, where they hold meetings."

"Do you know where their Lodge is?"

Woo shook his head. "No, that *is* secret. I am working on it. They change locations often, so it is difficult."

"How can I find this Li Xu Nan?"

"Hard to say," Woo said. "He frequents a couple of his night-clubs. We maybe try later tonight or tomorrow."

"Okay, tell me more about Thackeray."

"He is in late forties. Bachelor. Does not go out in public much. Lives on the Peak with all the rich *gweilo.*" *Gweilo* is a term meaning "ghost people"—often used by ethnic Chinese in reference to Westerners.

"Has there been any investigation since the drug bust in England?"

"Yes. My contact in police said they searched EurAsia's warehouse at Kwai Chung. They found nothing. Official company line is that they are shocked and dismayed that something like that could have happened with one of their ships. EurAsia spokesman denied all responsibility and blamed act on criminal enterprise."

"I'm going to want to take a look at that warehouse myself."

"We can do that."

"And I want to meet Guy Thackeray. Can you arrange it?"

"How's your game of *mahjong?*"

Bond had little experience with the game that was so popular in Hong Kong. "Not very good, I'm afraid. I've played one of the Western versions a bit." The game's rules and play varied from country to country.

"No problem. I give you quick lessons. Hong Kong version easier than Western version or Japanese version, uh huh?"

"When does he play?" Bond asked.

"He plays tonight! You have money? Big stakes. Thackeray is big winner. I do not know how he does it. Always wins. If we get there before he does, we have better chance at getting in game with him. Let us go, okay?"

"Sure. Just how much capital will I stand to lose?"

"Thackeray plays one hundred Hong Kong dollars per point," Woo said with eyes wide. "With a two-point minumum, ten-point maximum! Maximum Hand is worth 38,400 Hong Kong dollars!"

Bond frowned. That meant that Thackeray played a very challenging and very risky game. A winning hand must be worth at least two points or a stiff monetary penalty would be imposed. SIS might lose thousands of pounds. Nevertheless, closely observing Thackeray for a couple of hours over an intense game of chance just might be the best way for Bond to evaluate him. He believed that a man revealed every side of his personality during the course of any gaming contest in which a great deal of money was at stake.

"Fine," said Bond. "Let's do it."

Woo caught the waiter's attention and said, "*Mai dan*," miming the international scribble gesture. "I get this, James. You are now indoctrinated into our concept of *maijiang*."

Bond said, "I know all about *maijiang*. Face. Reciprocity. In other words, I'll get the next one. *Sikdjo*."

Woo grinned. "Ah, you been to Hong Kong before?"

"Yes, a few times. Japan, too."

Bond knew the Eastern philosophy of *maijiang* was very important to Asian people. It meant, quite literally, the selling of credit. *Maijiang* was used when a person gave or was given face and when reciprocity was implicitly understood and expected. If a person did a favor for one man, then that man was expected to do something in return. Saying *sikdjo* meant Bond agreed.

Woo paid the bill and the two men left the relatively tranquil ambience of the restaurant. They did not notice the strange albino Chinese man who sat reading a newspaper at the Harlequin Bar, just outside the entrance to the Man Wah. As soon as they left, he went to make a phone call.

6

The Prevailing Wind

The Viking 66 Sports Cruiser skipped along the waters away from the Causeway Bay docks and into Victoria Harbour. T. Y. Woo introduced the captain as his older brother, J.J. The elder Woo, when not assisting at the antique store on Cat Street, was a yachting enthusiast. T.Y. often used his brother's boat for official secret service business. Like T.Y., J.J. was very agreeable. He said little; when Bond addressed him, J.J. would just nod his head and smile. Bond assumed the man's English wasn't as good as his brother's.

The boat was built in the United Kingdom primarily for the American market with U.S. components, but J.J. managed to have a model shipped over to Hong Kong. Apparently the Woo family had been very wealthy, and J.J. and T.Y. had each inherited a private fortune. The 66 had a solid glass hull, twin 820-hp MANs, and the capability of topping out at 30 knots. The deep-V design gave the boat true offshore capabilities—and a smooth ride. T.Y. proudly told Bond that J.J. had bought the boat for a song—only 1.5 million Hong Kong dollars.

It was still broad daylight. The harbor was still extremely busy and full of all types of vessels. T.Y. told Bond that they had nothing to fear from the marine police—his boat was registered with them and would not be stopped. Even so, it was apparently not at all difficult to slip away from Hong Kong and over to Macau without Immigration finding out. The only trick was finding a discreet place to dock in Macau.

After twenty minutes, the boat was speeding through the strait north of Lantau Island and below the New Territories. Soon they were out in the open South China Sea. J.J. opened up the MANs, and the Viking reached maximum speed.

"We will be in Macau in another three-quarters hour, uh huh?" T.Y. said, grinning. The wind was blowing through his short dark hair, and Woo seemed to take great pleasure in the sensation. Bond was feeling the jet lag. He hoped some strong coffee would sharpen his wits enough to play a fast-paced game of *mahjong*, especially since he was not very familiar with it.

"Where are we going exactly?" Bond asked.

"Lisboa Hotel and Casino," Woo said. "Not one of my favorite establishments."

Bond knew the Lisboa. It was a prime tourist attraction in the legendary territory. Macau's history was almost as colorful as Hong Kong's. It predated the British colony by several centuries, its story part of the seaborne Age of Exploration that brought fifteenth-century Portugal to glory. Trade was the underlying catalyst for its development, specifically the immense wealth to be gained from the spices and silks of the Orient. The port of Macau was set up by the mid-1500s as a stop between Malacca and Japan. The territory flourished, especially during the early seventeenth century. By the twentieth century, however, it had declined and had developed a reputation as a hotbed of spies, vice, and intrigue. In 1987, the anticolonial Portuguese government signed an official agreement with China to hand over Macau on December 20, 1999. Unlike Hong Kong, Macau residents who gave up residency had the right to live in any EC country, including, ironically, Great Britain.

"You need quick *mahjong* reminder?" Woo asked Bond.

"That would be most helpful."

Woo gestured that they should get out of the wind and into the boat's cabin. They left the teak-covered deck, went below, and sat at a small table. Woo made some strong coffee and said, "Okay, tell me what you know."

"The game is a mixture of gin rummy, dominoes, and poker, you might say. There are four players who play against each other. There isn't much skill involved, mostly luck, and the trick is to play defensively and try to outguess what your opponents need. There are three suits—Bamboo Sticks, Circles, and Characters. There are four sets of tiles numbered one through nine in each of the three suits. There are also four Red Dragon tiles, four Green Dragon, four White Dragon, and four tiles of each 'wind'—the East Wind, West Wind, and so on."

"Yes, that is all true," Woo said. "There *is* skill, James. You must play fast and be creative in building your hand for most possible points. Every point worth a lot of money, uh huh?" Woo grinned. "We brought eighty thousand Hong Kong dollars of company's cash to lose. I already cleared it with M. She just said we better not lose it!" Woo laughed at that. "If Thackeray on a roll like he always is, M is in for big surprise!"

"Why is he so good?" Bond asked. "The game really does depend on the luck of the draw, doesn't it?"

Woo shrugged. "I do not know. If he cheats, I do not know how he does it. It is very hard to cheat at *mahjong*, uh huh? He wins thousands of dollars a night playing."

The Viking sailed around the southern tip of Macau and made its way up the western side of the peninsula. Woo explained that it was easier to dock unseen over there, and they could take a taxi to the casino. They found a decrepit wooden dock hidden in some overgrowth.

"We use this dock before," Woo said. "Be careful when you step on it. It not very safe. Oh, I almost forget. We cannot take guns in casino. They have high security. Metal detectors. We must leave them here."

Bond remembered that from previous visits, and it made him very uncomfortable. Reluctantly, he handed J.J. his Walther PPK. "I hope I'm not going to need that later," he said.

J.J. told T.Y. in Chinese that he would stay with the boat, then proceeded to stretch out on the bunk in the cabin. Bond and Woo carefully stepped onto the dock. It was a short walking distance to an urban area, and they found a taxi within minutes.

The Hotel Lisboa was a barrel-shaped concrete building painted mustard and white, with walls corrugated like a waffle and roofs fashioned to resemble roulette wheels. As they entered the lobby, Bond noticed a collection of oddities on display: a small dinosaur skeleton, giant junks of carved ivory and jade, and a tapestry of the Great Wall. After passing through an unusually stringent security check, Bond followed Woo into the noisy, gaudy casino, where he had gambled a few times before. He was always amazed by the joylessness of the Macau casinos. Gambling in Macau was taken very seriously, and the participants did not look like happy people.

Woo stopped at a slot machine. "I must feed Hungry Tiger first," he said. He slipped a 2 Hong Kong dollar coin into the contraption and pulled the handle. He got a cherry, a bar, and an orange. He shrugged. "Come on, let's go find *mahjong* game."

The Lisboa was built on several levels, with different games of baccarat, blackjack, roulette, fan-tan, and slot machines played on different floors. The main rotunda room of the first floor was full of smoke and sweat. Playing *mahjong* at a casino was highly unusual. Thackeray's game was a private affair, and was played in a rented, secluded room.

Bond and Woo took the stairs to the third floor, past the VIP baccarat room, and into a less crowded area. Woo spoke to a guard, who gestured to his right. Bond followed Woo to an archway covered by red curtains. "We are in luck," Woo said. "Thackeray not here yet." He moved through the curtains and was greeted by an Englishman in his late thirties with wavy blond hair.

"Mr. Woo!" the man said. "I thought you had lost all your money the last time you were here! Don't tell me you've come back for more punishment?"

"Ah, Mr. Sinclair, you know that I must save face and try again," Woo said with humor. "This is my friend and business acquaintance, Mr. Bond. He would like to play tonight, too. Is that all right?"

Sinclair scrutinized Bond and recognized a fellow Englishman. He held out his hand. "Simon Sinclair."

"James Bond." The man had a firm handshake.

"What brings you to Macau, Mr. Bond?" Sinclair asked.

"I'm a reporter for a Jamaican paper, the *Daily Gleaner*," he said. "I'm covering the handover of Hong Kong next week."

Sinclair rolled his eyes. "You and how many other thousand journalists? Well, come in, come in."

It was a small room with a square table in the center. Chairs stood at each of the four sides, and a set of *mahjong* tiles were spread out, facedown, on the table. A Chinese stood behind a fully stocked bar on one side of the room, preparing a concoction in a blender. An archway on the opposite wall led into a small foyer, presumably to a private washroom.

"Do you know Mr. Thackeray, Mr. Bond?" Sinclair asked.

"No, I'm looking forward to meeting him," Bond said. "Mr. Woo here tells me that he's quite a player."

Sinclair laughed. "He takes me to the cleaners twice a week. I don't know why I continue to play with him—some sort of masochistic streak in me, I suppose."

"What do you do, Mr. Sinclair?" Bond asked.

"I work for EurAsia Enterprises. I was . . . um, recently promoted to general manager."

As if on cue, the curtains parted and Guy Thackeray walked in, followed by two bulky men who looked like bodyguards. He stopped to survey the room, but for some reason became unsteady for just a moment. He regained his composure quickly.

"Hello, Guy," Sinclair said. "You remember Mr. Woo?"

Woo held out his hand. "Hello, Mr. Thackeray. I have come to lose my money again, uh huh?"

Thackeray shook his hand but didn't smile. "A pleasure to take it, Mr. Woo." There was a slight slur to his speech.

Woo turned to Bond. "And this is my friend from Jamaica, Mr. James Bond. He is a journalist covering the Hong Kong handover."

Thackeray looked at Bond, sizing him up. Bond held out his hand and said, "How do you do?"

There was a slight pause before Thackeray took his hand, almost as if he wasn't sure whether or not he wanted to do so. Thackeray's grip was firm and dry.

"Welcome to the Far East, Mr. Bond," Thackeray said. "I hope you're a better *mahjong* player than your friend Mr. Woo." Bond smelled alcohol. The man was very drunk.

"I'm afraid I'm mostly accustomed to Western rules, but I shall do my best," Bond said.

The man looked like his photograph. He was very handsome, even if his face was a bit severe. Bond did note that Thackeray appeared tired. He had the look of a man under a great deal of stress. After what happened to EurAsia's board of directors, the man must be dealing with a massive amount of red tape.

"What can I get you to drink?" he asked.

"Vodka martini, shaken, please. Not stirred."

For the first time since he entered the room, Thackeray displayed the hint of a smile. "I like a man who's particular," he said, then walked over to the bartender.

Over the next few minutes, the two bodyguards turned away other prospective *mahjong* players who had inquired about the game. Although the room was private, the bodyguards didn't prevent spectators from coming and going. By the time the men were ready to play, six or seven other Chinese men were standing around the edges, chattering quietly among themselves.

"Don't let my sycophants disturb your concentration, Mr.

Bond," Thackeray said. "They like to bet on the various hands during the game."

"The more the merrier," Bond said.

Thackeray had brought Bond his martini and placed an entire bottle of vodka on the table for himself. He sat down, poured a glass, then took a gulp.

"Shall we begin?" Thackeray said, standing next to the table. "Do you know the rules for our game?" Without waiting for an answer, he continued. "Two-point minimum, ten-point maximum, a hundred Hong Kong dollars a point, standard doubling, Maximum Hand is 38,400 dollars. No chicken hands allowed. Agreed?"

"Chicken hand?" Bond asked.

Woo explained. "Ah, in Hong Kong version of game, that is what we call a winning hand that has both types of sets—Chows *and* Pongs or Kongs. It is easiest type of winning hand to get. But remember, a chicken hand is okay if you have points from other things, like Flowers or Winds."

Bond knew what Woo meant. A winning hand in *mahjong* consisted of fourteen tiles in a combination of "sets." A Chow was a set of three consecutively numbered tiles from any suit, such as a 1-2-3 or a 6-7-8. A Pong was a set of three of the same-number tiles from any given suit, such as three 6s in the Circles suit. A Kong was a set of four of the same-number tiles from any given suit. To "go out," a player's hand must contain three or four Chows, Pongs, and/or Kongs, plus one Pair of the same tiles in any suit. Special hands consisting of a combination of specific tiles were worth more points.

"So, are we agreed?" Thackeray asked again.

"Certainly," Bond said, feeling as if he was signing a pact with the devil.

Each player was required to hand over 50,000 Hong Kong dollars for a cache of chips. A Chinese man working for the casino acted as moderator and banker. He stacked up four tiles facedown in the center of the table.

Thackeray handed Bond the dice. "I'll let you have the honor of rolling for the pick of Winds."

Bond quickly went over in his mind the process of the game. *Mahjong* was divided into four Rounds, each named after the four Winds. The Round's name was known as the "Prevailing Wind" for all the hands played within the Round. Each player's seating position was also named after one of the four Winds. Players picked Wind tiles in turn to determine which seat, or Wind, they were to play at the beginning. Whoever chose the East Wind was the dealer for the first hand in the East Round. A Round consisted of a minimum of four hands, with the deal being passed around the table. The game would end once each of the four Winds had been the "Prevailing Wind." There was a minimum of sixteen hands, usually more, in a complete game of *mahjong*. Fast players could complete a game in less than an hour.

Bond rolled the dice and counted the players around the table counterclockwise, ending on Woo. Woo drew one of the tiles on the table. It was the South Wind. Thackeray was next, drawing the East Wind. Sinclair drew the West, and Bond was left with North. Thackeray pulled up a chair. Bond sat to Thackeray's left. Sinclair sat facing Thackeray, and Woo was across from Bond. Thus, for the East Wind Round, Thackeray was the number 1 seat, East, and dealer for the first hand. Woo was number 2, South; Sinclair was number 3, West; and Bond was number 4, North.

All four men began mixing the 144 tiles facedown on the table. This was done with a tremendous clatter. Then each player proceeded to build their side of the "the wall," consisting of 36 tiles stacked two high.

Bond decided this was a good time to try to get his target to open up. "Mr. Thackeray," he said, "I would welcome the opportunity to interview you regarding the Hong Kong handover. I understand your company is successful and well-regarded. You're an important man in the colony, and I'd like to know what you think about living under Chinese rule."

"You're lucky, Mr. Bond," Thackeray said, building the second layer of his wall. "I'm giving a press conference the day after tomorrow at four P.M. It'll be at the corporate headquarters in Central. You're welcome to attend. I'll make sure your name gets on the list."

"Thank you, I appreciate the invitation," Bond said. He thought he would try to get some kind of reaction out of the man. "Terrible thing that happened at that restaurant. I imagine it left you and your company devastated?"

Thackeray's wall was finished. He looked up at Bond and stared at him. "Yes" was all he said.

Bond pushed the man further. "I've always thought luck comes in waves, both good and bad. Didn't something happen to your solicitor, too? I heard something—"

"Mr. Bond, did you come here to discuss my personal affairs or to play *mahjong*?" Thackeray growled. What little humor the man possessed was now totally gone. Bond was convinced he was a perpetually cantankerous alcoholic.

"Oh, I came to play *mahjong*," Bond said. "Forgive me."

The four completed walls formed a perfect square on the table. Thackeray took three small dice and rolled them in the center of the table. He got a 10. Starting with himself, he counted the sides of the wall counterclockwise, ending up on the South wall in front of Woo. Then, after counting ten tiles from the right end of the South wall, Thackeray "broke" the wall by separating the tiles at that point. He took the four tiles to the left of the break. Woo picked up the next four tiles, followed by Sinclair, and then Bond. This was repeated until each player had twelve tiles. Then Thackeray took two more tiles to make fourteen, and the other players each took one tile. East always began a hand by discarding his fourteenth tile.

Bond arranged his tiles in front of him. It was a terrible hand. He had two useless blue Flowers. The blue and red Flower tiles gave points to a player if the Flower's number matched his seat or the name of the Round. Flowers were immediately exposed for all to see, and the vacant spots in the hand were replaced by new tiles.

Thackeray had one Flower—a Red #1, which luckily matched his seat. This automatically gave him one point. Thackeray drew a tile from the dead wall and kept it. The other two players had no Flowers, which was worth a point if either of them won the hand and could avoid drawing any Flowers during its play. Bond drew two new tiles—they were both North Winds, which were helpful. His hand contained a 1 of Sticks (designated by the picture of a sparrow holding a stick), a 5 of Sticks, a 6 of Sticks, another 6 of Sticks, a 2 of Circles, a 3 of Circles, a 9 of Circles, a 3 of Characters, an 8 of Characters, a White Dragon, a South Wind, two North Winds, and the useless blue #2 and #3 Flowers.

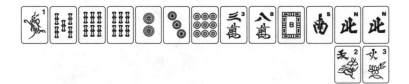

The most difficult thing about *mahjong* was deciding what kind of hand to go for and sticking with the objective. Good hands usually consisted of entirely Pongs and/or Kongs and the one Pair, or entirely Chows and a Pair. Bond's hand was almost impossible to predict. He had a pair of 6 of Sticks, and a possibility for a Chow of Circles. If he got another North Wind tile, he would have a Pong that matched his seat. This would automatically give him one point. Unless the draw was extremely favorable, he would have to go out with a chicken hand, so he needed to find a way to gain another point. Drawing the winning tile from the wall rather than from a discard would be worth a point as well as more money. Maybe he would get lucky.

Thackeray discarded a North Wind tile. Bond immediately said "Pong" and picked up the tile. It was unbelievable luck on the very first discard! Bond displayed the three North Wind tiles faceup on the table.

"Well, you're off to a good start, Mr. Bond," Thackeray said.

It was Bond's turn to discard. He got rid of the 1 of Sticks. It was then Thackeray's turn again, because turns resume to the right of any player that Chows, Pongs, or Kongs. Thackeray drew from the wall and discarded an 8 of Circles. Woo drew from the wall and discarded a North Wind tile, now useless because of Bond's Pong. Sinclair drew from the wall and discarded a 3 of Sticks. Bond drew a 2 of Sticks. Damn! If he hadn't discarded the 1 of Sticks earlier, he would have had a chance at making a Chow with another 3 of Sticks.

Play continued uneventfully around the table one more time until Sinclair discarded an East Wind. Thackeray said "Kong" and picked it up. He displayed four East Wind tiles, which automatically gave him two points—one point for possessing a Pong or Kong of Winds matching his seat, and one point for matching the Prevailing Wind. Along with his #1 Red Flower, he already had a total of three points. All he had to do now was win the hand in any possible manner.

Thackeray drew a tile, then discarded a 6 of Circles. Play continued around the table. Sinclair made a Pong from Woo's discard of a White Dragon. This made Bond's White Dragon useless, so he got rid of it with his next discard.

After a while, the discards were strewn haphazardly faceup in the middle of the table. When it was his turn, Thackeray reached across the table to draw a tile from the wall. He discarded a 4 of Circles. Bond could have used it to make a Chow, but a player can Chow only with the discard from the player on his immediate left. Besides, his Pong of North Winds had committed the hand to go for all Pongs or Kongs. If he had any Chows in his hand now, he would have a worthless chicken hand.

On Woo's discard of a 2 of Characters, Thackeray said "Kong" again and took it. The man had extraordinary luck.

After each player had drawn and discarded two more times, Bond was no better off than he was before. He discarded an 8 of Circles he had drawn, and Thackeray immediately said, "Out!" and picked up the tile.

All the players displayed their hands. Thackeray had a Full

House, a term given to any hand worth four, five, or six points. Thackeray had six. He got three points for having all Kongs or Pongs in his hand (plus the required Pair), two points for the East Winds matching his seat and the Prevailing Wind, and one point for the Flower. He won a total of $6400—Sinclair and Woo each paid $1600; Bond had to pay $3200 because Thackeray won with Bond's discard. Thackeray would have received a seventh point if he had picked the winning tile from the wall.

After each hand, the players' Wind assignment and the deal rotated counterclockwise, unless the East Wind player won the hand or the hand was a "dead hand," or draw. Once all four players had a turn at being the East Wind, then a new Round, the South Wind Round, would begin. Thackeray had the privilege of dealing again. During the deal, Thackeray asked, "Mr. Woo, what was it you said you do? I can't for the life of me remember what business you are in."

"I run antique shop on Cat Street," Woo said, smiling.

"And how do you two know each other?" Thackeray asked, gesturing to both Bond and Woo.

"T.Y. and I knew each other in London before I moved to Jamaica," Bond said casually.

Bond's new hand started off promising. He had three pairs. It was possible to build a hand of Pongs or Kongs, or he could try for seven pairs—a special hand worth four points.

It was about five minutes before Sinclair declared "Out" on a self-picked tile from the wall. He revealed a hand worth three points—one point for the self-pick, one point for a Pong of Red Dragons, and one point for a #3 Flower, which matched his seat. Everyone had to pay him $1600.

This time the seat/Wind assignments rotated. Woo was now East and Bond was West. Woo rolled the dice and started the deal. During this hand, Bond lit one of the cigarettes he kept in a wide gunmetal case. There was a time when Bond smoked sixty to seventy cigarettes a day. Around the time of the Thunderball case, he reduced his intake to twenty or twenty-five. Morlands of Grosvenor

Street had been the recipient of Bond's business for many years. They had made a special blend of Balkan and Turkish tobacco for Bond and decorated each cigarette with three gold bands. Recently, Bond switched companies and commissioned H. Simmons of Burlington Arcade to create a low-tar cigarette for him. These still retained the distinctive gold bands, along with a Simmons trademark. With this switch, he had managed to reduce his intake of tobacco even further, down to five or six cigarettes a day. He once joked to Bill Tanner that it was easy to quit—he had done it at least twelve times.

The play of the third hand went very quickly. Once, when Thackeray reached across the table to draw a tile from the wall, Bond thought he saw something strange. Was there a flash of the back of a tile in the man's hand? He couldn't be sure. He would watch the table a little more closely and pay less attention to his own hand from now on.

Thackeray won the third hand with a total of three points—one point for a self-picked winning tile, one point for having no Flowers, and one point for having a hand of all Chows and a pair. Everyone paid him $1600.

Seat/Wind assignments rotated again. Sinclair was East and dealer, and Bond was South. Bond was dealt what amounted to very close to a winning hand, even though it was a chicken hand containing a mixture of possible Chows and Pongs. Luckily, he drew no Flowers, which was worth one point. He had a chance of winning small. Play progressed five times around the table when Bond drew a tile from the wall that completed his hand. He declared "Out" and displayed his miserable hand. The self-picked tile saved him, as that was worth one point. His two points garnered him a measly $800 from each player.

While the men played, several people came and went through the red curtains. Some of the Chinese spectators were apparently winning a great deal of money. At one point, Bond was struck by a bizarre sight. Two Chinese men with pinkish-white skin and white hair came into the room, stood together against a wall, and watched. They were both wearing sunglasses and looked alike. Not only were they obviously siblings, but they were both albino! That was very unusual in this part of the world, Bond thought. In the past, Asian families would have considered such children to be "unnatural" and would have found a way to get rid of them.

The seat/Wind assignments rotated for the last time of this Round. Bond was now East and the dealer. He got a promising hand containing a complete Pong of the 6 of Circles, and two pairs. As they played, Bond thought he noticed something unusual again when Thackeray reached across the discarded tiles to draw a tile from the wall. Thackeray had Ponged with the 4 of Characters early in the hand. Bond decided to throw down Characters to see if Thackeray might be collecting them for a big hand. When it was his turn, Bond discarded a 6 of Characters near his side of the table. Sure enough, he noticed that the tile had mysteriously disappeared a few minutes later!

Thackeray went out for three points. He had a Semi-Pure hand, which meant that his hand was made up entirely of one suit with the exception of a Pong of Winds or Dragons—in this case a Pong of West Winds. Woo had thrown the winning discard, so he owed Thackeray $1800, and the others paid him $900. Bond saw that Thackeray's revealed hand contained a Pong of the 6 of Characters.

It was agreed that they stand, stretch, and refill their drinks in between the Rounds. Thackeray had polished off a third of the bottle of vodka. Bond and Woo stepped up to the bar and ordered doubles. Bond took a moment to look around the room. The albino brothers were gone.

"I told you he wins a lot," Woo whispered. "I think I will lose more money than usual, uh huh?"

"T.Y., there are two things I don't like about that man," whispered Bond.

"What?"

"He's a lousy drunk, and I believe the bastard's cheating."

7

Jade Dragon

The game resumed with the South Wind Round. Thackeray, as the East Wind seat, was dealer. Bond was determined to verify his suspicion that the man was a cheat. He recalled what he knew about Thackeray. The man had been a stage magician when he was younger. He might very well be adept at sleight of hand and parlor tricks. He was probably palming discarded tiles from the table as he reached over them to draw a tile from the wall. The big question was why would he cheat? He was very wealthy. He didn't need the money. Or did he? Could the obliteration of his board of directors have left his company in a bad state? Did the impending mainland takeover of Hong Kong have something to do with it? The alcohol, the cheating, and his belligerent manner all added up to something inherently reckless about him.

Bond drew a very good hand. His first discard was a lone East Wind tile. He had two Pongs and the possibility of one more. He was determined to find a way to beat Thackeray at his own game. To come out and accuse him of cheating would be unacceptable. Bond needed to gain Thackeray's confidence, not alienate him! If

Bond caused a scene here in the casino, he might blow his cover and permanently botch up the mission. He would have to find a way to cheat, too. As play progressed, he examined every angle. He didn't have the sleight-of-hand ability that Thackeray had, so that was out of the question. Perhaps at the next break he could enlist Woo's help.

Thackeray went out with a lucrative five points: three points for four Pongs, one point for holding no Flowers, and one point for a Pong of East Winds, matching his seat. Bond scanned the discarded tiles, looking for the East Wind tile he had discarded at the beginning of the game; he didn't see it. Thackeray had to have palmed it somehow. Poor Woo threw the winning discard, so he had to pay $3200. The others counted out chips worth $1600. Woo was no longer smiling.

The seat/Wind assignments did not change for the next hand. Now that the enormity of the dollar value for each hand was sinking in, a certain tension enveloped the entire room. Spectators were less animated and chatty. Whereas *mahjong* was usually a noisy, social game, this one had become deadly serious.

Sinclair won the hand on a self-pick with two points. The other players had to pay him $800 each.

Woo became the dealer for the next hand, which ended dead. The hand was played again, and this time Thackeray won small with two points on Sinclair's discard. Sinclair had to pay $800, the others $400 each.

Sinclair dealt the next hand. Woo got lucky and went out with three points on a self-pick. Everyone paid him $1600, which brought the smile back to his face.

Bond got the deal next and was determined to get through the rest of the South Round quickly so he could discuss his strategy with Woo. Thackeray won again, this time with three points on a self-pick. He was paid $1600 from each player.

They were halfway through the game. Bond had lost an enormous amount of money. He and Woo ordered doubles at the bar.

"What have we got into, James?" Woo said, shaking his head. "I did not expect to lose this badly."

"I have a plan," Bond said. "Let's go outside and get some fresh air."

The two men excused themselves.

Thackeray said, "Don't be long." He was sitting alone, sipping his vodka on the rocks. Despite his winnings, he wasn't smiling. In fact, he looked downright miserable.

Outside, Bond said, "I don't get it. Why is he so morose? He's just won a few thousand dollars and he's acting as if it's his last day on earth."

"Thackeray very private man," Woo said. "He has no friends or family, from what I can tell. I wonder if someone close to him was killed by bomb at restaurant."

"Well, we've got to beat him. He's definitely cheating. He was a stage magician when he was young, and obviously knows sleight of hand. He's palming tiles he wants from the dead pile. I'm going to need your help."

"Sure, James. What you want me to do?"

"Listen very carefully. You're going to have to throw me some tiles that I need, and I'm going to give you some signals to indicate what they are. You have to watch me closely."

"All right."

"I'm going to scratch areas on the left side of my face to indicate that I need tiles with numbers 1 to 4. If I scratch the left side of my nose, I need a 1. If I scratch my cheekbone just under my eye, I need a 2. I'll scratch my earlobe for a 3. And I'll scratch my neck for a 4. If I need a 5, I'll scratch the bridge of my nose. The same areas apply to the right side of my face for the numbers 6 to 9. The right side of my nose is a 6, the cheekbone is a 7, the earlobe is an 8, and the neck is a 9. Got it?"

"Okay. What about suits?"

"Immediately after I give you one of my scratching signals, I'll take a drink. If I take one sip, I need Circles. If I take two sips, I need Sticks. If I take three sips, I need Characters."

Woo repeated all of this to make sure he had it.

"For the special tiles, I'll rub my eyes as if I have a headache if I need a Red Dragon. If I cough twice, I need a Green Dragon. If I sigh heavily, I need a White Dragon. If I need Winds, I'll light a cigarette. I'll place the cigarette on the ashtray with the butt pointing to the player corresponding to the Wind I need. For instance, if I need an East Wind tile, I'll point the butt toward the player who is currently the East seat. Got it?"

"That is brilliant, James! We will win good, uh huh?"

"Well, we'll see. It still depends on the luck of the draw and if you even have the tiles I need, but this might give us an advantage. I may be winning on your discards, so you'll have to pay out a little more to me. I'll make sure you get it back."

"No problem, James."

"Come on, let's get back in there."

The West Round began with Thackeray as the East seat and dealer for the third time. Bond got a good hand. He had a Pong of the 3 of Circles, a pair of the 2 of Sticks, a pair of East Wind tiles, and a pair of South Wind tiles. During play, Bond nonchalantly scratched his left cheekbone, then took two sips from his martini. Amazingly, Woo had the 2 of Sticks, and he threw it. Bond said "Pong," and took it. He luckily drew another East Wind tile later, and managed to form another Pong on his own. He just needed a pair to complete his hand. He had a single White Dragon and an 8 of Characters. Bond let out a sigh, but apparently Woo didn't have a White Dragon tile. Bond went for the other one and scratched his right earlobe, then took three sips from his drink. Woo discarded an 8 of Characters. Bond went out with three points for his all-Pong hand. Woo had to pay $1600, the others $800.

Thackeray won the second hand with another Full House. He had three points for a Semi-Pure hand, one point from a self-picked winning tile, and one point for holding a Flower tile matching his seat. Everyone had to pay him $3200!

Woo looked quite pale after that one. Sinclair took up the deal, but the result was a dead hand. It was dealt again, and this time

Woo got lucky with another small win. He went out with two points. It was a chicken hand, but he self-picked the winning tile and had a Flower matching his seat. Everyone paid him $800.

Bond became the dealer for the last hand in the West Round. His hand was so bad that his signal system was useless. Thackeray managed to win with three points. He self-picked from the wall (one point), had four Chows (one point), and had no Flowers (one point). Everyone paid him $1600.

During the break before the last Round of the game, Woo whispered to Bond, "Is your plan going to work?"

Bond replied, "It has to this time. It's the damnedest game—even cheating depends on luck! In a situation that involves gambling, I never trust luck. I try to get by without it. But this is one time we need all the luck we can get. Just stick to what we agreed. I'm going for broke this time."

The North Round began with Thackeray as East and dealer. Bond drew a #4 Red Flower, which matched his seat. That was one point straightaway! The rest of his hand was very promising. He had a complete Pong of Green Dragons, a Red Dragon, and a White Dragon. If he could get two more of either of the Red or White Dragons and one of the other, he could go out with what was called a "Semi-Big Dragon" hand (two Dragon Pongs and a pair of the other Dragon), worth three points. If he could make the third Dragon a complete Pong, the hand would be worth six points. He also needed to complete another Pong or Kong out of some Circles or Sticks he held.

Play progressed uneventfully until Bond drew a Red Dragon from the wall. Now all he needed was a third Red Dragon and at least one White Dragon.

At his first opportunity, Bond rubbed his eyes. Woo acknowledged the signal with a slight nod of his head. A moment later, Bond sighed heavily. Thackeray looked up at Bond and said, "What's the matter, Mr. Bond? Are we boring you?"

"Oh no, I'm just starting to feel the jet lag," he explained. "I just arrived today."

When Thackeray reached across the table to draw from the wall, Bond noticed that the man palmed another tile. It was now a matter of time before one of them went out. Bond gave Woo the signals for a 6 of Sticks and the 3 of Circles, which might complete his third Pong.

Woo did a great job of pretending to agonize over what tile to discard. He threw a Red Dragon and Bond called "Pong!" Now if he could get the White one . . .

Play continued around the table until Sinclair discarded a White Dragon. Thackeray immediately said "Pong!" Damn! Thackeray had the other three White Dragons and now there was no way to make a pair with his single tile. Bond threw the useless tile when it was his turn to discard. There was still hope—he had two Dragon Pongs, worth a point each.

Thackeray Ponged again, this time with a 2 of Characters. Come on, Woo, Bond willed. Throw something good! It didn't happen. From the look on Woo's face, he was troubled by the lack of help he could give Bond.

Bond drew the #4 Blue Flower from the wall, adding another point to his possible score. On his next turn, he drew the badly needed 3 of Circles. Now all he lacked was to make a pair out of the two single tiles he had—the 4 of Characters or the 6 of Sticks. Bond gave the signals for the two tiles and Woo took a sip from his drink. On Bond's discard, though, Thackeray called "Pong!" again. He was ready to go out as well.

Woo drew from the wall and discarded the 4 of Characters. Bond called "Out!" and displayed his hand of four points—two Dragon Pongs (one point each) and two Flowers matching his seat. Woo had to pay $3200, the others $1600.

Woo became the dealer, and Bond got a terrible hand. Amazingly, Woo went out very quickly for two points on Thackeray's discard. He had a chicken hand, but he also had no Flower tiles, and a Pong of East Winds (matching his seat). Thackeray paid the $800 as if it was charity, and the others paid $400.

Sinclair got the deal next and the hand ended in a draw. It was redealt and Bond got another terrible hand. If he was going to beat Thackeray, he had only three more hands in which to do so. It wasn't to be this time, for Sinclair went out with Woo's discard. He got three points for holding four Pongs. Woo paid $1600, the others $800.

Bond got the deal. Bond couldn't believe the hand he drew. Of the thirteen tiles, ten of them were Circles that could be easily turned into sets. He signaled to Woo that he needed Circles. The problem was that he was only allowed to Chow from the player on his left, and that was Sinclair. Nevertheless, a chicken hand would be all right if the entire hand was made up of Circles. That would be a Pure Hand, which was worth six points.

I hackeray discarded one of the needed Circles. "Pong!" said Bond. A little later, Sinclair threw a tile Bond needed. "Chow!" he called. Thackeray looked at him. Now everyone knew Bond had a chicken hand. Thackeray's eyes were burning with curiosity. Bond was holding no Flowers, so he had at least one point. What else could he be holding?

Thackeray eventually discarded a Circle tile that Bond needed and he triumphantly called, "Out!" Thackeray raised his eyebrows when he saw Bond's Pure hand.

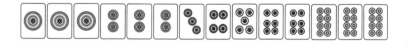

Including the point for no Flowers, Bond had a total of seven points—a Double Full House. It was the biggest win of the game so far. This time, Thackeray wasn't so pleased about turning over $6400 to Bond. The others had to pay $3200 each.

Since he won the hand, Bond kept the deal for the last hand of the game. It started off poorly, for Bond had a mixture of Sticks and Circles, and one Green Dragon. He wasn't sure what to go for. When he drew another Green Dragon from the wall, he wondered how possible it would be to get a special winning hand known as a "Jade Dragon." To do this he would need a Pong of the Green

Dragons, with the remainder of his hand made up entirely of Pongs of Sticks.

Bond gave Woo the signal for Sticks and coughed twice for the Green Dragon. Woo smiled when he threw the tile and Bond called "Pong!" Now all he needed was three Pongs of Sticks. He already had pairs of 2s and 7s. He slowly got rid of the Circles, and eventually drew another pair of the 8 of Sticks. Woo discarded a 2 of Sticks and Bond Ponged.

Thackeray clumsily knocked over some tiles from the wall when he reached across the table. Bond knew the man had dropped a tile he had palmed, but Thackeray quickly covered it and rebuilt the wall without anyone seeing the tiles. He was getting careless. The alcohol was finally getting to him. What made him so desperate to win? Was it a feeling of power that he desired? Bond had certainly seen it before in men like Hugo Drax, who had cheated at cards for no reason except to satisfy his own need to prove to himself he could do it.

Sinclair discarded an 8 of Sticks and Bond Ponged again. He needed a 7 and either a 9 or 1 of Sticks to complete the hand.

Woo discarded the 7 of Sticks and Bond Ponged. He had four Pongs revealed. Everyone knew all he needed was a pair to go out. It was Thackeray's turn, and for the first time he hesitated. Spectators around the room looked on with anticipation. Bond could very well have a Maximum Hand. Thackeray drew from the wall and looked at the tile. He considered it, unsure of whether to keep or discard it. He finally threw it down on the table. It was a 1 of Sticks.

Bond picked it up and coolly said, "Out." He revealed his hand and said, "Jade Dragon. Maximum Hand."

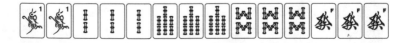

Thackeray's hand trembled when he handed Bond chips totaling $19,200. Sinclair's face had gone white as well—he had to pay

$9600. Woo gladly handed over his $9600. Bond thought the man's smile would split his face.

Thackeray stood up slowly. He turned to Bond and said with a thicker slur than usual, "You have luck on your side, Mr. Bond." He glanced at Woo. "Or . . . something." He then turned and walked toward the archway leading to the washroom. Bond collected his chips and turned them into the cashier who was standing eagerly near the table. He and Woo combined their cash and put it in a brown bag, which Woo stuffed into his jacket. They were ready to leave, but Bond wanted to speak with Thackeray one more time and confirm that he would see him at the EurAsia press conference on the twenty-fourth. The man was taking an awfully long time.

Three young Chinese men in business suits stepped into the room through the red curtains. They had a look in their eyes that Bond recognized only from years of experience. He thought later that a younger, greener agent would have been killed immediately.

Bond leaped at Woo, pulling him down behind the bar as the men revealed large butcher knives and meat cleavers they had concealed in their jackets. With lightning speed, they began to attack everyone in the room. They swung their blades like swords, slashing and chopping whatever piece of flesh got in their way. The room filled with the screams of the victims, and there was blood everywhere. Sinclair went down, as did the spectators and bartender. It was over as quickly as it had begun. The men turned and ran from the room.

"Are you all right?" Bond shouted to Woo.

"Yes!" Woo was stunned.

Bond jumped up. "Find Thackeray!" he ordered, then ran from the room. The crowded casino had become a frenzied panic. People were screaming and running for the doors. Bond scanned the crowd, looking for the three thugs in suits. They had slipped out. What was that all about? Were they after Thackeray? Was it an assassination attempt? Whatever it was, they had succeeded in killing or maiming at least a dozen people.

Bond returned to the gambling room. Woo was standing in the archway leading to the washroom. It was a gruesome mess. Bodies were strewn about, drenched in blood. Sinclair had been killed. Not everyone was dead—two or three men were crawling and crying for help. There were a few fingers and hands lying in puddles of blood. The killers had dropped the weapons in the room before fleeing.

"Thackeray gone," Woo said, bewildered.

"What?"

"No one in washroom!"

Bond went into the washroom. The two stalls were empty, and there was no window. How the hell did he get out? Bond examined the back wall of one of the stalls. He knocked on it and determined that it was hollow.

"It's a trapdoor," he said to Woo. He carefully felt the seams of the wall and finally found a minute depression. There was a tiny toggle switch there that, when flipped, activated a sliding door in the wall.

"Come on!" Bond commanded. He and Woo entered the dark corridor and ran twenty meters to another door. It opened easily—to the outside. They were behind the hotel, looking at a dark alleyway. Thackeray was nowhere in sight.

"What the hell . . . ?" Bond muttered.

They ran to the front of the casino. It was night now, and the neon from the building lit up the street. A black sedan tore out of the parking lot. Bond recognized the three killers in the front seat of the car. He started to draw his Walther PPK, but realized he had left it at the boat. The car sped away into the night.

The sound of approaching police sirens told them they should leave the premises. "Come on, James," Woo said. "There is nothing we can do. Let's go back to boat."

Bond nodded.

They hailed a taxi, went to the outskirts of town, walked quickly to the old pier, hopped on the Viking 66, and woke up J.J.

On the journey back to Hong Kong, they discussed what had happened.

"Were they Triad?" Bond asked.

Woo said, "Possibly. Probably. It was their method. I spoke to guard before we left. The men had picked up their weapons from kitchen before entering room. That is how they do it, so they do not have to bring weapons to scene of crime. They take whatever is available nearby."

"Were they after Thackeray?"

"It seem like it."

"He must have known they were coming. Why else would he run like that? How did he know there was a secret escape route from that room? What the hell is going on?"

"You tell me, James. I am tired."

Bond also felt fatigued. It was nearly ten P.M. He felt the jet lag. He would go to his hotel and sleep until late morning.

"You saved my life, James," Woo said. "Now I owe you big time."

Bond shook his head. "Forget that *maijiang* business, T.Y. I wasn't doing you a favor, I was doing my job."

"Still, I am very grateful and indebted," Woo said with great sincerity.

Bond smiled. "Don't worry about it. Be thankful we're returning to Hong Kong with all of our body parts."

Woo grinned widely and held up the brown bag. "Not only that, we return with helluva lot of money, uh huh?"

8

Private Dancer

James Bond slept until just before noon. He exercised, then ate a hearty brunch in one of the hotel's several restaurants, the Mandarin Grill. The Grill sported green decor on the walls, mirrors on rectangular columns, and a couple of large aquariums. Bond knew that the concept of *feng shui*, the art and science of positioning man-made structures in harmony with the vital cosmic energy coursing through the earth, was taken seriously in the East. Sometimes entire buildings had to be adjusted slightly in accordance with instructions from professional *feng shui* masters. Fish tanks were in abundance in restaurants, as these improved the *feng shui*. It was obvious that the Mandarin Grill was one of Hong Kong's carefully planned restaurants. Like the Man Wah, it was pleasantly subdued and quiet—a perfect place to collect one's thoughts. Bond had ordered scrambled eggs and toast with freshly squeezed orange juice, and now felt refreshed and alert.

Standing outside the Man Mo Temple in the Sheung Wan, or Western District, of the island, Bond marveled at the city around him. The people, mostly Chinese, seemed oblivious to the historical event that would occur in eight days. Everyone went about their business, completely ignoring the huge dragon to the north that was breathing down their necks. Bond wondered what would happen to some of Hong Kong's famous landmarks, such as the temple in front of him. Following the tourists, Bond stepped inside. The rich interior altar contained polished brass and pewter ritual vessels and a pair of shining yard-high brass deer symbolizing longevity and wealth. Brass statues of the Eight Immortals stood in front of the altar, each representing the different conditions of life: male, female, lord, peasant, age, youth, poverty, and wealth. A smaller room to the right contained images of Buddhist deities like Kwan Yum, Wong Tai Sin, and Kwan Ti, the god Mo himself. The temple was dedicated to two deities, Man and Mo, the first being the god of literature who controlled the destinies of mandarins and civil servants; the latter being the god of martial arts and war, who was the guardian deity of Hong Kong police but was favored just as much by the underworld. All day long, worshipers dropped in for a fast communication with the gods. Bond was fascinated watching people use the *chim*. These numbered bamboo sticks were used to answer important questions concerning business, family, or fortune. The narrow canister was shaken until a stick fell out; its number was used to predict the outcome. Of course, one could always try again if the answer wasn't favorable!

"You have question to ask gods, Ling Ling Chat?"

Bond turned toward the whisper and saw T. Y. Woo's smiling face. He was right on time.

Bond whispered in reply, "T.Y., I'm not sure the gods would appreciate the questions I have. And I probably wouldn't like the answers, either. Come on."

Bond and Woo left the temple and walked down Ladder Street from Hollywood Road. It was typical of the steep lanes paved with stone slabs for the convenience of sedan-chair bearers. They stepped down to Upper Lascar Row, which once housed foreign seamen known as lascars. The lane was lined with renowned brica-brac and antiques dealers. Also called "Cat Street," it got the nickname from the accompanying brothels.

Woo led him to a four-story building with a red facade surrounding picture windows. The legend "Woo Antiques and Curios Shop" was set into the facade, and the windows revealed a clutter of expensive antiques, art, and crafts. Two angry Chinese dragon-lions stood on either side of the single door, symbolically guarding the shop from evil.

"This is where J.J. and I live," Woo said. "This is safe house." Bond followed him inside and found J.J. polishing an antique bronze opium pipe. He looked up and nodded with a grin, then went back to work. The place was loaded with everything from inexpensive knickknacks to fine jade figurines and ivory objets d'art. He led Bond to the back of the store and showed him the code needed to punch into a numbered button pad on the wall. This unlocked a door, which revealed a set of stairs leading up to a large four-bedroom flat. Bond would never have guessed such a large space could exist within the narrow building he had seen from the outside.

Woo poured two glasses of cold Tsingtao beer, and they sat down at a table near the kitchen.

"I want to meet the Triad Dragon Head today, T.Y.," Bond said.

Woo rubbed his chin thoughtfully. "Will not be easy. Li Xu Nan very private man. Sometimes he can be found at one of his clubs, like I told you. He goes to Zipper a lot."

"What are my chances of finding him there today?"

"Fifty-fifty," Woo said. "Either he is there or he is not, uh huh?"

"T.Y., do you think this Triad is really involved in all this? What do you think about Thackeray's behavior last night?"

Woo shrugged. "Thackeray is hiding something. Maybe this press conference tomorrow will tell all. As for Triad, we know they somehow got into EurAsia's shipping business."

"Tell me more about them."

"Triad members believe they are on the right side of law and honor. You know, the original Triad was founded after seventeenth-century overthrow of Ming Dynasty by Manchus. Their motto was 'Restore Ming, Overthrow Ch'ing.' The name came from primal triad of Heaven, Earth, and Man. Members were like your Robin Hoods, taking wealth from rich and giving to poor. Triads originally were symbols of nationalism. Sun Yat-sen was Triad." Woo sighed. "Today they have degenerated into criminal underground. They put squeeze on many businesses. They control prostitution and illegal immigration. One of their big enterprises is emigrating young girls to West with promise of freedom and prosperity. In reality, girls become prisoners in brothels and are forced to work their way out of enslavement for several years before they are finally set free. Their largest business is drugs. They control maybe eighty percent of world's drug traffic. You think Central America is bad? They are peanuts compared to Triads."

"Where do the drugs come from?"

"From China, Thailand, Laos, Burma. Many places. Golden Triangle in Yunnan Province is major source."

Bond nodded. "What will happen to Triads once China takes over Hong Kong?"

Woo grinned. "There are some in Hong Kong who believe Triads will only become more powerful after takeover, not only because they are so ingrained in our culture but because they will find reason to reach back to their beginnings as political activists."

"They're anti-Communist, then?"

"Most definitely. If China decides to completely change Hong Kong and destroy democratic freedoms we have here, Triads will be first to oppose them. And they will be formidable foes. Other possibility is that they will corrupt China and continue as they are."

"Triads are outlawed in China, aren't they?"

"Yes, but they exist. Hong Kong, though, is center of all Triad activity in entire world."

"The analogy would be as Sicily is to the Mafia?"

"I suppose so, yes. You know, Triads are illegal in Hong Kong, too. Just being a member is illegal. If you possess any Triad materials you can go to jail, uh huh? That is why they are so secret."

"I think I better see some Triads firsthand, T.Y. Where is this nightclub?"

"In Tsim Sha Tsui East. Kowloon. The Zipper. Big fancy nightclub, very popular. Very expensive. Japanese businessmen especially like it. They have very beautiful girls working there."

"Are they prisoners of the Triads as well?"

"Some might be," Woo said.

Bond stood up. "Enough talk. Let's go. When we get there, T.Y., I want to go in alone. I'm curious to see how a *gweilo* is treated there."

During the Vietnam War, Lockhart Road in the Wanchai District of Hong Kong was immortalized as the haven for servicemen on R and R. This nightlife had diversified into other areas and was no longer completely isolated in Wanchai. Tsim Sha Tsui, one of the premier tourist areas of Kowloon, provided some of the flavor of the rowdy old days. It was virtually the Times Square of Hong Kong. There was a mix of British-style pubs, hostess clubs, karaoke bars, and noisy disco bars. There was the famous Bottoms Up club, a tame topless bar featuring waitresses who looked as if they'd been there since the place opened in the early seventies. There was the Adam's Apple, where half-naked hostesses pretended to make scintillating conversation while one drank. Hong Kong had something that appealed to the best and worst in everyone. In theory, strip clubs as such were illegal in Hong Kong—if girls removed their clothes, they did it privately out of public view.

Bond found The Zipper easily. It was a huge place, spanning an entire block of Tsim Sha Tsui East, an area of Kowloon that had more recently developed into an expensive tourist trap. Other high-class nightclubs, such as the Club B Boss and the China City

Club, were also in the vicinity. By six P.M., even before the sun had set, the brightly colored neon of the area rivaled anything in Las Vegas. There was a buzz of excitement in the air, and he could understand how the area had received such a glamorous reputation.

Bond casually approached the front door of The Zipper. Two Indian men wearing turbans stood outside the door. He heard loud American soft rock. The Zipper was a hostess club, which meant that patrons could "buy" time with a hostess. She could sit and have a drink with him, dance with him, talk with him . . . whatever they happened to arrange. What went on in private rooms was negotiated. Uninitiated visitors were often taken advantage of and overcharged. Simply having a drink with a hostess could be very expensive. Prostitution itself was not illegal in Hong Kong. Brothels and streetwalking were against the law, but straightforward solicitations and private arrangements between adults were legal.

He stepped inside and paid a cover charge of five hundred Hong Kong dollars, which included the first two drinks. Four lovely Chinese women in *cheongsams* sang out in English, "Welcome!" Then he entered a dark red room. It was large enough to feature a dance floor in the center, and had at least fifty tables and/ or divan–coffee table combinations scattered around its perimeter. The music was loud and a little irritating. A Chinese man flanked by three gorgeous women was on the dance floor, lip-synching an American rock tune in the karaoke style that was so popular. The place was not crowded, but it was very early in the evening. From what he could see, the hostesses were of various nationalities, and they were all young and attractive. There were a few Japanese businessmen snuggling with hostesses on divans. Two or three Caucasian men were sitting at tables with female companions. The place was devoid of any other clientele, but according to Woo, the club would be jam-packed by nine P.M.

Bond walked to the far side of the room and sat down at a table. He could see the entire club from this vantage point, including the archway leading to the front lobby. T.Y. had said that if Li

Xu Nan showed up at all, it would be in the early evening. Bond would just have to spend some money and wait and see. Within seconds, a lovely Chinese hostess approached his table. She, too, was wearing a *cheongsam*, high heels, and a smile. She sat down next to Bond and pulled her chair very close to his. Before she said a word, her bare leg emerged from the slit in the dress and pressed against his.

"Hello," she said. "What's your name?"

"James," Bond said, returning her smile. He couldn't help feeling a bit ridiculous in this situation. He played along, pretending to be the British tourist looking for a good time.

"Well, James," she said, "would you like a companion this evening?"

Surprisingly, her accent sounded American.

"Perhaps," Bond said. "Where are you from?"

"If you want to continue talking, it's two hundred and forty Hong Kong dollars for a drink and a quarter hour," she said with a straight face. Then she smiled again. "You're very handsome."

Bond said, "All right, I'd like a vodka martini. Please shake it—don't stir it. And get whatever you'd like." He paid her the cash.

The girl squeezed his arm. "I'll be right back, sweetheart."

He watched her walk toward the bar. She was probably in her late twenties, Bond thought, perhaps a bit older than some of the other girls he saw soliciting business in the place. She had straight, black shoulder-length hair, was unusually tall, and had long, wonderful legs. She returned, set down the drinks, and then sat beside him in extremely close proximity once again.

"I'm back," she said dreamily.

"I see that," Bond said. "What's your name?"

"Veronica. What's yours?"

"I said it was James."

"Oh yeah, you told me that," she said, then laughed. "Sorry, I'm a little out of it."

"Veronica" was either a little drunk or high on something else.

"Where are you from?" Bond asked again.

"Oh, you're wondering about the way I talk," she said. "I spent twelve years in California, living with my aunt and uncle. I went to grade school, middle school, and high school there. But I was born here in Hong Kong, and I'll probably die here in Hong Kong."

"Why do you say that?"

She shrugged. "I can't get out. I'm a Hong Kong citizen. You're English, aren't you? Why won't your country let us go there?"

Bond nodded and said, "It is pretty shameful, isn't it? England has watched over you for a hundred and fifty years and now she's turning her back on you. I know . . . I know . . ."

"What are you doing in Hong Kong?" she asked, taking a sip from some kind of frozen daiquiri.

"I'm a journalist. I'm here to cover the handover next week."

"I see. You live in England?"

"Jamaica, actually, though I'm originally from England."

"Wow, Jamaica. I've never been there."

"Most people think it's not what it used to be. It's fairly dangerous in some areas. I happen to love it, though."

She ran her fingers along his chin and looked at him seductively. Her almond eyes were lovely. There was intelligence behind them, and Bond felt sorry for her. He wondered if she knew Li Xu Nan, and if she was a member of the Triad. It was highly likely. Woo had told him that most of the girls who worked as hostesses were prostitutes involved with these organizations. The Triads "protected" them, even though they blatantly exploited them.

"Veronica," Bond said, "that's not your real name, is it?"

She smirked. "What do you think?"

"I thought so. Listen, can I interview you about the changeover? I'd love to have the perspective of a woman like you."

She laughed. "What, your paper will print the views of a night-club hostess?"

"Why not? You're as much a Hong Kong citizen as a wealthy banker."

"Don't count on that," she replied. "Wealthy bankers can buy

92

their way out of the colony. Many already have. Thousands of people have managed to leave over the past few years. With what's happened in the last couple of weeks, people who had decided to stay are now considering getting out. There is a lot of fear in the air."

"Fear of China?"

"Yes," she said. "You know that troops are lining up across the border from the New Territories?"

Bond nodded.

"Everyone is afraid that on July first the troops will pour in and take command of the city. There is going to be some violence."

"China has promised that Hong Kong will remain as it is for at least fifty years," Bond reminded her.

She scoffed. "Do you really believe that? Does the world believe that? They've already demanded changes in our governmental structure. The Legislative Council will be disbanded, you wait and see. They won't have any power. There will be a crackdown on places like this. Anything that appeals to the vices of Westerners will be banned—I know it will happen."

"But Hong Kong is Asia's cash cow," Bond said. "China cannot ignore that. They need Hong Kong. I honestly believe that they would lose face if they changed Hong Kong drastically."

Bond was surprised that he was having an intelligent conversation about politics with a girl he expected to have little gray matter. She was not only articulate, but she had eyes that could melt him if he allowed them to.

"Hey, listen," she said, "would you like a private dance? We can go back to one of those rooms. We'd have complete privacy."

"Maybe later," he said. "I'm enjoying our conversation."

She looked at him out of the corner of her eye. "You're not like most men who come in here. Usually, by now their hands are all over me."

Bond gave her a slight bow and said dryly, "I'm an English gentleman."

She laughed. "I can see that. You're also very handsome . . .

James." She leaned in close and whispered in his ear. "And I'd like to see what's in your pants, James."

It was a typical crude solicitation from this type of woman. For some reason, though, when she said it to Bond he became aroused. The girl was extremely sexy. He chalked it up to her genuine intelligence, usually conspicuously lacking in bar girls.

"Aren't I one of those *gweilo* who are treated with such disdain?" he asked.

"I lived in America for a few years, remember? I like *gweilo*."

"How much drinking have you done today?" he asked her.

"This is my third drink, James," she said. "Why, do I seem drunk?"

"You seem a little high on something."

She shrugged and sniffed, unwittingly revealing what her vice might be. "A girl's gotta do what she's gotta do to get through the working day, you know?" For a moment, she stared into her empty glass. Bond said nothing.

"I tell you what," she said. "I'm going to refill our drinks, all right?"

Bond said, "Fine." He gave her some more cash. She ran her fingers through his hair as she stood up, then sauntered back to the bar. He needed to ask her about Triads. Would she talk? She might open up to him if he played his cards right.

When she came back with new drinks, Bond asked her, "Would you leave Hong Kong if you could?"

"Are you kidding? I don't want to live in a communist country!"

"Can't you go back to your relatives in California? Take up residence with them?"

She shook her head. "They aren't there anymore. They were killed in an automobile accident. Besides, my mother is here. She's sick. I have to take care of her."

"If you had the right papers for the two of you, you would get out?"

"Of course!"

"Is that why you're with a Triad?"

She blinked. "What did you say?"

"You *are* with a Triad, right?" he said. "Aren't most women who work in places like this members of Triads?"

"You've been watching too many Chow Yun-Fat movies," she said, obviously attempting to gloss over the truth.

"Come on, Veronica," he said. "The Triads are acting as lifeboats for people opposed to living in a communist country. I know that they are illegally helping people to emigrate to other countries. You believe they will get you out, or at the very least protect you from . . . whatever. Am I right?"

"I don't know what you're talking about."

"Veronica, you can trust me. I know you're vowed to secrecy, but you have nothing to worry about. I already know everything about it, you see. I know that Mr. Li Xu Nan is the Cho Kun of the Dragon Wing Society."

Her eyes widened. She couldn't believe what Bond had just said. She was stunned and afraid.

"Veronica, it's all right," Bond said earnestly. "Really."

"Sunni," she said.

"What?"

"That's my real name. I shouldn't be telling you this. I could get in a lot of trouble."

"Sunni?"

She nodded. "Sunni Pei."

"That's a pretty name."

She leaned in to his ear again. "How about that private dance now?" She was attempting to change the subject and get back to business.

"Not yet, Sunni. I promise I'll pay you for a dance in a few minutes. But first I need a favor."

"I don't know . . ."

"I want to meet Mr. Li."

She shook her head almost violently. "That's impossible. No one meets the Cho Kun."

Bond was right. She *did* know him.

"Doesn't he come here every now and then? Will he come in here today?"

"I don't know. . . . Look, I don't know who you're talking about, anyway." She suddenly seemed very frightened. She looked around, hoping no one was near enough to hear what they were saying.

"Why not?" Bond asked. "Li Xu Nan is just another business-man."

Her jaw dropped. "Stop it! Be quiet!" she exclaimed in a whisper.

"You know him, don't you?"

"No," she said. "I know who he is, that's all. He comes in most afternoons. How do you know he's a Dragon Head?"

"I'm the media," Bond said. "I have my sources."

She was shaking with fear now. Bond was afraid he might have gone too far too soon.

"Look, Sunni," he said. "It's all right. You won't get into trouble. I want to interview him for my newspaper. I want to get his views on the handover and how it will affect his businesses. He can remain anonymous—it doesn't matter to me. All my headline has to read is 'Triad Leader Speaks Out'—it'll make a great story!"

"He will never admit being Cho Kun. Any association with a Triad is illegal in Hong Kong."

"I know that. I don't expect him to admit a thing."

"I don't know how I can help . . ."

"Just point him out to me when he comes in."

"He might not come in today."

"Well, I shall be here every day until he does. Now . . . how about that dance?"

When he said that, she smiled again. "You want to go to a private room?"

Bond nodded.

"It will cost you fourteen hundred Hong Kong dollars."

"I'm sure it will be worth every penny," he said.

Sunni seemed to forget the subject matter of their earlier conversation. She stood up, took hold of his hand, and led him to one side of the club and into a small room. She shut the door and gestured for him to sit in a chair against the wall. She took his money and tucked it into a small purse she placed on the floor.

"Just relax and enjoy the show," she said. She punched a button on a tape deck set into the wall. Music with a beat filled the room.

Sunni Pei then began a slow, sensuous dance in front of Bond. She stared into his eyes the entire time, smiling every now and then. She moved well. She might have had professional dance training, but she didn't need it for what she was doing. All she needed was sex appeal and attitude, and Sunni Pei had plenty of that.

Bond watched her, captivated. Never having gone in much for strippers, he admitted to himself that she was something special. Her beauty was extraordinary, and again, it was the intellect behind her seduction that made her so appealing. He found that he wasn't playing the British tourist in search of a good time anymore. He was really enjoying this.

Sunni deftly unsnapped the *cheongsam* and removed it. Underneath she had on nothing but a black satin bra and matching bikini panties. Her navel was pierced with a small, thin gold ring. She slipped the straps of her bra off her shoulders, unsnapped it and tossed it into Bond's lap. She laughed. Her breasts were the size of apples, firm and natural. Her nipples were erect; she frankly enjoyed playing the exhibitionist. A few beats later, she pulled her black panties down and lifted one long leg out of them. She stepped gracefully out of them, then stood over Bond. Her legs spread wide, she straddled his lap and moved her breasts within inches of his face. He could smell her sweet skin, which was lightly damp with sweat, and Bond felt an urge to touch her.

She brought her face up close to Bond's and blew lightly

around his left ear. Her lips touched him, giving him a light kiss. "You're not supposed to touch me," she whispered, "but I'll let you anyway."

Not refusing the invitation, Bond reached up with both hands and softly ran his palms and fingertips over her back. He felt goose pimples rise on her shoulders. Her skin was unbelievably soft and smooth. He pulled her to a sitting position on his lap. She began to run her fingers through his hair and along the back of his neck; he did the same with his own hands on her body. Her eyes never left his.

When his hands found her breasts, she gave a slight purr, then she pressed her mouth on his. They kissed, their tongues exploring each other's mouth with curiosity and delight. She pushed her pelvis forward into his and felt his hardness there. He wanted her, but this was not the time or place. For the time being, though, he allowed the "dance" to work its wonders on him and take him along the river of fantasy that was her primary intention. She seemed to be displaying sincere affection for him. Sometimes these girls were so good at what they did that it was difficult to tell if they were acting or not. Bond's instincts told him that she was honestly interested in him. She was having a good time, too.

When the music ended, Sunni gave him one last quick kiss on the lips, then stood up. She found her underclothes and put them back on. Bond sat there, a little dazed. This woman would be a powerhouse in bed, he thought.

"Did you like that?" she finally asked.

"Quite," Bond said. "Thank you."

She held out her hand. He took it and stood up. "Come on, let's go back out . . . unless you want another dance?"

Bond smiled. "Another time, Sunni."

"Better call me Veronica," she warned.

"All right."

She put the *cheongsam* back on, then they went back into the club and resumed sitting at their table.

"Can I refill your drink?" she asked. Bond told her yes. As she got up, she whispered, "Don't look now, but your man is sitting over there near the bar."

Sunni walked toward the bar, and Bond glanced over. Three or four tables were set inside a small section surrounded by a rail, apparently a "reserved" VIP area. At one of these tables sat a Chinese man in a business suit. On either side of him were two larger men in suits—the bodyguards.

From this distance, it was difficult to tell how old Li Xu Nan was. He appeared to be fairly young, perhaps in his early to mid thirties. He was sipping a drink and conversing with one of the hostesses.

Sunni brought back another martini and sat down.

"So that's Mr. Li," Bond said. "He seems young."

Sunni shrugged. "What did you expect? An aging don like in the Mafia?"

The door to the nightclub opened and three men entered. It wasn't until they entered the private section, removed their hats, and sat down at Li's table that Bond recognized them. Or rather, he recognized two of them.

All three men had white hair and pinkish-white skin. They all wore sunglasses. They were the albino Chinese he had seen in Macau! Now, *that* was interesting!

"Do you know those three men?" Bond asked.

Sunni glanced over at them. "No. They're strange, aren't they? Albino brothers, it looks like."

"That's unusual in this part of the world, isn't it?"

"I should say so." She turned back to him. "Sure you don't want another dance?"

"Later, Sunn—Veronica." Bond's attention was focused on Li and his visitors. He appeared to be giving them instructions of some kind. Who were these three men? Members of the Dragon Wing Society? Musclemen? Even though their backs were to him, Bond was able to discern some visual differences. They were each of different builds and weights. He thought of them as Tom, Dick, and Harry. Tom was the heaviest, probably about 240 pounds.

Dick was Bond's size—tall and slim. Harry was smaller in stature and was the most animated.

After a few minutes, the three albinos nodded, stood, and left the nightclub. Li remained sitting at the table with his two bodyguards.

Bond removed a business card and pen from his pocket. He wrote a message on the back.

"Sunni," he said. "Please deliver this to Mr. Li." He handed her 1000 Hong Kong dollars. "I appreciate everything you've done for me this evening." He gave her another $2000. "And this is for the dance."

She looked at the money in disbelief. "James, thank you! You don't . . ."

"Hush," he said. "You're wonderful. You're beautiful and a pleasure to talk to. I hope to see you again soon."

She nodded and said, "I do, too." She kissed him on the cheek, stood up, and walked slowly to Li Xu Nan's table with Bond's card in hand.

9

Interview with a Dragon

Sunni approached Li Xu Nan cautiously and handed him the card submissively. He looked at it and said something to her. She pointed to Bond. Li's gaze shifted over to him. It was cold and calculating. Bond could see that he could not believe that the Englishman would have the audacity to make contact with him. Li barked an order to one of his thugs. The large man nodded and walked across the dance floor toward Bond.

When he got to Bond's table, he said, "Mr. Li say you got big nose. But he also say you got big balls. He will talk to you. Come to table."

Bond followed the man to Li's table. The other bodyguard held a chair out and Bond sat across from the Cho Kun of the Dragon Wing Society. Li Xu Nan had neatly cut black hair and cold brown eyes. There was a two-inch scar above his left eyebrow, which managed to put years on his baby-faced features. With proper clothing and body posturing, Li Xu Nan could pass either as a man of forty or a young man of nineteen. Regardless of his age, Li exuded an aura of self-confidence, charisma, and great power.

Bond spoke in Cantonese. "Mr. Li, I am grateful for this opportunity to talk to you." He imagined that Li Xu Nan probably did not like to speak English.

"Your card says you would like to interview me for a story about Hong Kong businesses and the handover to China," replied Li in Cantonese. He had a pleasant voice. "I do not usually do this, Mr. Bond. If you were from a British paper I would have you thrown out of the club. But I have some things I would like to say. My name will be kept out of this?"

"Absolutely, if that's what you prefer," Bond said. He produced a small notepad and pen from his jacket pocket. "Let's begin with your business. I know you're a successful man here, but I'm not totally familiar with everything you do. Can you enlighten me?"

The man lit a cigarette and offered one to Bond. Bond politely refused, then Li began to talk. He clearly thought carefully about every phrase before he spoke.

"I am a businessman, Mr. Bond. My father, Li Chen Tam, was also a businessman. I inherited most of my enterprises from him. He came to Hong Kong in 1926 as a young boy, a refugee from the civil wars in China at that time. He worked very hard with humble beginnings. His first business was selling dumplings on the street. He fortunately joined forces with colleagues and created his own restaurant. A little later, he and his partners established a currency-exchange operation. He got into the entertainment industry in the 1950s, just when Hong Kong became the holiday spot for American GIs fighting the Korean War. It was with the opening of nightclubs and more restaurants that he made his fortune. By the time he died, he was a millionaire."

"And all of it is yours now?"

"That is correct."

"Are you the only son?"

"I am the only son," Li said.

"And I suppose your son will inherit from you?"

"I am not married."

Bond scribbled notes as the man spoke. He played the role of journalist well.

"How do you think the changeover will affect your business?" he asked.

"It is difficult to say. There are optimists who believe that things will remain the same. I hate the Communists, but I have to retain a positive outlook toward my own future. We all hope that the mainland Chinese will gain a new perspective on Hong Kong once they are in power."

"What do you mean?"

"Hong Kong is very capitalist. That goes against the very nature of China's doctrines. At the same time, Hong Kong offers a tremendous opportunity for China. If they allow Hong Kong to continue in its ways, it could be the first step toward democracy in China. China has promised to keep the structure in place for fifty years. What happens after that? Who knows. If they are happy with the wealth that Hong Kong will undoubtedly bring them, I imagine that nothing will change. On the other hand, China may feel that having a Westernized, capitalist port is hypocritical. They might think they have lost face and are selling out to the West. They may crush Hong Kong's capitalism. That would be a terrible thing."

"But *that's* what would cause China to lose face with the rest of the world, don't you think?" Bond asked.

"Yes, but they may not care. China has not cared much in the past what the rest of the world thought. As for those of us in Hong Kong . . . Mr. Bond, do you smell the fear outside? It is there if you sniff hard enough. The people of Hong Kong may be going about their business. They may have accepted the inevitable. What happens on July the first cannot be changed. But they are afraid. We all are. We can only hope that China will keep her promise and allow us to continue as we are."

"Why don't you leave?"

"My business is here, Mr. Bond. I cannot take my business

with me. I must stay and adjust to whatever happens. I am resigned to do that."

"Do you believe your businesses will be affected?"

"Not at first, certainly. Whether China allows establishments like this to flourish in Hong Kong remains to be seen. If hostess clubs are banned, then I will turn it into a restaurant. But I also believe that China will find it difficult to institute too many changes within the first fifty years."

"How so?"

"China will learn that societies exist in Hong Kong that go back centuries. They go back much further than communist China. I would imagine there might be new revolutions, more resistance, and more violence. Tiananmen Square was only the first of what might be many pro-democracy demonstrations."

Bond decided to get to the heart of the matter. "You're talking about Triads, aren't you?"

Li Xu Nan smiled slightly. He spoke softly in Chinese to his bodyguard. The Cantonese went very quickly, but Bond caught the word "girl" in the sentence. Had he got Sunni in trouble? The bodyguard got up and went to the bar. "I have ordered you a fresh drink, Mr. Bond, and one for myself."

"Thank you."

"Chiang Kai-shek was a Triad member. Did you know that?" he asked.

"Yes."

"I do not know much about Triads, Mr. Bond. I do know that the government of Taiwan was built on the backs of Triads resisting communist rule. Triads came into existence resisting an oppressive regime in China many, many years ago."

"So it's your contention, then, that Triads will become more powerful after the takeover? Aren't Triads outlawed in China, just as they are in Hong Kong? Don't you think they will crack down on organized crime?"

The bodyguard came back with the drinks. Li Xu Nan looked uncomfortable. He didn't like the way the conversation was going.

"Organized crime, Mr. Bond? I'm not sure I know what you mean," Li said.

"Come on, Mr. Li. You know that Triads today are not involved in patriotic activities. They're criminals."

"There are some Triads that have lost the honor of their ancestors, that is true, I suppose."

A strange answer, Bond thought. "I understand that Triads are instrumental in illegally getting people out of Hong Kong."

"That is probably true," Li said. "But is that really so bad? The British government has made it virtually impossible for a Hong Kong national to live anywhere else. Britain turned her back on the people who have lived under her rule for a hundred and fifty years. That is outright betrayal. If people want to leave, they should be able to. You speak of losing face. England has lost face with us. What was done may have been honorable to China—handing back a territory that was rightfully theirs. But not allowing the Hong Kong people an escape route was most *dis*honorable."

"Triads are involved with prostitution, too, aren't they?"

"I wouldn't know about that." The man was becoming angry.

"Come, come, Mr. Li. I know what goes on here in this very club."

Li slammed his hand down hard on the table, startling his men. The force of the blow knocked over all of the drinks. Bond remained calm.

"What is this?" Li demanded. "Did you come to talk about me and my business or about Triads? I know nothing about Triads! Go and talk to the police if you want to know about Triads! I resent the inference that what goes on here in my club has anything to do with a Triad. You have insulted me!"

"Forgive me, Mr. Li," Bond said. "Please accept my apologies. I merely thought you would have some insight into how these organizations have infiltrated the entertainment industry. I shan't take up any more of your time." Bond stood and bowed slightly, with respect. "Mr. Li, I would like to ask you one more question, if I may."

The Cho Kun of the Dragon Wing Society stared hard at Bond in disbelief. The *gweilo* had the audacity to continue speaking!

Through his pretense of humility, Bond stared back at Li. Both men knew that their facades had been torn away. The bodyguards were unsure what to do.

Bond finally spoke. "Mr. Li, recently there has been some violence in Hong Kong. Some terrorist acts have been committed against British citizens, and one on some visiting officials from Beijing. What is your opinion on the nature of these attacks?"

Li stood slowly, his face flush with anger. "I know nothing about those attacks. They were unfortunate and tragic. I hesitate to speculate on who might be involved with those incidents. This interview is over. You are lucky that I do not take away that notebook. Mr. Bond, my name had better not appear anywhere in your story."

"Are you threatening me, Mr. Li?"

Li leaned forward and whispered in English, his voice laced with menace. "Mr. Bond, I allow you to leave with your life. You are now in my debt. You have your story. Now, leave!"

Bond gave a slight bow of his head. "Thank you, Mr. Li." He stood up and walked away from the table. He walked around the dance floor to the club's exit. Sunni Pei was walking toward him, carrying a small tray of drinks to a trio of Chinese businessmen. She held out her hand and said a little too loudly, "Thank you for coming. We hope to see you again soon!"

Bond shook her hand and felt a small piece of paper. He palmed it and said, "Thank you, Veronica. I'll be back." She smiled nervously, then went on to serve the drinks as Bond left The Zipper. The neon lights from the street were blinding at first after the darkness of the club.

He unfolded the note and read: "Help me! Meet me on the street behind the club in five minutes! Please!"

Bond looked around to see if anyone was watching. He ripped the note into bits and let them scatter on the street, then walked around to the back of the large building. He waited in a small nook in the wall near an employee entrance. In precisely five minutes, Sunni came out of the door. She saw him and rushed to him, her eyes full of fear.

"James!" she said. "They think I told you that Li Xu Nan is Cho Kun of a Triad. This is considered a betrayal."

"So you *are* a member of the Triad?"

She nodded. "They will kill me. You don't understand."

"No, Sunni, I do understand."

"Please, can you hide me in your hotel until I can figure out what to do? I beg you!" She was truly frightened.

"Come on," he said, taking her hand. They rushed out of the alleyway and into the street.

10

Marked for Death

When they were clear of the club, Sunni said, "We need to go to Kwun Tong."

"I know a safer place," Bond said. He wanted to call Woo at the antiques store. They could get a car just by speaking a code word and an address into the phone.

"My mother," Sunni said. "They'll come to hurt my mother. We have to get her out of there."

"Can you phone her?" Bond asked.

"She never answers. She's not well."

Bond wanted to wash his hands of the woman right then and there. She was going to drag him into a situation with the Triad that he couldn't afford to be in. The mission could be compromised.

"Look," Bond said. "I'll help you. I'll get you to a place of safety. But we do it now, and we go where I say."

Sunni suddenly looked at him with a mixture of fear and anger. She swore at him. "Fine, I'll go alone. I should have known. You just want to get into bed with me." She started to run up the street. Bond let her go. She would only complicate things. He turned around and began to walk the other way when a black sedan tore up the street and screeched to a halt in front of the girl. Two young Chinese men jumped out of the car and grabbed her. Sunni screamed.

Bond immediately ran the half-block to the scene. She was putting up a great struggle as they attempted to push her into the backseat of the car. "Leave her alone!" Bond shouted at them. The men looked at him.

"James, help!" Sunni cried.

One man reached inside his jacket. Bond was a second ahead of him, drawing the Walther and taking a bead on the man's head.

"Let her go!" he shouted. "Keep your hands where I can see them!"

The other man must have had a pistol behind Sunni's back, for he rolled away from her and shot at Bond, just missing him.

Bond swung his aim to the shooter and fired. The bullet caught the gunman in the chest, knocking him to the pavement. The other man suddenly let Sunni go and got in the car. Sunni fell to the ground, terrified. The sedan's wheels squealed as it sped away, leaving the dead man for all to see.

Bond ran to Sunni and helped her up. "Are you all right?" he asked.

She nodded, visibly shaken.

"Come on," he said. "I'll take you to your mother. Is it close?"

"It's northeast, near the airport."

"Right, let's go."

They heard sirens in the distance, and Bond knew they needed to disappear before the police arrived. He grabbed her hand and ran into a side street, thinking they might be safe for the moment by mixing with the crowds in the streets. After they had sprinted a couple of blocks, he pushed her into a shop selling a variety of handmade bamboo birdcages. The screeches and whistles of the parakeets and budgies were extraordinarily disorienting.

"We'll rest here. Catch your breath," he said.

"Thank you," she said.

"It's all right," Bond said, but he was angry with himself. He shouldn't have got involved. Now he was in it up to his neck.

"Who are you really?" she asked.

He didn't answer.

"Are you a policeman? A detective?" she asked.

"Something like that," Bond said. "I work for the British government."

"Drug enforcement?"

He shook his head. "Just a troubleshooter, you might say."

"Right," she said. "Your shooting is certainly going to get us into trouble!"

"It was either him or me. Now, where is your flat?"

"Kwun Tong. We can take the MTR, that might be safe." The Mass Transit Railway was Hong Kong's efficient underground system.

Bond knew it was a risk taking her home, but he had already promised. "All right, show me."

She led him outside and down an MTR stairway.

The subway was impeccably clean. Bond was surprised by the shiny, unmarred surfaces of the trains and the lack of litter anywhere in the station. Unlike London, Hong Kong had no problems with graffiti and vandalism.

Sunni bought two tickets from a machine and led Bond through the turnstiles to the Tsuen Wan line. They had to wait only a few minutes for a train heading north. The rush hour was practically over, so it wasn't as crowded as it could have been. They left the train at Yaumatei station and changed to the Kwun Tong line, which would take them east.

Finally reaching their destination, Sunni and Bond got off at the Kwun Tong station. The area was a little different here, Bond thought. Kwun Tong was near the airport, so there was a mixture of industrial and residential streets. They walked to Hong Ning Road and into a housing complex called Connie Towers. It was a twenty-one-story structure that was modern, clean, and secure. The windows were "decorated" with laundry hanging on flagpoles, as was often the case in most Hong Kong tenement buildings.

"If you don't mind my asking, how much does a flat in a building like this cost in Hong Kong?"

"About three million Hong Kong dollars," she replied. Apparently she made good money working as a hostess.

They walked through an underground parking area to a lift. Chinese characters were painted above the doors, which Bond translated as "Come and go in peace." They got into the lift and stood there silently as they traveled to the eighteenth floor. Bond noted that she was apprehensive, a bit short of breath. The girl was truly beautiful, and although his better judgment told him he should mind his own business, his heart brought out the sometimes damnable chivalrous trait he possessed that had got him into trouble many times in the past.

Once they were on the eighteenth floor, Sunni moved to a door protected by a large, locked, metal sliding gate. She stood staring at it in fear. The lock mechanism had been scratched and obviously tampered with. She looked up at Bond, and his eyes told her to be quiet. He nodded to go ahead, so she used her key and opened the door. Bond drew his Walther PPK and preceded her into the flat.

It was a small place, modest but tastefully decorated. The living room contained a sectional sofa, coffee table, a stereo, and a few other pieces of furniture. A framed plaque on the table displayed a Chinese character meaning "Tolerance." There was a crucifix on the wall, indicating that Sunni was not Buddhist but one of the minority Chinese Catholics. A tiny kitchen was adjacent to the living room. A clothes dryer was in a nook by the kitchen, its exhaust pipe extending out of the window.

It was far too quiet. "Mother?" Sunni called out in Cantonese. She moved through an archway to a small hallway that led to two little bedrooms and a bathroom.

An elderly woman was lying on the bed in one of the bedrooms, seemingly asleep. Sunni approached her and called to her again. The woman didn't move. Sunni touched her and gasped. She recoiled and turned away. Bond knew immediately what was wrong. He felt the woman's forehead and grasped her wrist to search for a pulse. She was cold and lifeless.

"I'm sorry, Sunni," he said.

Sunni was sobbing, her back to Bond. "She . . . she had a bad heart," she managed to say.

Bond wondered if something happened that might have frightened the woman. There was also the possibility that she had simply died in her sleep. As he examined her further, he realized that rigor mortis had set in, indicating that she had been dead for some hours.

It was an awkward moment, and he wasn't sure how to comfort her. Bond put away his gun and reached out to her shoulders. She shrugged him off and said, "Please don't touch me." She turned to him, her eyes full of tears. "It's all your fault! They came here and scared her to death!" She pushed away from him and went into her bedroom, slamming the door behind her.

Bond spoke to her through the door. "Sunni, we don't know that for sure," he said gently. "She's been dead several hours. Her body is already stiff. When did you leave the flat today?"

"Around noon," she sniffed.

He nodded and said, "She's been dead more than two or three hours. Trust me." He opened the door slowly. She stood looking out of her window. Her bedroom was as small as her mother's. All told, the flat was about 80 square meters. Space was at a premium in Hong Kong.

The room was decidedly feminine. Bond noticed a small round charcoal burner plugged into the wall next to her bed. A red light was burning brightly on top of it. Sunni turned, wiping away her tears, and saw him looking at the contraption.

She managed a short laugh. "That's a little stove my mother gave me. It's a Chinese tradition. The red light means 'fire,' and it's supposed to bring me marriage . . . a husband. My mother was quite concerned that I'm nearly thirty and wasn't married." She started to cry again.

Bond held his arms out to her, and this time she allowed him to hold her. She sobbed quietly against his shoulder.

Then he heard a creaking noise. Damn! He hadn't closed and locked the front door! How could he have been so careless? He drew his gun. "Stay here," he commanded, then moved back into the living room.

As he entered the room, the front door slid open, revealing two young Chinese thugs in dark clothes. They were brandishing long, crude machetes. It all happened very quickly. The men rushed Bond and he shot them. They were both hit in the chest, but one of the men struck 007 hard on the left arm with his chopper. Bond yelped in pain but managed to fire at the man a second time at point-blank range.

He became aware that Sunni was screaming. He rushed to her and held his hand over her mouth. "Shhhhh, it's all right now," he said as calmly as he could. A few seconds passed and she started to calm down, but then she noticed Bond's shoulder. He was bleeding profusely through his jacket. He had a huge gash across his upper arm. He needed medical attention immediately.

"Lock the door, Sunni, quickly," he said sternly to jolt her out of her panic. She snapped out of it and ran to the door. Bond went into the bathroom and removed his jacket, shoulder holster, and shirt.

The cut was three inches long and a half-inch deep. Luckily, the muscle had not been severed, but blood was pouring from the wound. He quickly removed his right shoe and pulled the prying tool from under the tongue. He snapped off the heel and tipped the contents into the sink.

"Sunni, I need your help," Bond called. She hesitated at the door of the bathroom, not wanting to look. "Please," he said, "I need you to apply this antiseptic to the cut." He took the bottle and held it out in the palm of his right hand.

She looked at him. The same thought passed through both of their heads.

"Sunni," Bond said, "you're right. I suppose this is all my fault. I'm sorry."

"I should let you die, you know," she said. "I should grab a knife and cut you myself. I would regain face with them. It would cancel the death warrant on me."

"You don't really believe they can help you, Sunni? They're using you. You're a commodity."

"I am a Blue Lantern."

"What is that?"

"I've been accepted as a member but have not been formally initiated yet."

"Then you're not a member."

Sunni finally reached for the bottle of antiseptic and opened it. "You have to wash the wound first." Bond nodded. He moved to the shower stall and turned on the hot water. As he leaned into it, the blood swirled with the water down the drain. Sunni took a large white towel from a rack, wrapped it around Bond's arm, and held it tightly.

"According to the law, I am a member," she continued. "I could be arrested and jailed for simply being a Blue Lantern."

"I wouldn't have thought that they would allow women in Triads."

"It was once all-male, but in the last few years they've begun to admit women. Most of them stay Blue Lanterns and are never initiated."

"Then that should tell you what they think of you," Bond said. "Leave them."

She removed the towel and poured antiseptic onto the wound, which was still bleeding badly. Bond winced at the sting.

"Don't you see? I can't do anything! If I run, they'll eventually find me and kill me, or I'll be arrested and go to jail. My only way out of this is to kill you. Believe me, there are some other girls you could have met tonight who would have cut your hands off if you'd spoken to them about Triads."

"You're not going to try and kill me, are you, Sunni?"

She didn't answer. "You need stitches."

"Look," he said. "You need help, and I can help you. Come with me to a safe house. I can get medical treatment, and they won't find you there. I need to make a phone call. Then we could be on our way in minutes."

She wrapped some gauze around his arm very tightly, then covered it with the towel again. "There, that should hold you for a while. It's a good thing you had all that stuff in your shoe."

Bond stood up and put on his shirt. He slipped the shoulder holster back on. Extending or raising his left arm hurt like hell. He took two of the acetaminophen tablets and one antibiotic, swallowing them with water from the sink in his cupped right hand. He replaced the contents of the shoe and put it back on. Finally, he managed to put the bloody jacket back on, then walked into the living room and reached for the phone near the kitchen.

"I'm making that call. You can come with me or you can stay behind," he said. "If you're coming, you'd better pack a bag. You probably won't be coming back here."

"I can't leave my mother!"

He was dialing the number. "There's nothing you can do for her now, Sunni. You have to think of yourself. Do you want to come or not?"

He got a recording at the other end. He spoke into the phone, "Ling Ling Chat, need taxi immediately—repeat, immediately—at . . ." He turned to her. "What's the address?"

"One forty-seven Hong Ning Road, Kwun Tong."

Bond repeated it into the phone, then hung up. "You have five minutes to pack," he said. He understood what the poor girl was going through. In the space of one hour, she had suddenly been confronted with a life-or-death decision and the frightening prospect of abandoning any semblance of the life she had been living.

Finally she asked, "Can you get me out of Hong Kong?"

He said truthfully, "I can try."

"Legally?"

"I can try."

She hesitated another moment, then pulled out a carry-on bag, began to rummage through her bedroom, and threw clothing into the bag. She spent some time in the bathroom, dumping in supplies. Finally, she went to a bulletin board in the kitchen and removed some snapshots that captured some lost moments in her life. The last thing she did was to take a child's toy from the kitchen window. It was one of those petal-shaped pinwheels on a stick. She shoved it into the bag.

"It's for good luck," she said. She zipped up the bag and threw it on her shoulder. "I'm ready."

"Good girl," he said, then drew his gun. He moved to the front door and listened. He motioned her to follow him as he unlatched the bolt and slid the door open. The hallway was empty. They walked to the lift, and Bond noticed that it was moving up toward their floor.

"Let's take the stairs," he said.

With gun in hand, Bond led the way down, a flight at a time. At the twelfth floor, he heard footsteps hurrying up below them. He pressed Sunni back against the wall and waited. Sure enough, two more Chinese youths brandishing choppers appeared. Bond shouted "Freeze!" in Cantonese, but the thugs ignored him and charged. It left him no choice but to shoot. The gunfire reverberated loudly in the stairwell. The two Triads slammed back against the wall, then rolled down a flight of steps.

It wouldn't be long before the police arrived, he thought. They needed to get to the street and find Woo before that happened. His wounded arm felt as if it was on fire. Sunni was frozen in fear in a corner of the stairwell. He gestured for her to keep following him and continued down the stairs.

At the seventh floor they encountered four men. They rushed at Bond, attempting to overpower him. Bond got off one shot at point-blank range but had to duck to avoid the swings of the choppers. He rolled forward, through the three standing men, but couldn't avoid losing his balance and falling down the steps. The Walther flew out of his hand and fell to the landing below. One of the men charged at Sunni, his chopper raised. Instead of screaming and cowering, however, Sunni surprised Bond by performing an expert martial arts maneuver. She bent forward as the man swung, blocked his arm, and threw him over her back—a perfect *Yaridama*. The man crashed into the wall behind her. She immediately turned and delivered a crescent-moon kick to the man's chest and fast one-two spear-handed chops to his neck, breaking it.

By now Bond was on his feet, jumping toward the other two. They tried to swing the choppers at him, but he ducked, put his hands on the landing, and shot his legs straight out at them. The kick hit one man in the abdomen, knocking him into his partner. Sunni was behind them, and she grabbed one in a headlock, then brutally rammed him into the wall. In less than a second she was lashing out with a roundhouse kick to the other man's kidneys, sending him flying back toward Bond. Bond simply grabbed his shoulders as the man fell into him, then sent him sailing down the stairs. All four men were now down.

Bond looked up at Sunni with respect and smiled. "Nice work, Sunni."

She shrugged. "I grew up on the streets of Hong Kong before going to the States. I'm not totally helpless."

He retrieved the Walther as they continued down the stairs. They eventually reached the ground floor, and Bond stopped. "They probably have a car down here somewhere. There'll be at least a couple more of them."

He peered out into the covered parking area and saw the black sedan idling near the lot exit. There was only a driver, and he was peering over his shoulder at the lift door, waiting for the men to return. Bond realized that he would certainly see them when they came out of the stairwell.

"Stay here," Bond said. He took a breath, then bolted out of the stairwell. He performed an agile body roll and ended up behind a stone column. The driver of the car shouted something in Chinese. A shot rang out and a bullet broke away a chunk of the column.

Bond heard the car back up and turn toward him. Another shot demolished a chunk of the concrete dangerously close to his head. His left arm was throbbing with pain now, especially after the fight on the stairwell. He was thankful it wasn't his gun arm.

He carefully leaned out and shot toward the car, shattering the windshield, but the driver had opened the door and was squatting behind it for cover. It was going to be a standoff unless Bond could gain a better vantage point from which to fire.

He could hear police sirens in the distance. They'd arrive any minute. He was about to run back to the stairwell when he heard the screeching of tires from the direction of the parking entrance. A red taxi zoomed in and slammed into the driver's side of the black sedan. The driver was sandwiched between the vehicles, his body mangled like a broken doll. Chen Chen was driving the taxi, and his father was sitting beside him.

Bond called to Sunni, and they ran to the cab and got into the backseat. The taxi's only damage was a bent front bumper, so it maneuvered around the car and out of the parking lot just as a police car entered from the other side.

"You call for cab, mister?" said Woo, displaying his trademark grin.

"Sunni, meet my friend T.Y. and his son Chen Chen," Bond said. "Fellows, this is Sunni."

"Welcome and hello," T.Y. said to her. "We take you somewhere nice, uh huh?"

Sunni managed a smile, but she was still too shaken to speak. She was silent through the entire ride as Bond apprised Woo of the evening's events.

"There goes your cover," Woo said. "I do not know many journalists who carry guns and shoot Triads in residential housing, uh huh?"

"I'm just going to have to steer clear of the Dragon Wing boys

119

while I'm here. I hope I haven't compromised anything with Thackeray. I'll just need to watch my back on the street." He turned to Sunni. "Do you know a man named Guy Thackeray?"

She shook her head. He believed her.

"Any news from London?" he asked.

"Nothing," said Woo.

"What about Australia?"

"No one claim responsibility yet. Authorities are clueless. I got report from M. Section A's early findings indicate device was definitely homemade, probably created in crude laboratory. Sounds like someone independent. No affiliation with particular country. It could also be some stupid research lab, illegally experimenting with nuclear power."

Bond thought Woo's theories were sound. There were a lot of companies in the world that had the capability of harnessing nuclear power. The fact that no threats or extortion messages had been received by anyone was now turning out to be a positive sign. Perhaps it was an act of careless experimentation by an irresponsible energy company, with no intention of harm.

It was ten P.M. when the cab arrived at Upper Lascar Row on the island. They all entered the antiques shop and went up the stairs to the safe haven. Woo showed Sunni a room where she could be alone if she wanted. Bond poured himself a glass of straight vodka on ice and drank it quickly. "T.Y., I need to do something about this arm. And quickly."

"I already made call. I know good doctor, he is on his way now. Works for safe house."

Sure enough, a few minutes later a little Chinese man named Dr. Lo arrived. After a half hour, Bond's wound had been sterilized and stitched up. It still hurt, but he could live with it.

"I'm going to need some clothes from my hotel," he told Woo.

"No problem. All taken care of. Chen Chen will collect your things in morning, uh huh? Right now I fix some noodles for you and girl."

"T.Y., she's going to need a foreign passport. She's in danger, and I want to get her out."

Woo frowned. "M will not like that."

"Bad luck," Bond said. "Sunni provided some valuable information, and now we need to protect her. She damned near saved my life at that building. She's one hell of a fighter."

"I see what I can do," Woo said.

Bond finished his vodka. Shirtless, Bond knocked on Sunni's door. She said, "Come in."

She was lying in a fetal position on a double bed in the sparsely furnished room. "Are you hungry, Sunni? T.Y. is making us some dinner." She shook her head. Bond sat down on the bed beside her. "You're going to be okay. We're going to get you a foreign passport. You'll be able to stay here safely until you leave."

"Where am I going?" she asked quietly.

"Where would you like to go?"

"I don't know. I don't really care."

"Well, we'll try England for starters, all right?"

She shrugged. The poor girl had been through a lot—the realization that she was marked for death by the Triad, the discovery of her dead mother, and the traumatic escape from her building. It was enough to make anyone a complete wreck. Sunni had a great deal of fortitude. Bond leaned over and kissed her cheek, then stood up and left her alone.

It was later, after they had eaten a delicious meal of noodles and chicken (Sunni decided to join them but ate very little), and after they had all retired to their respective beds, that Sunni slipped into Bond's room.

He woke up when he felt her presence in the room. She was wearing a T-shirt and panties and stood barefoot by the bed, looking at him.

Without a word, he pulled the sheet down, offering her a place beside him. She slipped into the bed and snuggled next to him. Her body was warm and soft, and her legs felt smooth against his.

They kissed, slowly at first, then with more passion as their desire increased. After a few minutes, she pulled off her T-shirt and pressed her breasts against his chest. She enjoyed the feel of the hair there, as she wasn't used to it. Most Asian men lacked hair on their chests.

She opened up to him that night, over and over again. He filled her with strength and security, helping her achieve a release from the demons that had been tormenting her since the evening began. She needed the climaxes, for they allowed her to forget her troubles and lose herself in a floating world of ecstasy and passion. It was three or four hours later when the couple, totally spent, finally fell asleep in each other's arms.

Assassination

Shoot-out in Kowloon

Royal Hong Kong Police say that two incidents of gunfire in public yesterday may be related. The first occurred in Tsim Sha Tsui East near the nightclub Zipper, where a twenty-two-year-old man was shot by an unknown assassin. A little over an hour later, at a residential building in Kwun Tong, seven men were found dead and two seriously injured. Two of the men were found shot in a flat owned by Sunni Pei, who is reported missing. Her mother, Pui-Leng Pei, was also found dead in the flat, but it is believed she died of natural causes. Police suspect Triad activity is behind the two incidents. . . .

Zero Minus Seven: June 24, 1997, 3:55 P.M.

The newspapers were full of yesterday's news, for shoot-outs on the streets of Hong Kong were surprisingly uncommon. James Bond had made a point to examine SIS reports on the colony's crime status before leaving England. According to these, Hong

Kong was perhaps the most crime-free city in Asia. Gun control was very tight, and obtaining arms was difficult even for criminal organizations. The Royal Hong Kong Police was one of the most efficient forces in the world.

It was unfortunate that Sunni's name and picture were prominently displayed in the paper. Now she would definitely be a target. It would be even more problematic getting her out of Hong Kong. At least he hadn't been identified. Otherwise he would have to listen to M blame it on him for getting involved with "a tart."

Bond put the news behind him and concentrated on the task at hand. It was time for Guy Thackeray's mysterious press conference.

EurAsia Enterprises' corporate headquarters was located in a thirty-four-story building sitting in the heart of Hong Kong's busy Central District. Nearby were such landmarks as the Bank of China Building, the Hongkong and Shanghai Bank Building, Jardine House, Government House, and Statue Square.

James Bond arrived for the press conference early, just in time to learn that the event had been moved to nearby Statue Square for reasons unknown. It was a beautiful day, if a bit hot and humid. Perhaps Thackeray thought an outdoor setting would be more pleasant. The square was nondescript for the most part, save for the statue of Sir Thomas Jackson, a former manager of the Hongkong Bank. There was a time when it held several statues of British monarchs, but these had been removed long ago. A neoclassical domed building next to it housed the Legislative Council Chambers, the future of which would become uncertain in six days. Folding chairs had been set up in a roped-off area, and security guards were checking the identification of reporters desiring a seat.

Bond showed his journalist credentials to the security guard. The guard found his name on a list and let him through. He sat in the second row, near the outside end. There was a microphone stand on a small platform in front of the seats. A table had been set up along the side and complimentary glasses of wine were available. Looking around him, Bond remembered that the transition ceremony between the British and the Chinese was to take place in Statue Square at midnight on June 30, in a little less than a week's time.

About forty journalists were there, mostly from Hong Kong. There were a few Westerners present. One section of the audience was made up of EurAsia employees. From the look of them, they were the executives in charge of the company since the tragedy on the floating restaurant. They all looked apprehensive, not knowing what their CEO was about to announce to the world.

While waiting, Bond glanced up and admired the adjacent Hongkong and Shanghai Bank Building, popularly known as simply Hongkong Bank. It was one of the most striking pieces of architecture Bond had ever seen. Designed by the British architect Sir Norman Foster, its structure was based on the principles of bridge technology. Huge steel trusses were slung between two core towers, and the internal floors were suspended from these. Conventional support columns and concrete coverings were avoided by using a special cladding of super-quality aluminum. The see-through walls thus revealed all the inner workings of the lifts, escalators, and offices. The entrance to the bank was from a large open plaza underneath the first floor of the building. Standing guard in the plaza were two bronze Imperial Chinese lions similar to those flanking most important Hong Kong doorways. Dubbed Stephen and Stitt after two former chief managers, the lions served as mascots for all Hong Kong.

At precisely 4:00, Guy Thackeray entered the square followed by two other men, who were obviously bodyguards. They stood on either side of him as he approached the microphone.

Thackeray looked even more haggard than he did in Macau. There were dark circles under his eyes, and he appeared as if he hadn't slept for days. He was dressed in a sharp Armani business suit, though, and managed to exude an air of authority.

"Hello and welcome," he began. Bond again noted the lack of humor, and no trace of a smile. "I have called this press conference to make an important announcement about EurAsia Enterprises. As you know, our entire board of directors was killed recently. There have been a couple of recent attempts on my life as well. I have no idea why we became targets. Unfortunately, it's all had an effect on the company. Our privately held stock is at an all-time low. The future is uncertain, and I have no reason to believe that things will improve. Therefore, I am selling my family's fifty-nine percent of the holdings to the People's Republic of China, effective first of July, 1997."

There was a gasp from the crowd. Bond was surprised as well. The EurAsia executives had turned white and were dumbstruck.

"The remaining forty-one percent is owned by the families of the deceased members of the Board. Those shares will remain with the families, who will be joint owners with China. If they choose to sell their interests, that is up to them. I highly recommend that they do so. As for me, I plan to retire. I will leave Hong Kong and find a nice quiet place to live out the rest of my life. EurAsia Enterprises was begun a century and a half ago by my great-great-grandfather. It started out modestly but grew into an international trade organization. I have been proud to lead the company since I took it over from my own father twenty years ago. But like Hong Kong itself, all good things must come to an end. That is all. Thank you."

He started to leave the platform, but the mass of reporters raised their arms. "Mr. Thackeray! One question!" they called. Thackeray hesitated and said, "All right, I'll take a couple of questions. You, in the front row."

A woman stood and asked, "What made you decide to sell your company to the Chinese? Despite the troubles EurAsia has experienced recently, it's still a multibillion-dollar company!"

Murmurs from the crowd indicated that they all had the same question.

"Yes, you're right, it is still a multibillion-dollar company. The only comment I can make at this time is that I have no choice but to sell. One more question. The gentleman in the green jacket."

A man stood and asked, "Where are you planning to go?"

"I haven't decided. Certainly not England. I've never lived there, nor do I wish to. That's all. Thank you for coming."

He left the platform abruptly, and pandemonium broke out. The EurAsia people jumped up and ran toward Thackeray. The two bodyguards protected him, but Bond could feel their anger and dismay. This was all news to them. Very bad news.

"Mr. Thackeray! What is the meaning of this? How long have you known?"

Thackeray turned to them and said, "I'm sorry. You must make other arrangements with your lives. Most of you hold foreign passports. I suggest you use them. It's been a pleasure working with you all. Now I must leave."

It was a cold and cruel response. Despite the terseness of the announcement, Bond perceived that it had been very painful for Thackeray to make it. He was doing his best to remain stoic, though. Even the Englishman who hated Britain was keeping a stiff upper lip. He turned and walked out of Statue Square and got into the backseat of a black Mercedes waiting on Des Voeux Road. His window remained down as he looked out at the people and gave a little wave. He wasn't smiling.

Bond watched as the Mercedes pulled away and stopped at a red light. A truck moved into the lane between the car and the people, blocking the view for a moment. The light turned green, and the truck moved forward. The car moved into the intersection slowly. Thackeray's window was still down, but he had retreated into the darkness of the vehicle and couldn't be seen.

Suddenly, a young Chinese man dressed in black ran out into the intersection from the other side of the street. He passed by the open window of the Mercedes and threw something into it. Then he started running north across the square for all he was worth.

The car exploded into flames with such force that many of the people closest to it were injured. Bond felt the heat from the blast, and he was a hundred meters away. He quickly surveyed the scene—at least three pedestrians were lying on the ground, clutching their eyes. Everyone was screaming and running around in a panic. The Mercedes was totally destroyed. Only the smoking, charred chassis remained. Pieces of debris, possibly along with human body parts, lay in black, burning heaps on the street. Along with everyone else, Bond was shocked. The CEO of EurAsia Enterprises had been assassinated while the whole city was watching.

Bond turned to locate the running man and saw him leave the square and run into the plaza underneath the Hongkong and Shanghai Bank Building. He took off after him; no one else had been alert enough to follow him. Thackeray's bodyguards must have been blown to bits as well.

Access to the bank from the plaza was by way of what were claimed to be the longest freely supported escalators in the world. The entrance was set into a double glass ceiling above the plaza, and let visitors out on Level 3, the public banking business area. The assassin had disappeared up the escalator and was now inside the bank, probably hoping he could lose himself in the crowd and eventually sneak out. Determined to find him, Bond scrambled up the escalator.

Bond stepped onto the third level. He was struck by the spectacular atrium rising 170 feet through eleven levels of the building. The teller areas were situated on the north and south sides of the atrium. Other escalators went up to a fifth level, where more public banking services were available. Bond quickly scanned the place from the east end of the building.

Black was not an easy color to spot in a crowd. The bank was fairly busy, as it was near closing time. There was no sight of the assassin. Bond looked up to the fifth level and thought he saw a man in black moving along the right side of the atrium toward the west end of the building. He quickly ran up the next escalator and to the fifth level.

Attempting to look inconspicuous, Bond stepped up to a long counter where bank customers filled out forms and deposit slips. He surveyed the large room and found his prey. The assassin was moving toward a lift lobby on the west end of the building. He was looking around, trying to determine if he was being followed. Bond kept moving toward him, picking up the pace of his stride.

By now, police sirens and a fire truck had arrived outside. Many of the bank employees were looking out of the south-side windows at the chaos in the street below. A security guard who usually blocked access to the lifts was also curious and had wandered over to the windows to look. The assassin entered the lift lobby and pressed a button. Then he saw Bond moving toward him, and a look of panic crossed his face.

Bond started to run. There was a good eighty meters between them. The lift door opened and the assassin stepped inside quickly. Damn! Now Bond didn't care who saw him. He ran full speed to the bank of lifts and pressed the Up button. He watched the numbers on the assassin's lift, noting that it stopped on 12. Bond's lift came, and he got inside just as he heard the security guard shout at him to stop.

Level 12 was the top of the atrium. One could look out and survey all of the public areas from this impressive vantage point. Access to the higher floors was restricted to bank personnel only. A security guard stood in the center of the lift lobby to prevent people from wandering up. Bond's lift door opened just in time for him to see the assassin club the guard on the back of his head. The guard fell and the assassin ran to the left toward the stairwell enclosed in glass.

"Stop!" Bond shouted. He hesitated to draw his Walther PPK—he didn't want to start a panic inside the bank. But then the assassin opened the door to the stairwell. An alarm sounded, alerting everyone in the building to their presence.

The assassin began to run up the zigzagging flights of stairs. Bond followed him into the stairwell and took the steps two at a time. Three guards had joined the chase, and the city police were most likely on the way. They entered the stairwell after Bond had climbed two flights and shouted "Stop!" in Cantonese. One of the men then shouted the word in English.

Bond called down to them. "The man who blew up the car outside is running up the stairs! He's dressed in black!" Then he continued the chase.

Who could the assassin be? Was he Triad? Was he part of the Dragon Wing? Why was Guy Thackeray killed? Had he been the target of the floating-restaurant disaster after all, and was this a second attempt on his life? Was this some kind of vendetta? Perhaps someone in the organization knew about his intention to sell the company's stock to China and wanted to stop him. It was possible that the Triad wasn't involved at all. The puzzle was certainly becoming stranger. Bond wondered how he would get to the bottom of any of this now that Thackeray was dead.

He heard a door slam above him. The assassin had left the stairwell. Thanks to Bond's acute sense of hearing, he estimated that the sound couldn't have been more than fifty meters above him. Bond stepped onto the next landing and was met by the sound of gunfire. The assassin had shot a security guard in the doorway of the twentieth floor. Normally there was no exit from the stairwell without a card key. The guard must have opened the door from the inside, hoping to intercept the killer. Now his body was lying in the doorway, jamming it open. Bond leaped over the body and bolted through the door in pursuit.

He saw the killer running toward an open area full of desks and workers. The employees were cowering against the windows. The assassin leaped onto a desk, turned, and fired an automatic pistol at Bond, who dived for the floor just in time. Then, throwing caution to the wind, he drew his Walther, but the man had already leaped to another desk and was no longer a good target.

"Everyone get down!" Bond shouted. The people did as they were told, some of them translating Bond's orders into Cantonese for those who needed it.

The assassin jumped from desk to desk, flinging files and papers into the air, until he reached the other end of the floor. He ran through a door and into another office space leading back in the direction of the lift lobby and stairwell. Bond decided not to follow him through there, but instead to go back the way he had come in the hope of meeting him in the stairwell. The three security guards in pursuit burst into the room with their guns drawn. They shouted at Bond to halt.

"I'm a British policeman!" he shouted. "I'm not the man you're after. He's coming around through the room next door!" The guards looked confused, unsure whether to believe him or not. Suddenly, the assassin ran into the lift-lobby area. He had a frightened woman with him, a bank employee, and his gun was to her head.

He shouted in Cantonese. Bond didn't have to translate his words. The guards froze, as did Bond. Bond said in his best Cantonese, "You won't get away with this."

An empty lift opened behind the assassin, and he took the opportunity to step inside, taking the woman with him. The door closed and the lift started moving up toward the top of the building. Bond immediately pressed the Up button and waited for another lift. One guard was speaking in Cantonese into a walkie-talkie, informing other men where the assassin was headed. They had obviously decided to believe that Bond was on their side.

Just as another lift arrived, Bond noted that the assassin's lift had stopped on level 42. Bond and the guards took the lift up to the same level and stepped out. It was an executive conference room set up in a large space with a bar along the side.

"Oh, no," a guard muttered. He pointed toward an exit leading outside.

They could now see the assassin on a catwalk on the other side of the window. He was inching his way along the catwalk with the woman in tow. He looked as frightened as she did.

"What the hell does he think he's doing?" Bond asked. "He can't escape now!"

A guard said, "He could get on one of our hydraulic lifts on the extension. There is a ladder there he can use to climb down to another floor."

Bond could see what the guard meant. Extended on an aluminum-clad structure was a boxlike "cherry picker" that apparently could move up and down the building and was used to clean the windows. Sure enough, the assassin began to force the woman toward the box. She was too terrified to move. The man pointed his gun at her, shouting at her, but this only made her immobility worse.

"I'm going out there," Bond said, and moved toward the emergency exit. The killer, meanwhile, had abandoned the woman and was making his way toward the box alone. Bond stepped onto the catwalk and was surprised by the force of the wind. He didn't want to look down, for he would surely have difficulty maintaining his balance. All of Hong Kong lay before him. If it had not been from such a precarious perch, it would have been a spectacular view.

The woman was clutching a round beam that was part of the extension, holding on for dear life. Bond reached out to her. "Give me your hand!" he shouted. The woman cried but wouldn't move. "Please! He's gone!" Bond said. "The man is gone! Give me your hand and I'll help you get back inside!"

The woman looked at him through tears. She was about forty, Chinese, and very scared. She said something in Cantonese that Bond didn't understand, but he kept his hand outstretched. He smiled at her and nodded encouragingly. Finally, she nervously extended her arm and clutched Bond's hand. She was trembling furiously.

"All right, I'm going to count to three, then you let go of the beam! Do you understand?"

She nodded.

"One . . . two . . . three!" She let go of the beam, and Bond tugged on her arm. Luckily, she was very lightweight. She flew at Bond, and he grabbed her around the waist with his other arm. She clutched him, hugging him in a viselike grip. He held her, stroking her head, muttering soothing words in her ear. She looked up at him and kissed him several times on the cheek. He laughed, and she managed to smile too.

Bond got her back inside, but by then the assassin had made

his way down the ladder to another floor. There was no telling where he was now. He was probably already back in the building, trying to find a way out.

"Ever seen that man before?" he asked one of the guards as they ran back to the lifts. The guard shook his head.

They heard the sound of distant gunfire. "We should take the stairs," said the guard. Bond nodded. That way they could evaluate the situation on every floor as they went down. They entered the stairwell and flew down the steps, taking two at a time. The guard's intercom chirped when they reached the thirty-fourth floor. The assassin was spotted near the twelfth floor again.

"The lift!" Bond said. One of the guards used his card key to leave the stairwell, and he punched the Down button by the lifts. It came quickly, and the four men piled into the car.

Back on the twelfth floor, Bond found utter chaos. Civilians were lying on the floor, and one security guard was dead on the carpet. Two more guards were crouched against a rail and were aiming off in the distance. The killer had another hostage, a man, and was moving around the perimeter of the atrium on the east side. Bond looked down the atrium and saw that several Royal Hong Kong Policemen had arrived and were making their way into the building and toward the lifts. He thought that perhaps he should let them handle this. He had got himself too involved already. He wasn't sure what the status of his mission was anymore, now that Thackeray was dead. He needed to get back to the safe house and report to London. Yet he somehow felt a responsibility to the hostage and to the people of the bank. If he hadn't chased the man inside, there might not have been any casualties. There might even be more before this was finished. On the other hand, if he hadn't chased the assassin into the bank, he would have got away.

Bond decided that he wouldn't let that happen. The man was going down. Now. He quickly calculated the distance to the assassin. He needed to be no farther away than 180 feet away for the Walther to be effective.

"Talk to him. Distract him," Bond said to the guard. The guard shouted toward the assassin in Cantonese. Bond crouched down below the rail and moved around the side of the atrium, closer to the killer and his hostage. He darted to a desk and was ultimately able to take a position behind them. The killer was oblivious to Bond's approach, for the guard was successfully distracting him. Bond wouldn't need the gun after all. He tackled the man hard, causing him to release the hostage. Bond leaned him back over the rail, holding on to his gun arm. A shot went off into the air, and people screamed.

The two men struggled for the pistol as 007 attempted to keep the assassin's arm high so that no one would be endangered. Face-to-face, they looked at each other with venom. Bond had never seen him before. As a fighter, he wasn't much of a match. The man was exhausted from all the running and the stress from the chase. Bond used his right fist to hit him in the face. The assassin dropped the gun, and it fell the nine levels to the double-glass floor of the atrium. The man attempted to fight back but quickly realized it was no use. Bond hit him again. This time the man shoved Bond away from him, then performed a daredevil leap over the rail. Bond tried to grab his legs to stop him, but it was too late. He fell 170 feet to his death, slamming into the double-glass floor below. Surprisingly, the glass didn't break.

The man had killed himself rather than let himself be caught. Who had hired him? Where did he come from?

The guards all started down, and Bond followed them. They seemed to have forgotten all about him as the employees got up and began milling about. Bond couldn't afford to be questioned by the police. He needed to get away quickly and quietly. On his way toward the lift, he took a tan sports jacket and dark sunglasses from someone's desk and put them on. It wasn't much of a disguise, but it might work if he hurried. He rode the crowded lift down to the third level, where everyone was watching the police climb onto the glass floor to retrieve the killer's body. Bond surreptitiously moved through the crowd toward the escalator down to the plaza, and managed to get out without being seen.

Once on the street, he saw that the police were still at the scene of the explosion, talking to witnesses. He walked west, away from the area, and finally flagged down a taxi.

The cab took him to Upper Lascar Row. He paid the driver and walked up the street toward Woo's antiques shop. There he got another shock.

The front door of the shop was smashed, the lock broken. No one was inside minding the store. He made his way to the keypad at the back, punched in the numbers, and went upstairs. The place had been ransacked. Files were overturned, papers were scattered all over the floor, and the furniture had been ripped up. Bond recognized a thoroughly professional job.

"T.Y.?" Bond shouted. "Sunni?" He searched all the rooms and floors, but no one was there. The British Intelligence station in Hong Kong had been completely destroyed.

12

One of the Links

What had happened to the safe house? How was their security breached? Where were T. Y. Woo, his brother, and his son? Where was Sunni? Maybe they were all safe somewhere. Bond hadn't seen the company taxicab parked near the building.

Then he noticed his briefcase sitting undisturbed on the coffee table. It was still locked. Had someone tried to open it and left it there, or had T.Y. placed it on the table as some kind of message to Bond? Bond opened it, making sure it still contained the new transmitter and other important documents. The number 22 was displayed on the transmitter, which worked much like a telephone beeper with unlimited range. It was a command to call London. He didn't dare do it from the safe house. He quickly changed into a nondescript black polo shirt and black trousers, then left the safe house.

Bond wandered the streets, his mind turning over the events of the past few days. He needed to clear his head. The bright neon of Hong Kong was beginning to shine around him. Sticking to the narrow side streets, he walked past street vendors packing up their stalls for the evening. He strolled through the beautifully land-scaped Hong Kong Park, which was only a few years old. A spectac-ular walk-in aviary within the park contained 150 species of Asian birds, and this is where Bond chose to collect his thoughts.

How did the pieces of the puzzle fit together? What about himself? Were the police looking for him? Had his actions at the Hongkong Bank been documented by photographers or hidden video cameras? Was his face known? Would the Dragon Wing Society be looking for him, even though Sunni was the object of their hunt? Would they recognize him if they saw him? The unfor-tunate racist comment "All Chinese look alike" was also often said by the Chinese in reference to *gweilo*.

What about Guy Thackeray and his corporation? What the hell happened at that press conference? One minute the man was alive, delivering a bombshell to the world, and the next minute a bombshell was delivered to him. Who was responsible? Was it the Triad? Was it China? Thackeray had referred to other attempts on his life. Was he referring to the incident in Macau? If so, how did he know about the secret exit and when to leave by it? Bond wanted to know if the police had identified Thackeray's killer yet. If only Woo was around—he could talk to his contact with the Royal Hong Kong Police.

Bond decided to take a risk by going back to the Mandarin Oriental. A room there would provide some privacy for a phone call to London. When he left the aviary, he noticed nearly a hun-dred people, most of them Chinese, walking through the park carrying signs. The signs, written in Chinese and English, were pro-democracy slogans. One read "Stay out of our hair, China." Another read, "One country, two systems—remember your prom-ise, China." Yet another read, "No troops at the border." It re-minded Bond that Chinese troops had massed north of the New Territories. That alone would make any citizen of Hong Kong nervous.

Bond walked to the hotel, stopping only to eat a quick dinner in a fast-food Chinese restaurant. Woo had checked him out of the hotel, and Bond quickly learned that there were no rooms available. Bond asked the attractive girl at the reception desk to locate the manager. There really were no rooms available, but the manager allowed 007 to use a private office for a phone call, since he knew Bond personally.

He dialed the access number to get a secure line. When the duty officer answered, Bond said, "Predator," the code name that had been his for the last several years. The duty officer asked him to hold the line. After a few clicks, he heard the voice of Bill Tanner.

"James? Where the hell are you? M's beside herself!"

"I'm fine, Bill. I'm at the hotel at the moment, but I've really no place to stay. The safe house—"

"We know all about the safe house, James. Woo contacted us."

"Where is he?"

"He's all right, and so is his son. They are in hiding. I'm afraid the brother was killed."

"Christ. What about the girl?"

"Girl?"

"There was a girl at the safe house who helped me. We were going to try and get her to England."

"Oh yes, we got that request. You should have heard M's comments on that one. I won't repeat them here. I don't know about the girl. Maybe she's with Woo. As far as a passport is concerned, M is thinking about it."

Bond hoped so. "What happened? Do we know who was responsible?"

"Woo was out of the shop when it happened. He returned with his son to find his brother slashed to bits and the place in a shambles. He called a cleanup crew to dispose of the body and they got out fast. We're not sure where he is at the moment, but I imagine we will hear from him soon. Woo thought it was Triad."

Then it was possible Sunni wasn't with him after all.

"Do you know what happened to Thackeray?" Bond asked.

"Yes, it's all over the news already. Our morning television news programs have covered it. EurAsia Enterprises is the hot topic. There's a lot of speculation, and the P.M. is trying to contact China regarding the so-called sale of the company. It's all extremely bizarre."

"It doesn't make any sense to me either. I've been unable to find out a thing, I'm afraid. Do we know who the killer was?"

"It's still too early. According to the Royal Hong Kong Police, the man had no identification on him. No one knows who the hell he was. Anyway, M still wants you on the case. Just because Thackeray's no longer with us doesn't mean you can't still get to the bottom of it. Keep digging. If you can establish and prove the link between EurAsia and that Triad, you'll have done your job."

"All right, I know where to go next. What's happening in Australia?"

"Nothing new there," Tanner said with a sigh. "It's as if it never happened. If anyone knows anything about it, they're not talking. No one has come forward claiming responsibility. It's a big mystery."

"Great."

"The worry now is the transition. The number of Chinese troops at the border is increasing. Beijing is complaining about all the pro-democracy demonstrations that are taking place. They've asked the Hong Kong governor to put a stop to them, but he's refused. He's standing up for their rights. We all want the transition to be peaceful and dignified. Right now the air is full of distrust and near panic. I should probably tell you that we've sent a couple of warships your way."

"The Royal Navy?" Bond groaned. This was serious.

"You got it. Let's hope that their presence will act as a deterrent."

"Right. Anything else?"

"No. How's your arm? I heard you got cut."

"Hurts like hell, but I'll live."

"You always do. Keep in touch. We'll get you and Woo back together."

One of the Links

Tanner signed off and Bond suddenly felt very much alone, sitting in the middle of a powder keg just waiting to explode.

The Container Port at Kwai Chung was Bond's next stop. Woo had given him directions to EurAsia Enterprises' warehouse located within the huge complex. The only problem was that he would have to get over a barbed-wire fence, but he had encountered worse obstacles in his life.

Bond took a taxi to Kowloon and then farther north into the western New Territories. He had the driver let him off in front of the fenced Container Terminal on Kwai Chung Road. It was night now, and Bond's dark clothing would disappear into the shadows.

Hong Kong is one of the busiest shipping ports in the world. The Kwai Chung Container Port is one of many such terminals in the colony, but it is the largest and serves as a transshipment center for Chinese export goods because China's own transport infrastructure is inadequate. It is as important to China as it is to Hong Kong.

From where he stood, Bond could see hundreds of containers stacked high like colored building blocks. They all had labels and logos painted on the sides—EVERGREEN, UNIGLORY, HYUNDAI, K LINE, WAN HAI, CHO YANG, HANJIN, and others. Tall orange cranes loomed over the containers at strategic points around the port, along with equally tall blue barges. White warehouse buildings were scattered throughout the extended terminal. One could easily get lost, but Bond luckily was equipped with the map that Woo had prepared for him.

He removed his left shoe, pried open the heel, took out the small wire cutter, and replaced the shoe. He climbed the fence and easily snapped the barbed wire, slipped through and over the fence, and jumped down to the pavement on the other side. He took a moment to replace the wire cutter, then pulled the map from his pocket. The EurAsia Enterprises warehouse was at the southern end of the terminal.

Apparently the port never closed, for there were men working here and there, even after hours. The place was well-illuminated by tall floodlights. So much for dressing in dark clothes. . . . Bond darted from one pile of containers to another, hoping no one would see him. After ten minutes, he found the warehouse. It was fully lit and its loading doors were open.

The warehouse was near the shoreline, and Bond could see a large white cargo ship in Rambler Channel, the body of water adjoining the port. It was too far away to read the name on the side, but he assumed it was one of EurAsia's ships. A smaller lighter was traveling from the ship to the shoreline, where cranes were ready to unload cargo. It appeared that the lighter had already made a trip or two, for men were busy moving crates into the warehouse on forklifts. Bond moved closer to the building, looking for an entry somewhere at the back.

There was a door behind the warehouse, probably an emergency exit of some kind. Bond was sure it would be locked, but he tried it anyway. He was right. Twenty feet above him was an open window, but he had no way to scale the wall. Without a second thought, Bond snapped open the clasp on his belt buckle. Q Branch had devised this standard field-issue piece of equipment many years ago. A set of fiberglass lockpicks were hidden inside, undetectable by X ray. Bond squatted so that he was eye level with the doorknob, and slowly tried each pick until he found one that worked. In three minutes, the door was unlocked. He replaced the lockpicks and slowly inched open the door.

He was at the back of the dimly lit warehouse. There was a token crew working, perhaps three or four men. Bond slipped in and shut the door, then moved quickly to an area containing stacks of cardboard boxes. By peering around the boxes, he got a full view of the entire warehouse.

It was full of crates, boxes, forklifts, and other machinery. A prefabricated building serving as an office was built on scaffolding. Metal steps led up to the office. Its door was open, light pouring

out of it. Through the single window, Bond could see that someone was in there.

The most curious thing about the warehouse was the object
that sat upon a wheeled platform. It was a wooden sampan, a
simple boat with a hood covering. The word *sampan* means "three
planks," and that's practically all it was. What was it doing here?
Unlike the sampans one could see in Aberdeen Harbour, this one
looked brand new, as if it had just been built. Bond doubted that it
had ever been in the water. It was painted dark brown and had a
bright red hood. Red was the universal Chinese good luck color.

A figure emerged from the office and descended the steps.
Bond's jaw dropped when he saw who it was. The man was the
albino Chinese he had dubbed "Tom"—the heaviest of the three
men he had seen with Li Xu Nan at The Zipper. Tom spoke to the
workers and pointed outside. Immediately, the men moved to the
sampan and began to wheel it out of the warehouse. Tom followed
them.

Now was Bond's chance to get into that office. He ran up the
steps, knowing that he had a minute or two before Tom came
back. In addition to the window that faced the warehouse, there
was also one looking out at the harbor. On a desk beneath that
window was a stack of papers. Bond recognized a shipping itinerary
on top, printed on EurAsia Enterprises letterhead. Even though it
was written mostly in Chinese, Bond could translate the name of
the ship as the *Taitai*. A pair of binoculars lay on the desk. Bond
used them to look at the ship in the harbor. There was very little
light, but he could just make out the name of the vessel. Sure
enough, the word *Taitai* was painted on the bow. Bond put down
the binoculars and ran his finger down the itinerary, noting dates
and routes for the boat. Its next stop was Singapore, scheduled for
June 26, with a planned return on June 30.

A metal briefcase also lay on the desk. Bond found that it was
unlocked and looked inside. It was full of cash, all Hong Kong
currency, and a lot of it—thousands of dollars.

A map of Southeast Asia was tacked onto a cork bulletin board on the other side of the room. Bond studied it closely, for it was marked with yellow highlights. Several lines apparently charted different routes, over land and sea, from Hong Kong to a circled area in the Yunnan Province in China. Bond immediately recognized it as the "Golden Triangle," the infamous no-man's-land, the source of most of the world's heroin.

Bond glanced out of the window. Tom was still giving orders to the men. The sampan had been positioned under a crane. The lighter he had seen earlier was nearing the shoreline and was about to dock. Were they going to load the sampan onto the *Taitai*? Whatever for?

He knew he had only a few more minutes. He opened a file cabinet next to the desk and saw numerous manila folders. They were all marked with innocuous headings, certainly all pertaining to the shipping business. One, however, caught Bond's eye. It was marked "Australia."

He pulled out the folder and opened it. Oh yes, he remembered. EurAsia Enterprises owned a gold-mining operation in Western Australia. The material in the folder pertained to that. There was official letterhead reading, "EurAsia Enterprises Australia," and the address was in Kalgoorlie. Thumbing through the pages, Bond found nothing of interest until he came to a large sheet of paper folded three times. He opened it up and saw that it was a map of the Kalgoorlie facility. The gold mine was clearly drawn, showing the winding passages, entrances, and locations of the lodes. One amorphous shape in the mine was marked "Off Limits Area."

That was enough for Bond. He folded up the map and pocketed it. He then replaced the folder, shut the file cabinet, and took another look out of the window. Tom wasn't there! Bond moved to the doorway and peered out. Tom was standing at the warehouse loading doors, looking out at the harbor. If Bond moved slowly and silently, the man wouldn't see him. Bond stepped out of the door, swung his leg over the rail, heaved his body over, and carefully climbed down the scaffolding to the floor. He moved into the shadows back against the wall just as Tom turned and began to walk back toward the office. When the albino reached the room above him, Bond sprinted to the back of the warehouse, where he had been earlier.

A few moments later, Tom turned out the lights in the office, locked the door, and descended the stairs. He was carrying the metal briefcase. At that moment, a forklift entered the warehouse with one of the newly unloaded crates. Bond watched as Tom opened the crate with a crowbar, inspected the crate's contents, and pulled out a burlap bag. Another man wearing a suit entered and stood beside the forklift. Bond had never seen him before. Both he and Tom bent down to inspect the contents of the burlap bag. They seemed to be in agreement about what they saw. Tom handed the metal briefcase to the new man. He opened the case for verification, then closed and locked the case and shook hands with Tom. They walked out of the warehouse together, and the place was empty again.

Bond sprinted to the opened crate and took a quick look at the burlap bag. His suspicions were confirmed when he saw what was there. He didn't have to taste it to be certain that it was refined heroin. Without hesitating any longer, Bond hastened back to his position just as Tom and the other workmen returned to the warehouse. Bond slipped out of the back door, then moved around the side of the building so he could get a better view of the unloading.

Sure enough, the sampan was in the process of being lifted by crane onto the lighter. Why the hell were they shipping a sampan to Singapore?

A gray Rolls-Royce was parked near the entrance to the warehouse. The new man with the briefcase full of money was closer and plainly visible. He was Chinese and had a long scar that went across his nose and down his left cheek. Scarface opened the back door of the Rolls and got inside, joining another man sitting in the backseat.

It was Li Xu Nan.

At last, he had found one of the links to the puzzle! He had made the connection between EurAsia Enterprises and the Triad. Some kind of smuggling operation was being managed from this very warehouse. Guy Thackeray's assassination was now making more sense. He must have learned of the smuggling and tried to stop it. The Triad must have killed him to get him out of the way. That still didn't explain why he wanted to sell his company, though.

Bond had to follow that Rolls. He made his way back through the Container Port to the fence, through the barbed wire, as before, and jumped to the ground below. Sooner or later, the Rolls would leave the Port and drive down this road, but how could he follow it?

The answer came rolling down Kwai Chung Road in the form of a red and silver taxicab. Bond flagged it down and got in the backseat. He told the driver in Cantonese to wait: they were going to follow another car in a moment. He handed the driver fifty Hong Kong dollars, so he was happy to do what he was asked.

Sure enough, the Rolls-Royce soon appeared and headed for Kowloon. Bond made sure the taxi kept a safe distance.

13

Triad Ceremony

10:00 P.M.

The Rolls-Royce drove south to Boundary Street and then east across the peninsula. The road soon merged with West Prince Edward Road and the Rolls turned off into the area known as Kowloon City, not far from Kai Tak Airport. It pulled into a narrow, dingy alley and stopped. Bond told the taxi driver to let him out at the corner and managed to get out without being seen.

It was not a well-lit or inviting neighborhood. In fact, if Bond's memory served him correctly, he was near where the infamous "Walled City" used to be. This notorious pocket of vice and squalor was always an embarrassment. Long ago, before British rule, the enclave was a Chinese military outpost. After the British took over, a granite-walled fortress was constructed. The New Territories lease of 1898 left the area under Chinese jurisdiction due to an administrative error, and it remained unregulated by the Hong Kong government. By the mid-sixties, the Walled City was a cesspool of crime, the haven of drug smugglers, prostitutes, thieves, and murderers. Britain and China finally reached an agreement in 1987 to rid themselves of this sewer, and in 1993 the Walled City was demolished. A park was now being developed on the site. Nevertheless, Bond thought the absence of the Walled City didn't make the neighborhood seem much friendlier. The side streets south of the proposed park were just as sinister. It was just the place for Triads to operate, and it was precisely where James Bond now found himself.

Bond watched the men get out of the Rolls. They entered a shabby building, and then the Rolls drove away. He waited a minute, then stealthily crept toward the middle of the alley. Li Xu Nan and Scarface had entered what appeared to be an abandoned building. The door was loose on its hinges, and the windows were broken and, in some cases, completely missing.

Bond decided to climb up another level and perhaps slip into one of the second-floor windows. It wasn't difficult to get a foothold, but once inside, he found himself in a dark room with a wooden floor. The slats in the floor were loose, allowing some light from the level below to seep through. If he wasn't careful, the floor would creak. Bond got down on his stomach and snaked along the floor, distributing his weight so that the noise would be minimized. Through the slats, he could see several men milling around, preparing for some kind of meeting. They were dressed in black robes resembling those worn by Buddhist monks, with white sashes serving as belts. They also wore strange headbands made of red cloth, with the free ends hanging down over the front of the body. There were a number of large loops, or knots, in the bands around their head.

Bond searched his memory for what he knew about Triads and their sacred initiation ceremonies. If they were about to perform a rite, then he could very possibly be the only Westerner to ever witness it. He had to make sure he was completely silent, as they would surely kill him if they found him.

An altar was constructed at the west end of the room, illuminated entirely by candlelight. A large wooden tub painted red and filled with rice was in front of the altar. Four Chinese characters adorned the outer circumference of the bucket; Bond translated them as "pine," "cedar" (both of which signified "longevity" to the Chinese), and "peach" and "plum" (both of which denoted "loyalty").

He remembered that the bucket was called the "Tau," and contained various precious objects of the society, including five sets of four triangular flags, or pennants, which represented the names of legendary "ancestors" of the five "Lodges" of Triad societies.

More important were the "Warrant Flags," which were used by Triad officials during the ceremony. The name "Dragon Wing" was written in Chinese down the side of the Warrant Flag of the Society Leader, and the main character "Ling" ("warrant") was in the center. An upright, oblong-shaped flag bore the characters meaning "Order of the Commander of the Three Armies," another reference to the complex legendary history of the Triads. Most of the flags had two red pennons attached to the top bearing the characters meaning "Act According to the Will of Heaven: Overthrow Ch'ing, Restore Ming."

The main altar had a number of peculiar items on and around it. Above the Tau and its contents, which stood in front of the altar, hung a sheet of red paper. It bore characters indicating the hope that the society would flourish throughout the country. Among the other items present were brass lamps, a pot of wine and five wine bowls, an incense pot for holding joss sticks, dishes of fresh fruit and flowers, and a large mixing bowl. Finally, there was a sheet of yellow paper bearing the names of the Triad's recruits hanging above the altar, and five small triangular flags. Characters meaning "wood," "fire," "metal," "earth," and "water" were written on these five flags.

Bond heard a drumbeat a few times and the room became silent. Li Xu Nan, dressed in a red robe, entered the room and sat to the left of the altar. As he was Cho Kun, the Dragon Head, his was the only robe decorated with characters. On his left arm was a white circle containing the Chinese character meaning "Heaven." On his right arm was the character meaning "Earth." On his back were two characters meaning "Sun" and "Moon," respectively, but when combined they meant "Ming." On the front of the robe was an octagonal symbol of the Pat Kwa, or "Eight Diagrams." In the center of the octagon was the yin and yang symbol of opposing yet complementary forces upon which the major portion of Chinese philosophical thought was based. Magical powers were ascribed to this venerated emblem, and for this reason it was frequently employed by priests, necromancers, geomancers, and ordinary people as a good luck or protective charm.

The man Bond referred to as Scarface entered the room and sat to the right of the altar. He was wearing a white robe, and was the only man with a string of prayer beads around his neck. Bond didn't know much about Triad ceremonies, but he did know that they were usually led by an official known as the Heung Chu, or "Incense Master," who acted as a spiritual leader and sometimes second in command of the society. Scarface was obviously the Incense Master.

Two men in black robes stood at the extreme east end of the room, holding swords to block the entrance to the Lodge. Another official in a black robe, the recruiting officer, moved from the altar down to the east end and began the ceremony. Bond noted that four Chinese teenagers stood outside the swords. They were not dressed in black robes, but rather in simple white shirts and trousers. These were the recruits.

The recruiting officer turned his right shoulder to the "guards" and called out in Cantonese, "Lower the net!" He made a sign with his left hand, denoting his rank within the organization. The two men in black robes then performed the secret handshake of the society out of view of the recruits. After performing this ritual, the recruiting officer was allowed through the swords.

The first official then addressed the recruits in Cantonese, "Why do you come here?"

The recruits replied in unison, "We come to enlist and obtain rations."

"There are no rations for our army."

"We bring our own."

"The red rice of our army contains sand and stones. Can you eat it?"

"If our brothers can eat it, so can we."

"When you see the beauty of our sworn sisters and sisters-in-law, will you have adulterous ideas?"

"No," the recruits replied in unison. "We would not dare to."

"If offered a reward by the government, even as much as ten thousand taels of gold, to arrest your brothers, would you do so?"

"No. We would not dare to."

"If you have spoken truly, you are loyal and righteous and may enter the city to swear allegiance and protect the country with your concerted efforts."

The recruits each handed the official some money, and in return received a joss stick, which they held in both hands. The recruits then got on their hands and knees and crawled under the raised swords, symbolizing that they were "passing through a mountain of knives."

Scarface, the Incense Master, stood and picked up the Warrant Flag of the Leader from the Tau and displayed it to everyone in the room.

"The Five Founders bestow on me the banner of authority," he said. "With it I will bring fresh troops into the city. We will pledge fraternity according to the will of Heaven. None must reveal the secrets that may be disclosed to him. The brethren have elected me to take charge of the Lodge, and have entrusted the seal of authority to my care. I am determined to exercise my authority."

The Incense Master then turned to three minor officials present near the altar. Bond recognized them as the three officials who were next in the chain of command of the organization. They were known respectively as the White Paper Fan, who acted as an adviser or counselor; the Red Pole, who was a fighter and trainer; and the Straw Sandal, who acted as messenger and communications officer.

The Incense Master said to the Straw Sandal, "An order has

been issued from the Five Ancestors Altar. Investigation must be made around the Lodge. If police are present to spy on us, they must be relentlessly washed." With that, he handed the Straw Sandal a warrant flag and a sword.

Bond knew that "washed" meant "killed." The Straw Sandal went around the room, checking the identities and hand signs of everyone present. When he was finished, he returned and handed back the flag and sword, saying, "I now return the order flag in front of the Five Ancestors Altar. Thorough search has been made of the Lodge. Everywhere was searched. All are surnamed Hung."

This confused Bond until he remembered that "Hung Mun" was a universal surname meaning "Triad Society," and was used by all Triads. The ceremony was clearly going to be a difficult test of Bond's knowledge of Cantonese!

The Incense Master then lit two tall single-stemmed brass lamps on the altar, saying, "Two old trees, one on either side, will bring stability to the nation. Heroes are recruited from all parts of the country. Tonight we pledge fraternity in the Red Flower Pavilion." Next he lit five joss sticks, then held them in both hands. He began to recite a lengthy poem.

"We worship Heaven and Earth by the three lights. Our Ancestors arose to support the Ming. The Hung door is open wide and our brothers are many. Hung children are taught to remember the oaths and rules. Politeness, Righteousness, Wisdom, Faithfulness, and Virtue are our fundamental rules. The three talents—Heaven, Earth, and Man—combine to establish the nation. We dedicate ourselves by the drawing of blood. Our Ancestors showed their loyalty by sacrificing themselves for the Emperor."

Bond watched and listened in fascination as the Incense Master continued his recitation. After several minutes, Scarface placed the five joss sticks in the main incense pot on the altar at the five cardinal points—north, east, south, west, and center. As he did this, he said, "The smoke of the incense sticks reaches the Heavenly Court, penetrates the earth, rises to the center, rises to the

Triad Ceremony

Flower Pavilion, and reaches the city of Willows. We pledge fraternity in a union to overthrow Ch'ing—to bring an end to the decadent Ch'ing Dynasty and restore the rivers and mountains to Ming."

Next, the Incense Master took the dishes of fruit and flowers and a cup of wine and placed them in front of the memorial tablet on the wall. He recited a similar poem, then poured the cup of wine onto the floor.

The recruits knelt before the Incense Master and rolled up their trouser legs. The left trouser leg was rolled three times outward to signify the resurgence of Ming, and the right was rolled three times inward to signify the disappearance of Ch'ing. Then they removed their shoes and put one straw sandal on their left feet. The Incense Master said, "Straw sandals were originally of five strands. In a battle at Wu Lung River they were lost. Only one was saved and retrieved at Chung Chau."

Next, he poured wine into cups and emptied them onto the floor. "Wine is offered to the souls of our Ancestors and to those who died for our cause. Our fraternal spirit will last forever. The heroes in heaven will protect us. We swear we will kill all the traitors, so that Hung brothers can enjoy happiness and peace."

At this point, two officials in black robes brought in three life-size paper figures in a kneeling position. They were placed on the floor, and a label was attached to each figure bearing one of the names of three historical Triad traitors. An official known as the Sin Fung, or Vanguard, took a long sword from the Tau and approached the figures. He placed the five elemental flags around them and said, "A big flag is erected in the Lodge. All heroes come here to worship. When our troops move out onto the plain, this sword will first stab Ma Ning Yee." With that, he swiftly cut off the paper head of the first figure.

"When the sword is turned back, it is used to stab Chan Man Yiu." He then cut off the head of the second paper figure.

"On the third occasion, it stabs the bad Emperor of Ch'ing."

He then cut off the head of the third paper figure and called out, "Brothers assembled here, will you give help when the need arises?"

Everyone in the room shouted, "We will!" so loudly that it startled Bond.

At this point, the Incense Master took each of the items in the Tau, one by one, and recited a short poem about each. Following this was a long, drawn-out question-and-answer session between the Incense Master and the Vanguard, "proving" the identity and validity of the Vanguard and his role in the ceremony.

It was time for the actual initiation of the recruits. Each potential Triad member was given a joss stick, which was lit and held pointed down with both hands. The Vanguard asked them, "Which is the harder, the sword or your neck?"

The recruits all answered, "My neck." Bond deduced that this was an indication that even the threat of death would not cause them to reveal the society secrets. Then the Vanguard began to read the Thirty-six Oaths of the Society. As each oath was proclaimed, a new joss stick was lit and handed to each recruit. The recruits repeated the oath and then extinguished the joss stick on the ground in front of them, symbolizing that they, too, would be similarly extinguished if they broke the oath.

"After having entered the Hung gates I must treat the parents and relatives of my sworn brothers as my own kin. I shall suffer death by five thunderbolts if I do not keep this oath.

"When Hung brothers visit my house, I shall provide them with board and lodging. I shall be killed by myriads of swords if I treat them as strangers.

"I will always acknowledge my Hung brothers when they identify themselves. If I ignore them I will be killed by myriads of swords.

"I shall never betray my sworn brothers. If, through a misunderstanding, I have caused the arrest of one of my brothers I must release him immediately. If I break this oath I will be killed by five thunderbolts."

Triad Ceremony

The oaths continued in this fashion, mostly dealing with subjects regarding honor, betrayal, loyalty, and defending other members of the society. Several of the oaths were promises not to commit adultery or harm the other brothers' family members. Finally, the Vanguard reached the last two oaths.

"I must never reveal Hung secrets or signs when speaking to outsiders. If I do so I will be killed by myriads of swords.

"After entering the Hung gates I shall be loyal and faithful and shall endeavor to overthrow Ch'ing and restore Ming by coordinating my efforts with those of my sworn brethren even though my brethren and I may not be in the same professions. Our common aim is to avenge our Five Ancestors."

The Vanguard called out, "Will you swear to obey the oaths?"

"We swear to obey!" the recruits replied.

"Those who obey will be prosperous to the end. Those who do not will die as laid down in the oaths."

During this recitation, the large yellow paper at the front of the altar was held up high and then set on fire. The ashes were placed in the large bowl, to which was added rice wine, sugar, and cinnabar.

An official entered the room carrying a live chicken and a china bowl. He passed in front of each recruit, allowing them to touch the chicken's head and the bowl. The Vanguard, who was holding the long sword, said, "The lotus flower signifies wealth and nobility. Loyally and faithfully we perpetuate the Hung family. The wicked and treacherous will be broken into pieces, in the same manner as this particular lotus flower." That said, the Vanguard took the china bowl, tossed it in the air, and deftly smashed it to pieces with the sword. The official then handed over the chicken to the Vanguard and helped him tie its legs together. They placed the chicken's head on a chopping block, with the bowl of ashes, wine, sugar, and cinnabar on the floor next to the block.

"The chicken's head sheds fresh blood. Here there is loyalty and righteousness. We will all live long lives."

The Vanguard stood and, with great show, cut off the chicken's head with one swift blow of the sword. There was an immense amount of blood, and the headless body jerked grotesquely as if it were still struggling to get away. The Vanguard took the head and dipped it into the bowl, mixing the blood with the other ingredients. The carcass was then taken away, and the recruits all held up their left hands, palm out. The Incense Master approached them, holding a needle and red thread.

He said, "The silver needle brings blood from the finger. Do not reveal our secrets to others. If any secrets are disclosed, blood will be shed from the five holes of your body."

The Incense Master then pricked the middle finger of each recruit's left hand and added their blood to the bowl's mixture. Each recruit touched the mixture with the pricked finger, then placed the finger in his mouth to taste the substance. "It is sweet," they all said, one by one. Next, the Incense Master poured a little of the mixture into cups and handed one to each recruit.

"After drinking the Red Flower wine, you will live for ninety-nine years. When nine is added to this number, you will live for one hundred and eight years."

Bond's stomach turned as the recruits drank from their respective cups.

The Incense Master then formed a signal with his left hand, designating the recruits' ranks in the society. The recruits stood and bowed to the Incense Master, the Dragon Head, the Vanguard, and to each other.

The entire assembly stood and recited, "Old and new brothers gather here tonight. Loyalty and faithfulness will ensure us longevity. Wicked and treacherous will perish like the incense sticks."

Officials began to dismantle the altar as the chant continued, "The city is being dismantled from East to West, from the South Gate to Peking City. No firecrackers are fired in celebration, the metropolis is reduced to ashes."

The ceremony was over. The entire rite took a little more than two hours. The recruits joined the ranks of the other members as

Triad Ceremony

Li Xu Nan, the Cho Kun, the Dragon Head, stood and addressed the society.

"We will gather again in three days to perform the final phase of the initiation ceremony—in which your faces shall be cleansed. We welcome our new brothers to the Dragon Wing. We have one more piece of business to conduct tonight. One of our Blue Lanterns has broken her oaths. We must decide her fate." He turned to the Vanguard. "Bring out the traitor."

The Vanguard motioned toward a door. Two officials brought in a girl. She was blindfolded, and her hands were tied behind her back.

Bond's heart jumped into his throat. It was Sunni!

"Our sister here has betrayed the society, not only to a stranger but to a *gweilo*. She has sought refuge with the enemy. She has sought to leave the fraternity. What must we do with her?"

The group shouted, "She must die!"

Li stood for a moment in silence. He walked around Sunni, who was now on her knees on the floor. He inspected her as if he were evaluating prized livestock.

"I agree with my younger brothers," he said, "but we shall wait. The traitor may be useful in an enterprise valuable to the society. For the time being, she will be kept in isolation." He nodded to the two guards, who pulled Sunni up and led her out of the room. It took every ounce of Bond's strength not to burst through the dilapidated ceiling and attempt to rescue her.

Li Xu Nan and Scarface stood side by side in front of the Triad and gave the hand signs for their ranks. Scarface said a final prayer and dismissed the group. The meeting was over. The members left silently and, after a few minutes, Li, Scarface, and the official who was the Vanguard were alone. They took off their robes.

Scarface took the metal briefcase from behind the altar. Scarface handed it to the Vanguard, who apparently was the Chan So, or Treasurer, of the organization.

Li said, "This month's earnings. Make sure it is properly distributed. The families of our brothers who were killed at the girl's residence must receive special consideration."

The Vanguard bowed. "Yes, Cho Kun." He took the case and left. Bond watched as Scarface extinguished the rest of the lighting, and he and Li walked out of the Lodge.

Bond waited a full ten minutes before moving. He had to find Sunni. He crawled forward so that he was directly above where the altar had been. There was a loose board there through which he could drop. He pulled it up, then jumped down to the floor below. He waited a few seconds to allow his eyes to adjust to the darkness. Then he moved toward the door where they had taken Sunni and stepped through it.

He was met by myriads of swords, all pointing at his chest.

14

Bedtime Story

The speed with which Bond was disarmed was startling. He felt as if he were moving in slow motion and that everything else was happening too fast. The Triads with the choppers marched him to the adjacent building, one that was obviously still in use. One of them unlocked the door and roughly shoved Bond inside. He was led down a hallway to another locked steel door. Behind it was a dark staircase leading to a basement. Bond was pushed inside, and the door slammed and locked behind him.

Bond crept down the stairs in the dim light to a small, bare room containing a cot and a toilet. It was, to all intents and purposes, a jail cell.

Sunni Pei was sitting on the cot. When she saw him, she jumped up and ran to him. "James! My God, James!" she cried, then fell into his arms and held him tightly.

Bond stroked her head and embraced her. "It's all right, Sunni. We'll get you out of this."

"They're going to kill me, James, I know it!" She said this with anger and spite, not with the tears he had expected. "And after all I've done for them!"

She released him and led him to the cot.

"I told you before that they've merely used you," he said. "They never made you a full member."

"The oaths still apply to me, though," she said. "And I was taking just as much of a risk with regard to the law in Hong Kong."

She stood up and started pacing the cell. "I can't tell you how I hate myself, James! I was their goddamned *whore*! I sold my body to put money in *their* pockets!"

"Sunni," he said, "you did it because you believed in them. I understand. You believed they would get you out of Hong Kong. You believed they were your brothers and sisters. You believed they would take care of you."

She sat down again. "Well, in many ways they did take care of me. I couldn't have afforded that flat otherwise. They paid for most of it. They gave me a social life, such as it was."

"Sunni, you know that if you hadn't received an American education, that if you had grown up entirely as a Hong Kong Chinese, then you would be thinking quite differently. You *would* have killed me the other day. You would have been loyal to the Triad. Your cultural background would have prevented you from even considering associating with a *gweilo*."

"Oh, I still have a strong Chinese cultural heritage," she said. "I just happen to speak like an American." She used an exaggerated accent on the last word, then she pouted. "You're right, though. It's surprising that they even allowed me into the Triad with my Westernized habits."

"You had other assets that they deemed valuable."

"And what might those be?"

"You're beautiful and you're intelligent."

She smirked. "Oh right, I'm the perfect hostess. I can go with Chinese, American, Japanese, German, *English* . . . you name it."

Bedtime Story

"I didn't mean it that way," he said.

The sound of keys in the door interrupted them. It opened and two Triads stepped in. They gestured for Bond to come with them. Sunni stood up, too, but one of the men roughly pushed her back onto the cot.

Bond shoved the thug against the wall. The other man brutally delivered a spear-handed chop between Bond's shoulder blades, sending him to his knees. The blow had hit the nerve center below his neck, and for a moment Bond saw nothing but stars. The man shouted at Bond in Chinese, then kicked him. 007 weakly got to his feet and followed the men out of the room.

He was brought upstairs, down a hall, and up another flight of stairs. He was finally able to take in more of his surroundings as he walked. The building was a modern business office. It might have been the corporate headquarters of a small real-estate or insurance company. They passed open offices containing new, expensive-looking black and white leather furniture. In many ways, the place reminded him of the way the new M had refurnished SIS head-quarters.

He was finally led into a large, plush office and left alone. It was decorated in the same fashion as the other rooms he had seen, but with a distinctive Chinese flavor. Along with the high-tech, modern furniture, there was a bamboo screen against the wall, painted brightly with a scene of Chinese fishermen snaring a dragon. A small Buddhist altar was in a corner, with a small idol of the god Kwan Ti, or Mo, on it. Bond remembered that not only was Mo the god of policemen, he was also the favored deity of the underworld. There was nothing else in the room that would suggest that the office belonged to the Dragon Head of a Triad. It must have been Li Xu Nan's legitimate office.

Before Bond could sit down, Li entered the room and shut the door behind him. They were alone.

"We meet again, Mr. Bond," Li said in Cantonese. "I am sorry that it is under unfortunate circumstances."

"You can't hold me, Mr. Li," Bond said. "I'm a British citizen. My newspaper will be trying to find me when they've realized I've gone missing." His Cantonese had improved since arriving in Hong Kong.

"Oh, dispense with your crap, Mr. Bond," he said. "You are no journalist. I know who you are."

"I work for the *Daily Gleaner* . . ."

"*Please*, Mr. Bond! I am no fool!" Li walked to his large oak desk and took a cigarette out of a gunmetal case not unlike Bond's own. He lit it without offering one to his captive. "You are James Bond, an agent with the British Secret Service. It was not difficult to ascertain this. You see, I know Mr. T. Y. Woo and what he does. I have known for years that his shop on Cat Street is a front for your station here in Hong Kong. You were followed from Miss Pei's flat the other day. When we saw Mr. Woo's private taxi pick you up, it all fell into place."

"Then it was you who killed J. J. Woo? It was you who ransacked the place?"

Li shrugged. "We wanted the girl. She is a traitor. We deal with traitors most severely. We only messed up the place to leave a message. The elder Woo attempted to stop us. He was an obstacle that we had to overcome. It was not personal."

"Where are T.Y. and his son?"

Li said, "I honestly do not know. They were not there when we raided the building."

"Don't you see that he knows who *you* are and what you do? He can have the Hong Kong Police down on you at any minute."

"He cannot prove a thing. You're the only one who has witnessed anything," Li said. "Let me make this perfectly clear, Mr. Bond. You are a *gweilo*. We don't like you. You are not welcome here. Our ceremonies are sacred and secret. You have seen something no other *gweilo* has ever seen. You are a dead man, Mr. Bond. If I had not stopped them, my brothers would have already killed you."

"Why did you stop them, then?"

Li paused a moment, walked to the drinks cupboard, and removed a couple of glasses. "Drink, Mr. Bond?"

He wanted to refuse, but the drink would actually do him a lot of good. "All right. Bourbon, straight."

Li filled the glasses and handed one to Bond. "Do you remember the other day when you 'interviewed' me? I told you that you were in my debt."

"I remember."

"The time has come for you to repay the debt."

"Why should I?"

"Hear me out, Mr. Bond. You have no other choice."

Bond settled onto the couch. "All right, Li, I'll listen."

"I'll have to tell you a story," Li said, sitting across from Bond in a leather armchair. "A little bedtime story. It involves someone else you know . . . Mr. Guy Thackeray."

Bond interrupted Li. "Did you kill him?"

Li paused a moment and shook his head. "No. We had nothing to do with that. Let me tell you something. I hated Guy Thackeray. He and I were mortal enemies. But I wanted him alive. I needed him alive. And the story I'm about to tell you will explain why. No, he was killed by General Wong, a lunatic up in Guangzhou. You have heard of him?"

Bond nodded. "Are you sure? Why would he do that?"

Li held out his hands tolerantly. "Patience, Mr. Bond. Hear me out. And then you will understand."

The Dragon Head paused a moment, then spoke evenly and calmly. "The year was 1836. A twenty-six-year-old man named James Thackeray had sailed from his home in Britain two years earlier to the Pearl River Delta in southern China. He had heard a fortune could be made trading goods to the Chinese, but it was a difficult time and place to make a living. *Gweilo* were not welcome in southern China. You see, Mr. Bond, China needed nothing from the West, but she was quick to believe that the West needed

China's tea, among other commodities. Therefore, the government grudgingly allowed the 'white devils' to trade on the outer fringes of her empire."

Bond interjected, "It seems to me that each side treated the other as inferior."

"Yes," Li said. "Anyway . . . James Thackeray had originally attempted to trade manufactured goods and had made a meager living with silver, but it wasn't enough to feed his wife and young son, neither of whom was allowed into Guangzhou, or Canton, as it was called then. Other British traders were in the same predicament, and it appeared for a while that trade with China would be a failure.

"No one was quite sure when it happened, but eventually some ingenious trader discovered that the English did possess a commodity that the Chinese wanted. It was opium. The merchants had no qualms against peddling opium to wealthy Chinese, and it soon became the most valuable resource in that part of the world at the time. China was quick to ban the substance, but the British managed to find a way to smuggle it in anyway."

"And the opium trade became big business," Bond said.

"Correct. In 1836, James Thackeray began trading opium and quickly developed a small clientele which provided him with more money than he had ever dreamed of. Thackeray's best customer was an extremely wealthy Chinese warlord and government official residing in Guangzhou. His name was Li Wei Tam." Li paused again, then added, "He was my great-great-grandfather."

Bond sat up straighter. The story was getting interesting.

"My honorable ancestor was a warlord who was ten years older than Thackeray. He had tremendous influence in Guangzhou and the area around the Pearl River Delta. Although the Ch'ing Dynasty was in power, Li's loyalties were with the Mings, who had been overthrown in the seventeenth century. Of course, he would never have admitted this publicly. If he had done so, he would have been arrested and most likely put to death. Li Wei Tam was part of a secret society that had pledged to overthrow the Ch'ing Dynasty.

Bedtime Story

"It was pure luck, really, that James Thackeray had found an audience with the warlord and was able to establish a relationship with him. In fact, the two men grew to respect each other. Although they probably wouldn't admit it to other members of their respective races, they became friends. This was due in part, no doubt, to Li Wei Tam's physical dependence on the drug that James Thackeray so happily supplied." This last bit was said with a certain amount of venom.

Li went on. "In 1839, things started to change. The emperor decided to end the opium trade once and for all. The governor of Hunan Province was ordered to confiscate all of Guangzhou's foreign traders' opium, thus igniting the First Opium War. For the next three years, James Thackeray found it extremely difficult to get his opium into China and to his favored customer. Likewise, Li Wei Tam had to go through unpleasant stretches of withdrawal from the drug. Finally, my great-great-grandfather used his influence in his secret society to establish an illegal pipeline from Thackeray to Guangzhou. In one of the first, albeit unethical, cooperative efforts between a British citizen and a Chinese warlord, James Thackeray was allowed to continue his lucrative opium trade and Li Wei Tam was able to perpetuate his comfortable, horizontal life on an opium bed. I suppose you know what happened in 1842?"

Bond answered, "The war had ended, and Hong Kong Island was ceded to the British."

"Yes. The ban on opium still existed, however. The Chinese government, as a result of what they viewed as an unfair and unequal treaty, made trade an even more challenging endeavor despite the fact that the treaty had guaranteed Britain's right to trade openly and freely."

Bond added, "In China's view, the ceding of Hong Kong Island was a humiliating experience and was never wholly forgotten nor forgiven."

"You are an intelligent man, Mr. Bond," Li said. "I can almost forget you are a *gweilo*. Shall I continue?"

"Please do."

"While companies like Jardine Matheson were allowed to build headquarters on Hong Kong Island, James Thackeray still found himself dealing independently and without an established, legal structure with which to conduct business. He, too, needed a legitimate enterprise that he could call his own. Even though he had made what some men might call a fortune over the last few years, Thackeray needed more capital. It was Li Wei Tam who came to his rescue. One night in 1850, over an exquisite meal, a tremendous amount of rice wine, and quite a bit of opium smoke, a deal was struck that would have repercussions for both men's future generations. My honorable ancestor offered to 'loan' Thackeray the much-needed capital to start his own trading company. Thackeray, who was basically an honest man, was flabbergasted. He said he would accept the money only on the condition that they made a provision by which Li could be repaid.

"My great-great-grandfather was drunk and high from the amount of wine and drugs consumed that night, and thought whimsically about Thackeray's request. For the sake of *xinyong*, a term that means 'trust' in our language, Li Wei Tam attempted to think of a ridiculous demand which Thackeray could never fill as a gesture of his own generosity. After all, his primary motivation was the continuing supply of opium. James Thackeray was his friend, and he hadn't many friends—Chinese or otherwise.

"The ceding of Hong Kong happened to be a much-discussed and extremely controversial topic in southern China at the time. The treaty signed at Nanking had provided that Hong Kong be handed over to the British in 'perpetuity.' "

Bond added, "There were even British citizens who thought the treaty was absurd."

"Yes. At that time, no one could predict that it would one day be the Manhattan of the Far East. Therefore, with a sly grin, my great-great-grandfather told his friend, 'Mr. Thackeray, you may have the money for your company on one condition. You must sign an agreement with me. Should Hong Kong ever come under

Chinese rule again, then your assets in the company shall be handed over to me. It would then become *my* company.'

"Thackeray, who believed that Hong Kong would *never* leave British rule, laughed and agreed. The two men drew up official legal documents. James Thackeray signed them, and Li Wei Tam applied his *chop*, our official family seal, alongside the signature. It was *maijiang* of the highest order. Thus, EurAsia Enterprises was born."

My God, Bond thought, the roots of this whole mess went back a century and a half!

Li continued. "Opium was legalized in 1856 as the Second Opium War began, and during the following years James Thackeray became one of Hong Kong's wealthiest men. EurAsia Enterprises flourished, and even London recognized his and the company's importance. The Kowloon peninsula was ceded to Britain in 1860, and finally, in 1898, the New Territories was leased to Britain for ninety-nine years. Little did anyone know at the time that this last treaty, signed at the Second Convention of Peking, would have a direct effect on Hong Kong Island and Kowloon as well."

"What happened to Thackeray and your great-great-grandfather?" Bond asked.

"James Thackeray died in 1871. His son Richard took over EurAsia Enterprises and continued to trade opium to Li Wei Tam, who had reached a ripe old age. The company expanded, opening branches all over the world. My great-great-grandfather finally succumbed to the gods in 1877, and the partnership between the Thackeray family and the Li family ended. My great-grandfather, Li's only son, never approved of his father's addiction to opium, nor of the *gweilo* who sold it to him. He did, however, make sure that the agreement signed by the elder Thackeray and his father remained intact and safe. Perhaps someday it would come in useful."

Li stood and refilled Bond's glass, then resumed his place in the leather armchair to continue the story. "Now the tale gets a little complicated," he said with a smile. "To make a long story short, in 1911, civil war broke out in China. You may know that an ambitious, Western-educated revolutionary named Dr. Sun Yat-sen initiated a rebellion dedicated to establishing a republican government in China. He succeeded; by 1912, the Ch'ing Dynasty was no more."

Bond was quite familiar with China's tortured twentieth-century history, but he allowed Li to tell it in his own words.

"It was a period of great turmoil. During a skirmish in Guangzhou, my great-grandfather was killed, leaving *his* son Li Pei Wu, my grandfather, to look after the family fortune. Unfortunately, the republican government was extremely unstable; between 1912 and 1949, there were times when it didn't exist at all and the country was a . . ." Again he searched for the right word, and finally said in English, ". . . a free-for-all!" Li smiled at his choice of phrasing.

Bond continued the history lesson. "As for Sun Yat-sen, he formed the Kuomintang party in an attempt to limit the republicans' power. The government outlawed the Kuomintang and Sun Yat-sen was forced into exile."

"You are well informed, Mr. Bond," Li said. "Ambiguous warlords vied for leadership for more than a decade. In 1921, the Communists organized in Shanghai, with Mao Zedong among their original members. They made bids for power in the turbulent country, and in 1923, Sun Yat-sen agreed to admit them to Kuomintang membership. But after Sun's death in 1925, the young general Chiang Kai-shek took over the leadership of the Kuomintang and set about reunifying China under its rule, ridding the country of imperialists and warlords, and exercising a bloody purge of the party's communist membership."

Bond wondered what all this had to do with Li's family. In answer to his thought, Li said, "My grandfather's family got caught up in the maelstrom that ravaged China during this period of unrest. The family fortune was lost to the Communists in 1926, and my grandfather was murdered for having 'secret society' connections. My grandmother and her two young children became refugees and fled across the border into Kowloon. The eldest of the children was a boy of seven named Li Chen Tam."

"Your father."

Li nodded. "The Communists had seized all of my family's property, amongst which was the document of antiquity signed by James Thackeray and my great-great-grandfather, Li Wei Tam. The document was considered lost for all time. I've already told you a little about my father. Li Chen Tam fell into the hard life in which many Hong Kong Chinese refugees found themselves during the years between the two world wars. He supported his mother and baby sister by selling food on the street. When he became a teenager, he made the acquaintance of several other young Chinese boys who belonged to a fraternal organization. They offered to help him financially and protect his family. In exchange, he had to pledge allegiance, as well as secrecy, to their organization. This organization was the San Yee On, which you know as one of the largest and most powerful Triads in Southeast Asia.

"My father rose rapidly through the ranks, especially after entering the lucrative entertainment business in the 1950s. Along the way, like so many of the Triad leaders at the time, he made a few enemies even within his own organization. In the early 1960s, when he was approaching age fifty, my father broke off from the San Yee On and formed his own Triad, the Dragon Wing Society.

"He was quite aware of his great-grandfather's agreement with EurAsia Enterprises but was unable to do anything about it. So my father concocted an underhanded scheme to get his own back. By putting the squeeze on EurAsia's shipping department heads, the Dragon Wing Society infiltrated the company's interior workings. Nothing was shipped out of Hong Kong without the Triad's intervention. Things came to a head, and eventually news of the squeeze went all the way to the top of the company."

"Who must have been, let's see . . . James Thackeray's great-grandson?" Bond asked.

"Correct. Thomas Thackeray, then the current *taipan* of Eur-

Asia Enterprises, and Guy Thackeray's father. While being a shrewd businessman, Thomas Thackeray had inherited his great-grandfather's trait of greediness. If there was an opportunity to add to his fortune, then he would brush ethics aside and encourage the moneymaking to continue. It was with this attitude that Thomas Thackeray justified entering into a business alliance with my father. The two men met in person only once, and secretly, at one of my father's nightclubs. It was agreed that EurAsia Enterprises would provide the means, the Dragon Wing Society would provide the goods and muscle, and together they would share in the profits. Thus, EurAsia Enterprises began distributing heroin all over the world as couriers for the Dragon Wing Society."

Bond noted, "It seems the story has come full circle, practically a reverse of the partnership that existed in the mid nineteenth century."

"Ironically, that is true," Li said. "There was, however, another piece of the alliance. The smuggled heroin had to come from somewhere, and that was the Golden Triangle. A certain young Chinese official in Guangzhou had influence over the operations of the poppy fields there. His name was Wong Tsu Kam. Extremely militaristic and a staunch Communist, Colonel Wong also happened to be even greedier than Thomas Thackeray! He was the unseen, silent partner of Thackeray and my father. He maintained the poppy fields. He refined the opium into heroin in his own laboratories located on site in the Golden Triangle. He cleared the way for the heroin to be safely smuggled into Hong Kong so that the Dragon Wing Society could get it onto EurAsia's ships. For his efforts, Wong received a tremendous kickback. A man with those kinds of assets in China wielded great power, and he used it to advance within the Communist party until he became a full-fledged general in 1978.

"A year before Wong Tsu Kam became a general, Guy Thackeray took over EurAsia Enterprises. I had succeeded my father as Cho Kun of the Dragon Wing Society. Our uneasy partnership continued through the eighties and into the nineties. All along, my father knew of the ancient agreement that would have given us control of EurAsia Enterprises should the Hong Kong colony ever be handed back to China. In 1984, the speculation came to an end when the treaty was signed to do that very thing in 1997. The rage that my father felt at the Thackeray family and at the Communists who had stolen *his* father's assets eventually killed him. He died of heart failure shortly after the news was made public. I carried on, but now a bitter rift existed between me and Guy Thackeray. Our partnership continued, but it was purely a business transaction. It had ceased being personal long ago.

"It was in 1985 that General Wong made his move. One afternoon, his people made an appointment to see Guy Thackeray at EurAsia Enterprises' corporate headquarters in Central. With a Chinese lawyer in tow, General Wong met Thackeray in the company's luxurious boardroom and pulled out a tattered document written in both English and Chinese. General Wong was in possession of the original agreement made between James Thackeray and my great-great-grandfather! According to Chinese law, the state now owned the document and what it represented. Li Wei Tam's heirs had fled China and their assets were seized by the Communist government. Therefore, as the representative of that Chinese government, General Wong informed Guy Thackeray that the fifty-nine percent of stock owned by Thackeray would automatically transfer to China at midnight on June 30, 1997, just as the colony itself would be handed over after a hundred and fifty years of British rule. General Wong had been given full authority to execute the transition and implement whatever new management system he desired. Whatever he decided to do, Guy Thackeray was out. In essence, not only would General Wong gain control of a multibillion-dollar corporation, but he would also increase his profit margin in the drug-smuggling operation by one-third. He would have the monopoly over me and the Society, too! General Wong would be able to call all the shots. As for Thackeray, he would be left high and dry. It made no difference that forty-one percent of the stock was owned by other British citizens. Wong implicitly made it clear that they would be persuaded to sell their shares and leave Hong Kong forever."

"What happened?" Bond asked.

"Guy Thackeray never told a soul about this meeting apart from his own English solicitor, Gregory Donaldson. He spent the following five years consulting Donaldson about the matter. Donaldson was sworn to secrecy, and they searched for a way out. But it was hopeless. Once China took over the colony, their law would reign supreme and the original agreement would be deemed legal. For the next seven years, Guy Thackeray lived with the knowledge that he would have to give up his family's company and there wasn't a damn thing he could do about it. He became a bitter, unhappy man—a friendless recluse prone to gambling for high stakes in Macau."

Bond realized that this explained the man's eccentric behavior and the alcoholism.

"Thackeray arranged a meeting with me one rainy night in 1995 and told me the news. At first, I was ecstatic that my great-great-grandfather's agreement still existed. Then, as the truth of the matter sunk in, I was filled with hatred and the desire for revenge. I hated the Thackeray family for their role in the history of the mess, and I detested General Wong for stealing what was rightfully mine."

Li smiled wryly as he ended the extraordinary story. "Since then, the drug-smuggling partnership has kept operating—it was business as usual. After all, a profit could still be made until things changed in 1997."

James Bond had listened to Li Xu Nan's story, fascinated and repelled at the same time. It was a classic case of injustice and irony. A vicious criminal was being cheated out of something of great value that was rightfully his, and Bond found himself feeling the man's outrage, too.

"So you see, Mr. Bond," Li said, "Mr. Thackeray and I had a mutual interest in keeping Wong from taking over the company. Thackeray and I were not friends. We were enemies, but we had a common goal. I did not kill him."

"But why would General Wong kill him?" Bond asked. "If he was going to gain the company on July the first anyway, why murder Thackeray?"

Li shrugged. "I do not know. You will have to ask him."

"And why was the solicitor, Donaldson, killed? And the other directors?"

"Perhaps they were going to get in the way legally," Li suggested. "Maybe there was a loophole, and that was the only way Wong could close it. General Wong may be a Communist, but he is one of the most corrupt capitalist pigs I know."

It made sense. It was Thackeray's murder that was the big question mark.

"The other night we were in Macau. Some Triads chopped up a *mahjong* game at the Lisboa Casino. Were they your men?"

"No. I give you my word," Li said.

Bond sat in thought. A big piece of the puzzle was still missing.

"Now we come to the task I must ask you to do, Mr. Bond," Li said. "As I mentioned earlier, you are in my debt. If you perform this task for me and succeed, I will release you from my debt and also spare your life."

"I don't know what it is you want me to do, Li," Bond said, "but I can tell you right now I don't work for criminals. You can kill me now. I've lived my entire life with the prospect of death coming at any moment."

Li nodded. "Brave words, Mr. Bond. Why don't you hear me out first?"

Bond sighed. "All right. What is it you want?"

"I want you to go to Guangzhou and pay a little visit to General Wong."

"And then what?"

"Steal my great-great-grandfather's agreement. Wong keeps it in a safe in his office. Bring it back to me. If you have to eliminate the good general in the process . . ." Li shrugged his shoulders.

Bond laughed. "You must be joking, Li! How the hell do you think a *gweilo* like me could get anywhere near this general, much less break into his bloody safe? Don't you think I would stick out like a sore thumb in China?"

"Hear me out, Mr. Bond. I have a plan." Bond raised his hand, gesturing for Li to continue, but he knew the very thought was absurd. "You are skeptical, Mr. Bond, I see that, but listen to me. We have learned that a new lawyer from London will be arriving in Hong Kong later this morning after the sun rises. He is Gregory Donaldson's replacement as EurAsia Enterprises' solicitor. Since Mr. Thackeray's untimely demise, this new lawyer will be handling things. He has an appointment in Guangzhou tomorrow with General Wong himself. I propose that you go to Guangzhou in his place. My organization has contacts at the airport. We can do a switch before the man even enters Immigration. You will be hand-delivered to General Wong by EurAsia executives. You will meet Wong privately. He will most certainly show you the original document. You will have the perfect, and probably the only, chance to get it. Then my brothers will help you get out of Guangzhou and back to Hong Kong."

"Not on your life, Li."

"I'm afraid you'll have to die, then."

"I've heard worse threats."

Li said, "Very well, I will offer you another incentive—the life of that girl, the traitor. She can leave with you, and I will call off the death warrant on her head."

Bond closed his eyes. The man had played the trump card.

15

Day Trip to China

The British Airways flight that carried James Pickard, Esquire, of Fitch, Donaldson, and Patrick, arrived on time at Kai Tak Airport. "Representatives" from EurAsia Enterprises were waiting, not in the gate area or in the Greeting Hall beyond Immigration, but right in the movable jetbridge that attached to the door of the aircraft.

Two Chinese men in business suits stopped Pickard as he stepped off the aircraft.

"Mr. Pickard?"

"Yes?"

"Come with us, please. We take you to hotel."

The men opened a service door in the jetbridge and gestured toward a set of metal steps leading down to the tarmac. Pickard was confused.

"Don't I have to go through Immigration?" he asked.

"That already taken care of," one of the men said in broken English.

Pickard shrugged, chalked it up to Chinese efficiency, and was pleased he was getting the VIP treatment. He happily walked down the steps and into a waiting limousine. As soon as the car was away, James Bond ascended the same set of steps and entered the jet-bridge. He walked through it and into the terminal. As he had not got much sleep the night before anyway, he looked and felt as if he really had just flown the long haul from London. He was dressed in an Armani suit borrowed from Li Xu Nan, and he carried a briefcase full of law books. He was unarmed, having reluctantly left his Walther PPK with Li.

The passport and travel documents with which Li's people provided him were top-notch forgeries. As James Pickard, British citizen, he sailed through Immigration and Customs, and was met in the Greeting Hall by an attractive blond woman and a Chinese man, both in their thirties.

"Mr. Pickard?" the woman said. She was English.

"Yes?"

"I'm Corinne Bates from the public relations office at EurAsia Enterprises." She held out her hand.

Bond shook it. "Hello. James Pickard."

"How was your flight?"

"Long."

"Isn't it, though? I find it dreadful. This is Johnny Leung, assistant to the interim general manager."

"How do you do?" Bond said, and shook the man's hand.

"Fine, thank you," Leung said. "We have a car waiting."

Bond allowed himself to be guided outside and into a Rolls-Royce. So far, the operation was going smoothly.

"All the hotels were booked because of the July the first transition," Corinne Bates said. "We're putting you up for the night in a corporate flat in the Mid-Levels. Is that all right?"

"Sounds fine," Bond said.

The car drove through the Cross-Harbour Tunnel to the island, made its way through Central and up into the Mid-Levels, an area of prominence but just a step down from the elite Victoria

Peak. It finally entered a complex on Po Shan Road, just off Conduit Road.

They let him into the flat, a lovely two-bedroom affair with a parquet floor and a view of Central.

"We'll pick you up at six-thirty in the morning, Mr. Pickard. The train leaves from Kowloon at seven-fifty," Ms. Bates said.

"We're taking the train?" Bond asked.

"It's the easiest way," she said. "And that way you can see a bit of the Chinese countryside. It's about a two-and-a-half-hour ride to Guangzhou."

Bond nodded. After the couple made sure he had everything he needed, they left him alone. He picked up the phone and dialed a number that Li had given him. Li answered the line himself.

"How is the view from Po Shan Road?" Li asked.

His men must have followed them from the airport. They were very efficient. Bond thought that for a criminal organization they were as well-organized and effective as any major intelligence outfit in the world.

"It's fine, Li. Just make sure your men watch my back, all right?"

"Don't you worry, Mr. Bond. Just bring back my document in one piece." ,

"Mr. Li?"

"Yes, Mr. Bond?"

"I'd like to know what happened to T. Y. Woo and his son. Can you find them?"

"As a matter of fact, we found the boy safe and sound at one of Mr. Woo's private flats. We did not bother him. Mr. Woo is probably attempting to find you, so we left word with the boy that you are safe. I would hate for Mr. Woo to blow the whistle to your government before your job for me is completed. Do not worry about him, Mr. Bond. Have a nice trip tomorrow. Enjoy southern China."

Li hung up before Bond could say anything else. Bond stood in the center of the living room and stared out the window at the postcard view. He could easily get away from this place, but it would jeopardize Sunni. At times, Bond wanted to kick himself. Why did he have such a soft spot for women? Sunni meant nothing to him, really. She was just another in a long line of affairs that provided a few fireworks for a while and would eventually fizzle out. His pattern with women was so predictable that he could chart the liaison's progress on a blackboard. He intentionally stayed as far away as possible from any kind of commitment with a woman. It seemed that whenever he allowed himself to get seriously involved, something terrible happened. He would never forget Vesper Lynd, the first woman he had ever really loved. She had tried to accept his love for her, but that affair ended in guilt and tragedy. There were others he had lost in recent years because of their association with him, including fellow agents and companions Fredericka von Grüsse, Harriet Horner, and Easy St. John. By far the worst disaster was when his lovely wife of fifteen minutes, Tracy di Vicenzo, was gunned down by bullets meant for him. Now here was Sunni Pei, a damned Triad member looking for a way out of her wretched life. Bond could easily walk away from this job and from her.

"Bloody hell," he said aloud. He knew he wouldn't do that. He had already put himself on the line for Sunni. Bond stubbornly justified his actions by telling himself that this little visit to General Wong in Guangzhou was an essential part of his mission. After all, he had learned that Wong was involved with Thackeray and Li. Wong was the number-one suspect in Thackeray's murder. Wong was now calling the shots with regard to the EurAsia/Triad connection. It *was* an essential step in his mission. He wasn't veering off on some wild-goose chase just to save a female. This was business, and the journey just might provide him with the means to complete his job in Hong Kong.

Bond searched the kitchen and found a bottle of vodka. Pouring a double helped him accept the fact that he was *really* doing this for that lovely girl with the almond eyes.

Day Trip to China

The Kowloon-Guangzhou Express left precisely on time. Corinne Bates and Johnny Leung saw James Pickard to the station and made sure Bond got through Immigration and aboard the right train. Apparently General Wong had insisted that the new solicitor from Fitch, Donaldson, and Patrick come to China alone. The train was surprisingly comfortable, with plenty of room in the aisles. Bond sat by the window and watched as the several stops within the New Territories came and went, and they finally crossed the border into southern China.

Shenzhen was the first major city just beyond the border, and at first glance it appeared to be just another part of Hong Kong. Something was different, though, and Bond couldn't put his finger on it until the train had traveled a few minutes into the country: there was a lack of English signs. Throughout most of Hong Kong, public signs were written in both Chinese and English. Here, the world was strictly Chinese.

A large portion of southern China had become a "Special Economic Zone." This meant that the Chinese government was allowing free enterprise to exist to a certain extent. If a family was able to make a living selling their own goods, then they were welcome to do so. Only eligible people were permitted to live in the Special Economic Zone. For example, in the city of Shekou, women outnumbered men eight to one. This was because it was primarily a manufacturing community in which intricate work could be performed only by small hands. When Hong Kong became part of China on July 1, it, too, would be a part of the Special Economic Zone. Whether or not it would retain any semblance of autonomy remained to be seen.

Shenzhen looked extremely commercial and urbanized. Bond expected to see an obligatory McDonald's or two along the way, but when he saw the famous rabbit logo of *Playboy* on a building, he was quite surprised.

179

The train stopped briefly to let passengers on and off, then continued northwest toward Guangzhou. The scenery flashing by the train window curiously alternated every few seconds—one moment it was rural farmland that looked archaic, and in a flash there was a sudden patch of built-up suburbia. It was not uncommon to see a wood shanty alongside a newly built tenement high-rise. Bond's impression of the farmlands was that time had stopped. The rich, green rice paddy fields were still being irrigated by handheld water poles or crude machines pulled by water buffalo. Yet a hundred meters away from the farm were fifteen- or twenty-story brick buildings, many with an uninteresting mosaic tile pattern decorating the exteriors. Bond had read that the government was making room for more high-rises. China's one billion people needed homes.

Bond couldn't help feeling that it was a world of incongruities. The urban areas were stark, white, and depressingly drab. He was sometimes unsure if many of the buildings he saw were empty or abandoned, or if they were simply not yet completed. They were either soulless ghost towns or they were isolated pieces of a soon-to-be booming metropolis that was not yet occupied. It was quite strange. Just when Bond thought that many of the homes reminded him of what he had seen in poor Latin American countries, or Mexico, a large, modern warehouse or factory would suddenly dominate a circle of shacks made of plywood and grass.

The train sped through smaller cities like Pinghu and Shilong, and finally pulled into Guangzhou Station, a sprawling monstrosity built in the 1960s. As Bond stepped off the train, he was met by a soldier wearing a light blue tunic, navy trousers, a red armband on his left arm, and a navy cap with a gold star on a red circle. He held a sign that was poorly scribbled: "James Pickard, EurAsia Enterprises." The man didn't speak English, and Bond's Mandarin was terrible, so they compromised with Cantonese—which the soldier blatantly regarded as an inferior language. The soldier saw Bond through Immigration and into a government minibus. As he walked through the railway station, Bond was struck by the hundreds of rural migrants camped on the station's vast courtyard, surrounded by bundles of clothing and bedding. Some of them looked as if they had lived there for months or even years, eating, sleeping, and carving out a niche for themselves right there on the pavement. Some were peddling goods and services to tourists. It was a stark contrast to the clean, metropolitan station in Kowloon.

Guangzhou itself is the sixth-largest city in China, with an estimated population of three and a half million. It is the transportation, industrial, and trade center of south China. It has shipyards, a steel complex, and factories that produce many heavy and light industrial products. It had been the seat of Sun Yat-sen's revolutionary movement and was a Nationalist center in the 1920s until its fall in 1950 to the communist armies. Hong Kong was crowded, but it was nothing compared to Guangzhou. The streets were packed with vehicles and there was a traffic jam at every intersection. However, most of the people got around on bicycles, and there were hundreds zipping along the major roads in specially marked bike lanes. Open-air markets were in abundance. Also prominent were huge billboards displaying images of united workers, looking off in the distance toward a bright, bold future.

Bond found himself thinking that it was a world terribly behind the times, and that the people had absolutely no idea that the rest of civilization had passed them by. Over the years he had attempted to become more tolerant of governments such as China's, but the imperialist blood of long-forgotten generations welled up inside of him when he saw the squalor and the misguided complacency of the humanity around him. He had spent most of his career battling communism. These days he had to concentrate on suppressing his own personal prejudices against it.

The minibus drove along Jeifang Beilu down to Dongfeng Zhonglu and passed a large octagonal building designed in traditional Chinese palace–style architecture. It was the Dr. Sun Yat-sen Memorial Hall, an auditorium built between 1929 and 1931. The building was in a graceful park with a magnificent garden in front of it. A bronze statue of Sun Yat-sen overlooked the garden and faced conspicuous government buildings across the busy main road. The Hall itself had a solemn outer appearance with red walls and panels and a roof made of blue Shiwan tiles with four tiers of rolled, protruding eaves. It was simultaneously ornate and gaudy.

The minibus turned into the intimidating gate of the main and largest government building, a tan seven-story structure with a red roof. The gate was set within a brick facade with a blue roof, and was connected to a high fence that surrounded the building. The driver spoke to a guard, the gate opened, and the minibus pulled into a parking lot full of military vehicles—jeeps, a couple of troop transports, and one tank.

When they got out of the minibus, the guard pointed across the road. "Dr. Sun Yat-sen Memorial Hall," he said. "Nice tourist attraction." He gestured to the building in front of them. "This is our local government building. General Wong will see you here."

The guard escorted Bond into the building, where he had to sign a visitors' book under the watchful eyes of other soldiers. The next thing they did was curious—Bond was frisked from head to toe. Why would they do that to a visiting solicitor? He attributed it to the rigors of communist China. He was then led to a lift and taken to the third floor, where the guard let Bond into a small office.

"Wait here," the guard said, then left him alone.

Bond sat down in a straight-back chair. The room was bare except for a conference table and a few chairs. A water cooler sat in the corner. It was very hot. The air-conditioning was either off or broken, or they didn't have it at all. The weather outside had finally hit the humid summer temperature for which south China was known. Bond had to wipe his forehead with a handkerchief.

After a moment, a man entered and stood in the doorway. He was dressed in full Chinese military regalia and appeared to be about sixty years old. He was short, probably no more than five and a half feet, but was broad-shouldered and muscular. He had white hair cut short to the scalp, a pug nose, and he wore spectacles with round lenses.

"Mr. Pickard?" he asked in English. "I am General Wong."

Bond stood up and shook his hand. "How do you do?"

The man didn't smile. "I trust you had pleasant journey."

"It was fine, thank you."

General Wong's expression remained sour. "We get down to business. You know about my takeover of EurAsia Enterprises."

"Yes, of course. I must admit, though, this document of yours took us all by surprise at Fitch, Donaldson, and Patrick."

"Guy Thackeray was fool," Wong said. "He kept it secret. He should have told you in 1985 when I first saw him. He was idiot. He should not have held press conference to tell world he was selling company. He was not selling at all! What happened to him?"

"He was killed by a car bomb."

Wong's eyes narrowed. "I know that. Why? Who did it?"

The general did not have a pleasant disposition. It was as if he was doing Pickard a favor by stepping down from his pedestal to speak with him.

"No one knows, General," Bond said politely. He smiled in an attempt to bring levity to their conversation. "There are quite a few people who believe you had something to do with it."

"Me?" the general shouted. "You accuse me?"

"I didn't accuse you, General. I merely said that there is speculation in Hong Kong that the People's Republic was behind the act. But that's not why I'm here, is it? Aren't we going to talk about your claim to Thackeray's company?"

"Why would I kill Thackeray? His death spoiled everything! Market value of EurAsia Enterprises went down! Company is losing money! He deliberately made announcement to bring value of company down! Why would I want him dead? You tell your friends I did not do it."

"General, I assure you, they are not my friends. I just got here from England."

The general took a deep breath and tried to control his temper. The insinuation had ruffled his feathers. Bond's instincts that

Wong had no motive for killing Thackeray seemed to be sound, but he still could have been behind the murder of Donaldson and the tragedy at the floating restaurant.

"General, my colleagues at Fitch, Donaldson, and Patrick have yet to see the document that gives you the right to take over EurAsia Enterprises. My first task is to see that document and make photocopies of it to take back to England."

"Document very fragile. I keep it in plastic inside safe."

"I understand that. Still, I must see the original. I must ascertain that it is genuine."

"Very well. Come." He stood up. "You want water? Very hot today."

Bond would have loved to drink some water, but he was wary of its purity. "No, thank you, I'm fine."

He followed the general into what was presumably his private office. In contrast to the rest of the building, it was full of expensive furniture, antiques, and fine art. A tiger's head was mounted on the wall, and there were objets d'art scattered around the room. What appeared to be a gold-plated bust of Mao Zedong sat on a bookshelf. The most impressive artifact in the room was a life-size terra-cotta horse and soldier. Bond imagined that it had been part of a fantastic, archaeological dig around the tomb of Ch'ing Dynasty emperor Qin Shi Huang near the city of Xian, where over six thousand clay soldiers and horses had been unearthed and found arrayed in an oblong battle formation as an artistic reflection of the emperor's great army. Most of the terra-cotta figures were left in place, but a few made it to museums around China. General Wong must have spent a fortune in order to obtain one. Anyone who saw this opulent office would not have believed its inhabitant was a Communist.

General Wong pushed back a curtain behind his desk and revealed a safe. He twisted the knob a few times, unlocked it, and carefully removed a large parchment enclosed in a transparent plastic cover.

The document was brown with age, but the lettering was still intact. One side was written in English and the other in Chinese. The wording and legality of the agreement seemed to be in order.

"This is quite an artifact," Bond said. "I'll need a photocopy to take back to England."

At that moment, the phone buzzed. Wong answered it and listened. He looked at Bond suspiciously, then barked an order in Mandarin. He hung up the phone and said, "Forgive me. There is matter I must take care of."

Bond heard footsteps in the hallway approaching the office, followed by a loud knock on the door. Wong snarled an order to come in.

Two guards entered carrying a man who had been recently beaten. His clothes were tattered and torn, and his face was bruised and bloody. They threw him on the floor, where he curled into a fetal position and groaned. Wong walked over to the man and roughly turned him onto his back.

Bond was horrified to see that it was T. Y. Woo!

"Mr. Pickard," Wong said. "This man was caught spying. Do you know him?"

Bond had to lie. If he gave the slightest indication that he knew Woo, then his cover would be blown and they would both die. The lesson he had taught Stephanie Lane in Jamaica just days ago hit home with a vengeance.

"I've never seen him before in my life," Bond said. "Who is he? What happened to him?" He played the shocked British civilian unaccustomed to such violence.

"Never mind what happened to him," Wong said. He gave an order to the guards, who pulled Woo up by the shoulders and started to haul him out of the room. For a brief moment, Woo's eyes met Bond's. There was sadness there, but also a sign that he understood what Bond did and why. Bond turned away, feigning repulsion. He really felt rage and despair. He might as well have aimed the gun at Woo's head and fired it himself.

After they were gone, Bond said, "I'm sorry. I'm not used to seeing things like that."

Wong just stared at him. There was an awkward moment of silence.

"Maybe I will have that glass of water now," Bond said.

Wong didn't say a word. He took the ancient document off the table and replaced it in his safe. Then he picked up his phone and pushed a button. He spoke into the receiver and hung up. Once again, Bond heard the footsteps in the hall. This time the guards didn't knock. They came straight into the room and stood on either side of Bond.

Wong said, "You are impostor. You are not lawyer. You are spy."

"Now wait just a minute . . ." Bond began, but one of the guards punched him hard in the stomach. Bond doubled over and fell to his knees.

"Who are you? Who do you work for?" Wong demanded.

Bond didn't say anything. What had happened? Had Woo talked? No, that was impossible. He was as professional as they come. Where had something gone wrong?

"I got phone call before you arrive," Wong said. "Mr. James Pickard never step into Hong Kong Airport. My people were there." He held up a photo of the real James Pickard. "You are not this man."

Bond didn't move.

"Are you going to tell me who you are? Talk! I give you one more chance. Who do you work for?"

Bond stood silent and at attention, like a soldier.

"Very well," the general said. "We move on to next step."

16

Agony and Anger

"Remove your clothes," Wong commanded in Cantonese.

My God, Bond thought. What were they going to do? He felt cold fear. He suddenly had total recall of another time long ago when he had been tortured with nothing on. It had been hours of excruciating agony, and it damn near killed him.

"You heard me!" Wong shouted.

Bond did as he was told. As he undressed, Wong opened a cabinet behind the desk and removed a white bedsheet. He walked to the middle of the room and spread out the sheet. It floated down and settled neatly onto the carpet. It wasn't completely white. There were several suspicious stains on it.

When Bond was naked, Wong gestured for him to stand in the middle of the sheet. Bond stood at attention in front of him. Wong slowly walked around him, inspecting him, admiring the man's body.

"You think you are fit, Mr. Englishman," Wong said. "We shall see how fit you really are."

A guard trained an AK-47 on Bond while General Wong returned to the cabinet and removed a long, white stick with ridges. He held it in front of the vulnerable man. For the first time since Bond arrived, Wong smiled. In fact, he had become a completely different person. The sour face and unpleasant demeanor were completely gone.

"This is rattan cane, Mr. Pickard, or whoever you are," he said. "I have friends in Singapore who not only employ it for punishment, but swear that it is also effective persuader. Now, I ask again. Who do you work for?"

Bond said nothing. He knew he was in for a great deal of pain. In Singapore, the maximum number of strokes with the cane was usually five; ten for extreme cases. What kind of damage could it do? He knew that the lashes would leave welts on his skin, possibly permanent scars. What if he was caned many, many times? Could he force himself to pass out, as he had trained himself to do? It was one of the most difficult tests of willpower that he knew of.

"Bend over and grab ankles," Wong said.

Bond did so. He felt humiliated and dangerously exposed.

Wong took a position on Bond's left side and held the cane to 007's buttocks. He rubbed the rough stick against the skin there, indicating to Bond how the cane might feel if it struck him hard.

"Who are you and who do you work for?" Wong asked again, his voice trembling with excitement.

Bond kept his mouth shut. He closed his eyes tightly and gritted his teeth. Concentrate! Focus on something! He opened his eyes and saw a dark stain on the bedsheet a few inches from his face. It was probably dried blood. Bond stared at it, willing himself to fall deep within the confines of that dark, shapeless haven.

The cane struck him with such force that he nearly lost his balance and fell forward. There was an intense, burning pain across the middle of his buttocks. They felt as if they were on fire.

Bond gritted his teeth harder and continued to stare at the spot. He had begun to sweat profusely; a drop slid down his forehead, onto his nose, then fell onto the sheet.

Agony and Anger

"You see what it can do now?" Wong asked pleasantly. "Now will you talk?"

Bond concentrated on the spot in front of him, attempting to conjure up whatever peaceful thoughts he could manage. My God, give me something of beauty to look at. Give me something pure. Give me . . .

The cane struck again, slightly lower than the first blow. Christ, it hurt! He kept up his internal litany, forming a mental picture in his mind of the image he invoked. Give me my house in Jamaica . . . Give me my flat in Chelsea . . .

The third blow slashed Bond across the tops of his thighs. It was dangerously close to more vulnerable parts of his body. God, not that again! He might not be able to take that. Give me . . . give me . . . Sunni. . . .

The fourth blow landed on the buttocks again, overlapping the first red mark.

Sunni . . . Bond thought of the girl with the almond eyes. The spot on the sheet became her lovely face. . . . Those lips . . . those eyes . . .

A fifth stroke tore his skin an inch below the last one.

Sweat was now rolling off his face in a constant flow. His heart was pounding. He wanted to scream, but he dared not. He knew that the general took pleasure in the torture. The more the victim suffered, the more the sadist enjoyed it. Bond was determined to be the most disappointing whipping boy General Wong had ever had.

The sixth stroke nearly knocked Bond over again. The madman was putting his weight into it now. He was breathing heavily. "Well?" he asked. "Have you had enough?"

Bond sensed that the general was surprised and perturbed that Bond's reaction to the torture was not what he was expecting.

Bond turned his head to the left and spat, "Please . . . sir. May . . . I have . . . another, you . . . bloody . . . bastard . . . ?"

The seventh blow knocked Bond forward and onto the sheet.

He curled up in a ball on his right side and felt the blood seeping down the backs of his thighs.

"Get up!" Wong shouted.

He brutally whacked Bond across his left arm, directly over the stitches of his previous wound. Oh, bloody hell! Bond screamed to himself. He didn't want to be hit there again. Getting lashed on the backside was immeasurably preferable, mainly because he was beginning to grow numb there. He weakly pulled himself up and assumed the position again.

The ninth blow seared his thighs once more. Again, Bond wanted to yell, simply to release the anger, humiliation, and tension that enveloped his body. He remained stubbornly silent.

The tenth stroke sent Bond to the sheet again. It was the hardest, most savage blow yet. He didn't know if he could manage to pull himself up off the floor.

At that moment, there was a loud knock on the door. Wong shouted something in Mandarin. The guard with the gun opened the door slightly and listened to a hurried whisper from another man in the hallway. He closed the door and whispered something to Wong.

Suddenly, Wong threw down the cane. "Bah!" he shouted. He said something in Mandarin that implied that Bond was nothing but excrement. He said something to the guard, retrieved the cane, and put it back in the cabinet.

"I have appointment," Wong said. "We will continue in little while." With that, he left the room.

The guard lifted Bond from the bloodied sheet. He stood weakly, his legs shaking like mad. The guard threw Bond's clothes at his feet and said something in Mandarin. Bond picked up the sheet and wrapped it around himself, soaking up the blood and pressing his wounds. It was going to be a while before he could sit comfortably.

The guard shouted at him, indicating with the machine gun that he should get moving. Bond swore at the man in English, dropped the sheet, and pulled on his clothes. Contact with his trousers was excruciating. Unable to sit to put on his shoes, Bond went down on his left knee. He got the right shoe on, then painfully changed positions and rested on his right knee. The guard was looking out of the door into the hallway, the gun half trained at Bond.

Bond quickly removed the pry tool from his left shoe. He snapped open the heel and removed the plastic dagger. He slipped on the shoe, snapping the heel back in place as he did so. He tucked the dagger under the Rolex flexible watchband on his left wrist, then slowly raised himself up off the floor.

The guard gestured with the AK-47 for Bond to leave the room. Another guard stood in the hall and moved toward the lift.

The lift descended to the basement level. They came out into a stark white hallway, at the end of which was a locked steel door. The lead man unlocked it and held it open for Bond and the other man to go through, into another long hallway lined with five or six other steel doors. Each of these contained a small barred window at eye level, obviously opening into cells. He wondered how many individuals entered this building and never came out.

If he was going to make a move, Bond knew it had to be now or never.

The guards turned right and led him to the end of the hall. The first man unlocked the door there and held it open. Bond reached for his left wrist and firmly grasped the small handle of the plastic dagger. He knew that his timing had to be perfect or he would be a dead man.

Bond turned to the man holding the AK-47 behind him and said in Cantonese, "Would you mind not pushing that thing into my back?" The guard relaxed, giving 007 the space he needed. He pushed the AK-47 away from his body with his left hand and simultaneously swung the dagger straight up with his right. The three-inch blade pierced the soft skin of the man's jaw just under the chin, thrusting up and into the mouth. In the next half-second, Bond grasped the machine gun and chopped the man's arm with a right spear-hand, causing the guard to release his grip on the weapon. By now, the other guard had begun to react by pulling a pistol out of a holster on his belt. Bond swung the AK-47 around and fired one quick burst at the second man, throwing him back into the open cell. The first guard was now clutching at the dagger in his jaw, an expression of surprise, pain, and horror on his face. Bond used the butt of the machine gun to smash the man's nose, knocking him unconscious. He moved quickly into the cell to inspect the guard he had shot. The four bullets had caught him in the chest. He was quite dead. Bond retrieved his plastic dagger, wiped it clean on the man's shirt, then replaced it under his wrist-watch band. He prayed that there were no other guards in the basement. The burst of gunfire had been quick. He hoped that the noise had not penetrated the upper levels of the building.

Bond had to get out and find Li Xu Nan's men, who must be watching the building. It was not going to be an easy escape. First, however, he had to accomplish the task he came to perform. He had to go back to the third floor and get that bloody document.

He was still bleeding, and the pain was nearly unbearable. He stepped into the cell and removed his trousers again. He slipped off the right shoe and once again pried open the heel. He used a sheet from a cot to wipe himself, then did his best to apply antiseptic to the wounds. He ripped the sheet into strips and layered them around his thighs and buttocks. It would have to do until he could get medical attention. Bond then swallowed a couple of painkill-ers, replaced the items, and put his shoe back on.

He stepped over the bodies of the guards and went into the hallway. He looked through the barred windows of each door on his way out. A body, covered by a sheet, lay on top of a stretcher in one of the cells. Could it be . . . ?

Bond tried the door, but it was locked. He went back and searched the pockets of the dead guard who had held the keys. He found them and went back to the locked door, unlocked it, and stepped inside. He approached the body quietly, all too sure of what he would find underneath the sheet.

It was T. Y. Woo. He was lying on his stomach with his head

turned to the side. He had been shot in the back of the skull. The entire front of his face was blown away.

Bond was overcome with an immense feeling of guilt and rage. He slammed his fist down on the stretcher. The bastards actually did it. Woo had probably been tailing him, keeping an eye on him, watching his back, and Bond had betrayed him. They had executed him, and it was he who had helped to send his friend and ally to his death.

Damn it, get ahold of yourself! he screamed silently. It was unavoidable. It was a matter of keeping one's cover. Any good agent would have done the same thing. Woo would have turned his back on Bond, too, if it had been the other way around. It was part of the job. It was part of the risk.

Despite these rationalizations, Bond's anger overcame him. Now he had not only to get that document and get out alive, but he had to avenge Woo's death. After suffering the degrading torture Wong inflicted upon him, and now having discovered the extent of the general's frenzy, Bond saw red. He knew he should stay objective and keep his emotions out of it. This wasn't a vendetta, he tried to tell himself, but all he wanted to do was wring the mad general's neck.

Bond left the cell, holding the AK-47, prepared to blast the first obstacle that stood in his way. He used the guard's keys to open the main door and enter the hallway leading to the lift.

Once he was back on the third floor, Bond made his way quietly toward Wong's office. The place was unusually quiet and empty. The good general's staff was obviously not a large one.

The office door was closed. Bond put his ear to it and heard a woman moaning with pleasure. The general was having a little afternoon delight. Good, Bond thought. Now it was his turn to catch the general with his pants down.

Bond burst into the room and trained the machine gun on the couple behind the desk. General Wong was sitting in his large leather rocking chair, and a woman in her thirties was sitting on his lap, facing him. Her skirt was pulled up above her waist, and her legs were bare. Wong's trousers were around his ankles, and the look on his face was priceless.

The woman gasped, frozen. She was dressed in a military uniform and the front of her blouse was unbuttoned, revealing small breasts in a white brassiere.

Bond closed the door behind him. "Get up," he said to the woman. When she didn't move, he shouted, "Now!" The woman jumped up and hurriedly put herself back together. Wong sat there, exposed.

"What's the matter, General?" Bond asked in Cantonese. "Is it the humidity that's causing you to wilt?"

"What do you want?" Wong said through his teeth.

"Open the safe, and be quick."

Wong stood up. "I pull pants up?"

"Slowly. First place your pistol on the desk with your left hand."

The general carefully took a pistol from the holster on his belt and laid it on the desk. It looked like a Russian Tokarev, but was most likely a Chinese copy. Then he bent over, pulled his trousers up, and fastened them, before turning to the safe in the wall and opening it.

"The document," Bond said. "Put it on the desk." The general did as he was told.

Nearly a week before in Jamaica, James Bond had taught Stephanie Lane always to expect the unexpected, but he was so intent on making General Wong pay for what he did to Woo that he made a near-fatal mistake and broke the rule. He didn't expect the woman to come to the general's defense.

She attacked Bond, screaming a bloodcurdling war cry. The move so surprised him that he lost his balance. The woman successfully tackled him, and they fell to the carpet where only a little while ago Bond had been lying in agony. She went for the gun, obviously quite prepared not only to sleep with her general but to die for him as well. Wong moved around the desk and kicked Bond hard in the face. The woman managed to wrestle away the

AK-47 as Bond rolled away. Wong took the machine gun from her and pointed it at Bond.

In one swift, graceful maneuver, Bond took hold of the plastic dagger, rocked back onto his shoulders, lunged forward, and threw the knife at the general. The blade spun across the room and lodged in Wong's throat, directly below his Adam's apple. His eyes widened, and for a moment he stood as stationary as a statue. The AK-47 fell to the carpet as he reached for his neck with both hands. He made choking, gurgling noises as blood gushed out of his mouth.

Bond took no chances. He grabbed hold of Wong's shirt to steady him, then punched the man hard in the jaw. Wong fell back across the desk and rolled over onto the floor. Bond turned to the now-terrified woman. He was so full of violence and fury that he might have killed her, too, had he not been unarmed. Instead, he backhanded her, knocking her unconscious.

The general was still writhing on the floor. He had pulled the knife out of his throat and was struggling for air. His trachea had been severed and his lungs were filling with blood. Bond stood over him and watched him die. It took three long, excruciating minutes.

Now Bond had to act fast. He grabbed the document and stuffed it into the briefcase he had brought with him from Hong Kong, which was still sitting on the floor by an armchair where he had left it earlier. He took the AK-47, then picked up the dagger and returned it to its position in his shoe.

His trousers were wet with blood. The sheet strips had not lasted long.

How the hell was he going to leave? He glanced out of a window. It overlooked the front of the building. He counted four guards outside by the gate. Across the street was the Sun Yat-sen Memorial Building. Maybe he could make it over there somehow and hope that Li's men were close by.

Bond opened the office door and looked into the hallway. It was all clear. Bond crept to the lift and pushed the button. When it opened, a guard stepped out. Bond killed him swiftly and quietly and entered the lift. At the ground floor, flattening himself against the side of the car, he pressed the Open Door button and held it.

The ruse worked. When the lone guard got curious and decided to see why the lift door hadn't closed, Bond brought the man's head down hard on his right knee, then hit him on the back of the neck with the butt of the AK-47.

Two armed guards stood in the building foyer. They saw Bond and immediately pulled their pistols. Bond acted with split-second timing, boosted by the adrenaline rushing through his body. He opened fire and the two guards slammed back against the wall, leaving a bloody trail as they slid to the floor.

Bond stood there a moment, breathing heavily. He was still filled with rage, an emotion he usually tried to avoid because it could cause recklessness. This time, however, it served as a goad. Blasting away the guards had actually felt good. My God, he thought. This is what he lived for. It was no wonder that he inevitably became restless and bored when he was between assignments. Living so close to death was what invigorated him and gave him the edge that had managed to keep him alive for so many years.

Feeling invincible, Bond walked outside into the broad daylight of the courtyard. He didn't care that his clothes were wet and bloody. He didn't care if the entire Chinese army was waiting for him. He was quite prepared to blast his way out of Guangzhou until he had no more ammunition or he was dead, whichever came first.

There were only the four guards at the gate. They looked up and saw Bond. Their jaws dropped, so stupefied at the *gweilo*'s appearance that they were unsure what to do. Bond trained the machine gun on them. They slowly raised their hands above their heads.

"Open the gate," Bond said to one of them. The guard nodded furiously, then did as he was told. Bond walked backwards out of the gate, keeping the gun trained on the soldiers.

Agony and Anger

It was midafternoon and traffic on Dongfeng Zhonglu was quite heavy. Bond looked in both directions and quickly calculated when he might make a mad dash across the street. When the moment came, he turned and ran. The guards immediately began to chase him. Their timing wasn't as good, as they had to dart between vehicles to get across.

Bond ran up the steps past the statue of Sun Yat-sen and into the Memorial Hall. The interior lobby was narrow and dimly lit. He went straight into the arena-style auditorium, which had two balconies and a stage at one end. It was dilapidated and had a decidedly musty smell, and it was empty and dark.

He ran down the center aisle to the stage. He jumped onto the apron and ran stage right into the wings. A staircase led down to what was some sort of green room. It was probably meant to be a dressing room for performers or speakers. He heard the guards enter the auditorium above, for they called out to each other in Mandarin. Sooner or later they would find him.

Bond made his way to the other side of the auditorium basement, then slowly climbed up the staircase there to the other side of the stage. The guards were still searching the aisles. He slid along a counterweight system to the back of the stage behind a faded, torn cyclorama. What he was looking for was there—a loading door for bringing scenery in and out. Bond pushed back the bolt and kicked it open. He jumped down to the pavement and ran around the side of the building to a parking lot. Tourists were walking from their vehicles to the front of the building. Many of them stopped and stared at the bloody figure of a Caucasian running across the pavement.

It was then that a black sedan screeched into the parking lot and stopped in front of him. A Chinese man in a business suit jumped out and held the back door open.

"Get in, Mr. Bond!" he said in English. "Hurry!"

Bond dived into the backseat, and the car squealed out of the parking lot and into the busy street. There were two of them—the driver and the man who had spoken. Bond thought they looked familiar. He had seen them at the initiation ceremony in Kowloon City.

The one in the passenger seat looked back at Bond. His brow was creased.

"What happened to you?"

Bond was not sitting down. He was on his knees, facing out the rear window.

"They gave me a beating," Bond said. "Where are we going?"

"Back to Kowloon, of course. Try to relax. It's a three-hour drive."

He didn't know how he could possibly relax in this position, but he had to admit he felt a hundred times better just being out of the hellhole from which he had escaped.

Bond watched the traffic behind the sedan and saw no signs of pursuit. It was curious that there hadn't been many soldiers at Wong's building. He counted himself extremely lucky. If an entire regiment had been there, he would probably be dead by now.

The man in the passenger seat used a cellular phone and spoke Cantonese into it. Bond heard him say that they had picked up the gweilo. The man turned to Bond.

"Mr. Li wants to know if you got it."

Bond said, "Tell him I've got what he wants."

The car spent the next half hour navigating the crowded thruways of Guangzhou and finally made it out onto the open highway southeast toward Dongguang and Shekou.

Bond thought of his friend T.Y. The man's death couldn't have been prevented, and Bond had merely done his duty and played by the rules.

He thought of the ironic parallel of the situation. England, in agreeing to hand over Hong Kong to China, had also acted honorably and dutifully. In doing so, however, she had turned her back on the people of Hong Kong.

17

Men of Honor

9:00 P.M.

By the time the hovercraft from Shekou arrived at the China Ferry Terminal in Tsim Sha Tsui, the world's governments had learned of Bond's actions that day. The story relayed over hot lines all around the globe was that General Wong Tsu Kam had been murdered by a "mysterious" Brit. There was speculation that it was the same "Brit" who had killed the two visiting officials in Hong Kong on June 13. China was accusing England of espionage and murder. At least four witnesses in the Chinese military force testified that they had been forced by an armed but wounded Caucasian to let him leave the governmental building located in the heart of Guangzhou. Several soldiers had been killed inside the building. For the time being, China was keeping the news from the press, but there was no telling when it might be leaked.

The Prime Minister attempted to assure China that no British "hit man" was operating on their soil. The idea was absurd — England didn't want a confrontation with China. China refused to listen.

Adding fuel to the fire was the release of James Pickard, Esquire, at six P.M. He had been blindfolded and taken from an undisclosed location in Kowloon to Kai Tak Airport to be left standing on the Departures level. He was unharmed, but he immediately went to the police and reported what had happened to him. An hour later, he was surrounded by reporters and photographers. He would receive fifteen minutes of fame, and then would be shipped back to London in the morning. This bit of public spectacle only added to the series of mysteries that had plagued Hong Kong over the past month.

Government officials in Hong Kong were seriously alarmed. What if the allegations were true? The Chinese troops lining the border were under new command within the hour, and word had it that tanks were now moving up to the line. An early takeover was a frightening possibility. It was important to keep the people in the dark, but it was entirely likely that some reporter would stumble across the news at any time and splash it across the papers. A colony-wide panic had to be avoided at all costs.

The Royal Navy was due to move into Victoria Harbour within twenty-four hours, joining the Hong Kong naval forces. Britain had sent a Destroyer and two Duke-class Type 23 Frigates to join the three RN Peacock-class patrol craft permanently deployed in Hong Kong. The colony's own naval force was operated by the Marine Region of the Royal Hong Kong Police, mostly a Coast Guard Force responsible for the territorial waters of Hong Kong and all of the surrounding islands. As far as the public was concerned, the Royal Navy's presence was simply to be on hand for the transition, but in reality they were on full alert. The Royal Marines had been dispatched and would be forming a line south of the Chinese border. The United States issued a private statement urging restraint, but her nearby fleets were watching and waiting. The Japanese government offered to mediate, but China refused to acknowledge the gesture.

As for James Bond, getting out of China had been relatively simple. The car had been driven to Dongguan, where they stopped at a small hotel so James Bond could shower, dress his wounds, and change clothes. Li had sent yet another Armani suit for 007 to wear. After a stand-up meal at a food stall, the group continued along the superhighway to the rapidly expanding Shekou. There they boarded a hovercraft to Kowloon. A new passport had been prepared for Bond (complete with a false exit stamp from Hong Kong Immigration), this time in the name of John Hunter. The presence of the other ethnic Chinese deflected any suspicions on the part of Chinese Immigration that Bond might be the man wanted for General Wong's murder.

A car drove Bond from the hovercraft terminal to Li's office building in Kowloon City. The Cho Kun greeted him as an old friend. He smiled broadly and clasped Bond's hand.

Bond handed over the document without saying a word. He was tired and in pain, and didn't relish the idea that he had done something to help a Triad. He was angry with himself.

"Here it is," Bond said. "I can't imagine it's worth much now."

Li inspected the document with awe and wonder. He held it gingerly, as if it were a newborn baby. Bond could swear that tears came to the man's eyes.

"Thank you, Mr. Bond," he said. He meant it.

Bond didn't wait for Li to offer to make him a drink. He went to the cabinet and poured himself a glass of vodka.

"You know, Mr. Li, the Hong Kong police will catch up with you sooner than you think," Bond said in Cantonese.

"I have taken some action to avoid that. I have not been passive while you were in China sticking your neck out for me. At approximately eight-thirty this evening, the EurAsia Enterprises warehouse at Kwai Chung Container Terminal was destroyed."

"What?"

He shrugged. "There was a fire . . . or something. It blew up. There is nothing left there. No evidence at all."

"I see. . . ."

"The police were already onto something. One of the shipping employees talked after learning he would be laid off after the handover. A story was already due to hit the papers tomorrow.

EurAsia Enterprises will be accused of participating in drug smuggling. If our friend Guy Thackeray were still alive, he would probably be under indictment. It is lucky I have friends in the press. I thought it best to obliterate any incriminating evidence."

"So your little drug-running operation is dead?"

"That one is, certainly. It is all right; I do not mind. To tell the truth, I have been searching for a way to end that vicious circle. It was very profitable, but I have other means of income. I can find another method."

"You mean you'll just find another way to prey on the weaknesses of the human condition."

Li ignored the insult. Instead he grinned broadly. "Oh, have you heard the latest news from China? I have a source who works at Government House. Beijing has issued a demand! If the British government does not turn over the so-called murderer, there will be . . . trouble." Li looked like a Cheshire cat.

"Why does that make you so happy, Li?" snapped Bond. "Do you realize what my government will do to me when they learn I was responsible? It would be nice if we could discredit General Wong somehow."

"You are right," Li said. "After you left this morning, I received something that will help your case. It is the result of a plan I set in operation months ago. The god Kwan Ti has been good to us. It is no coincidence that this came into my hands today of all days."

Li opened a desk drawer and pulled out a brown envelope. Bond opened it and found several photographs and a cassette audiotape inside.

"Those were taken by some of my men at General Wong's facilities in the Golden Triangle. For . . . insurance, in case I ever needed it. It is unfortunate that two brothers died getting me that material."

There were several black-and-white photos, taken by a hidden camera, of Wong inspecting poppies in a field, looking in a microscope in a lab, and holding bags of heroin. There was also a series of photos of Wong speaking with another Chinese man. They were standing inside the lab, near the desk of a chemist.

"Look at the photo. There is Wong, speaking to one of his lieutenants. Do you see the man sitting next to him? With the microscope? He is a brother. The conversation was recorded. It is all in Cantonese. They speak about the entire operation. Wong names not only EurAsia Enterprises as the carrier, but proudly states that he was the mastermind of the scheme. Egotistical bastard. Another brother had a camera in a pack of cigarettes and got this picture. An old trick, but it worked."

"My God, Li," Bond said. "This could save Hong Kong! We must get this to your friends in the press tonight!"

"It shall be done. In twenty-four hours, China will be eating her words and will be apologizing. Imagine . . . one of their top generals involved in drug smuggling! They will need to save much face! Now, what can I do for you, Mr. Bond? What can I do to dispel this notion you have that I am some kind of evil person?"

"I'll think about it," he said. "First I need to ring London and face my boss's wrath. Then I'd like to see Sunni."

Bond was shown into a private office with a phone. He dialed the access number and was connected to a secure line. After a moment, he heard the familiar voice of Bill Tanner.

"James! Where the hell have you been? M is about to have a stroke!"

"It's a long story, Bill."

"You're going to have to tell it to her. Hold on. She wanted to speak to you as soon as we heard from you."

"Great. All right, put her on."

There were a few pips, and then he heard the voice of the woman who would not be happy to hear what he had to say.

"Bond?" she asked.

"Yes, ma'am. I'm here."

"Where are you?"

"I'm in Kowloon."

"What the hell is going on, 007? Do you know anything about this general who was killed in Guangzhou?"

"Yes, ma'am."

There was a pause at the other end of the line. "And what do you know about it?"

"The general was involved with Guy Thackeray and the Dragon Wing Society in a drug-smuggling scheme. It was as we suspected, ma'am. EurAsia Enterprises was connected with the Triad, but it looks as though this Chinese general was as much a part of it as anyone. A story is going to break in the next couple of days, complete with photos. The man was as corrupt as they come. I have good reason to believe he was behind the terrorist acts and might have been the instigator of Guy Thackeray's murder."

"007, were you in Guangzhou today?"

"Yes, ma'am."

"I see." Bond could imagine her eyes narrowing as she sat in her office in London.

She continued, "The P.M. has been all over my back today. I will cover for you the best I can, 007. I hope you can tell me you were not caught on surveillance cameras."

"I don't think so, ma'am. If it's any consolation, Wong was responsible for the death of T. Y. Woo and he damn near killed me. I couldn't have completed the mission without going to Guangzhou, ma'am."

"I don't doubt your motives, Bond. I have a problem with your temerity. You've always had a reputation of being a loose cannon, 007, and now I have the privilege of experiencing your foolhardiness firsthand. I want you to stay put, Bond. Don't leave the colony. Captain Charles Plante of the Royal Navy will contact you at the safe house on the thirtieth of June. He will get you out and back home. The front door of the safe house has been repaired and the place cleaned up. The key will be taped inside the mouth of one of the Chinese lions in front of the shop. We've got Woo's son out of the colony already. He's on his way to England, where he'll live with a foster family."

"Yes, ma'am," he said. He was under virtual house arrest! What the hell was he going to do for three days?

"Oh, and 007?"

"Yes?"

"You had requested a British passport for some tart, a Chinese girl?"

Bond tensed at the word "tart." "That's right, ma'am. She helped me. Saved my life, actually."

"Well, forget her." With that, M rang off.

Bond walked out of the room and back into Li's office. He sat down on a large leather armchair. It still hurt to sit, but he was beginning to get used to it.

"You need some medical attention, Mr. Bond," Li said. "I will have my doctor take a look at you."

"Thanks," Bond said, lost in thought. He was forgetting something, and he was struggling to remember what it was.

"Where are the clothes I was wearing when I first came here?" he asked.

"They are here in the closet. Why?"

Bond got up and looked through them. He found what he was looking for in the trouser pocket. It was the map of EurAsia Enterprises' Kalgoorlie gold mine. "Here it is," he said. "I found this at the warehouse. Before spending the last two glorious days in your employ, Li, I had planned on leaving Hong Kong to take a look at this."

Li took a look at it. "Australia?"

"I've got a nagging feeling that there's something there that I need to see. That facility is part of this whole thing. The only problem now is how I'm going to get there."

"I can get you to Perth," Li said.

"You can?"

"I have two restaurants there. I have my own airplane. I travel to Singapore, Tokyo, Australia, Thailand . . . wherever my businesses take me. No problem with Immigration."

"How long is the flight?"

"A good ten hours to Perth."

"Then we've got to get going. I want Sunni to come with me."

"I shall be happy to provide this service for you, Mr. Bond. What you have done and endured for my sake has gone beyond the call of duty. You have acted most honorably. For this, I am in your debt. You and the girl are free to go, of course, and I shall call off the death warrant. We can provide you with false passports, as before."

"What are you going to do with that document? EurAsia Enterprises is finished anyway."

"I will probably go public and tell the true story about the company's history. It will further discredit General Wong. He was attempting to acquire the company on his own, you know. Beijing is unaware of what he was doing. It will appear to them that he was straying even further toward capitalism. I will take over EurAsia Enterprises. There is still a powerful shipping organization in place there. I will rebuild it and make sure it stays legitimate. The important thing is that I have restored face with my ancestors. I have got back what belongs to my family. If nothing else comes of it, that alone is enough. Now, let us hurry if we are going to get you to Australia. I am anxious to repay you for your honorable act of courage today."

"Let's get one thing straight, Mr. Li," Bond said. "You don't owe me a bloody thing. You can talk all you like about honor, but let's call a spade a spade. You're nothing but a gangster, and I despise you and everything you stand for."

"I feel the same way about you, Mr. Bond," Li said with a wry smile. "Any business I have done with *gweilo* in the past was out of necessity. If I had ever been given a choice in the matter, I would not have done it. Your people came to our land and assumed superiority. It is now time for you to leave. I cannot say that I am sorry. But I must impress upon you something to think about. You must surely realize that if Hong Kong is to remain the capitalist moneymaker in fifty years that it is now, it will be up to the Triads to keep a check on the Communists' regulation of the territory's economy. We will be the underground defense against human rights violations and any attempts to undermine the autonomy of Hong Kong."

"You're concerned with human rights? A man who peddles drugs and women? Spare me, please. I believe the Hong Kong people will do quite well on their own, Mr. Li. They are honest and hardworking. They will stand up to oppression."

"You are correct, Mr. Bond. The Hong Kong people are among the world's strongest. Yes, I have made money illegally. You and I believe in opposing creeds. We are from different cultures. Yet we are dedicated to our respective tenets, the doctrines that are our articles of faith, you might say. I would never betray mine, as you would never betray yours. I have killed men. So have you, Mr. Bond. Are we not a little alike? Are we not both men of honor? I may not like you, Mr. Bond, but I trust you. It may be foolish to say this, but I would trust you with my life. I want you to know that from this point forward, you can trust me with yours."

Bond shook the man's hand. The grip was firm and strong. He said, "I appreciate what you've said. I can't forget that you and I are enemies on principle, Li. That doesn't mean, however, that you don't have my . . . respect." It was the strongest compliment Bond could manage.

Zero Minus Four: June 27, 1997, 12:01 A.M.

Avoiding the Immigration authorities once again, James Bond and Sunni Pei boarded Li Xu Nan's private British Aerospace 125 Corporate 800B jet at Kai Tak Airport. As soon as it was in the air, a bomb exploded on one of the Star Ferries in Victoria Harbour. It had been placed in the machine room, and a hole was subsequently blown in the hull. The boat sank rapidly. Luckily, the ferry wasn't crowded and most people made it onto life rafts or were able to grab life belts. Marine Police were magnificently efficient in responding to the incident in record time and saved the lives of everyone aboard. The only casualty was the boat itself.

The Royal Hong Kong Police received three claims of responsibility within the hour, two of which were discounted as pranks. The third reportedly came from an anonymous caller in China. The message simply stated that the bombing was in retaliation for the murder of General Wong. However, the caller went on to say, since no lives were lost on the ferry, another attack somewhere in the colony was imminent.

18

The Golden Mile

Perth is the fastest-growing city in Australia, the capital of the
largest and wealthiest state in the country. Western Australia, covering a third of the continent, is composed of harsh, desolate ex-
panses of the Great Sandy, Gibson, and Great Victoria deserts,
caught between the Kimberley Plateau and the Nullarbor Plain—
two and a half million square kilometers in total. Yet within all this
space are a mere one and a half million inhabitants, most of them
in or around the relatively youthful city of Perth, located in the
southwest coastal region.

Li Xu Wan's private jet flew into Perth International Airport at
midmorning. It was a pleasant, sunny day. James Bond, with Sunni
Pei at his side, had no problem with their counterfeit visas and
passports. They passed through Immigration as John Hunter and
Mary Ling, then went straight to the Hertz Rent-a-Car counter.
Bond asked for their best four-wheel-drive. Li had even provided
Bond with an American Express credit card in the name of John
Hunter.

"It's about a seven-hour drive to Kalgoorlie," he said to Sunni.

His backside was still sore, especially after the long flight, but the herbal treatment Li's doctor had given him had worked wonders. Besides, Bond wanted the feel of driving on the open highway—it would do him more good than another plane flight.

"Oh, James," she said. "This is going to be fun. I haven't taken a road trip since I lived in California!"

"I imagine we'll find a decent motel in Kalgoorlie, have a good dinner, and rest until early tomorrow. Then I'll take a look at the EurAsia mining facility."

"I'm going with you," she said. "I'm not letting you out of my sight anymore."

Bond wasn't sure he wanted her along while he was working. Instead of replying, he leaned over and kissed her forehead. She looked fresh, rested, and very pretty. She was wearing a white blouse with the lower buttons undone and the bottom tied in a knot, exposing her pierced navel. Her blue-jean cutoffs were short, exposing the full length of her splendid legs. As they walked through the airport, Bond noticed other men turning their heads to look at her. He had known many beautiful women in his lifetime, but Sunni was surely one of the most striking.

As for Bond, he had dressed for the warmer climate in a cotton, short-sleeved, light blue polo shirt, and navy blue trousers. Although sitting for long periods of time was still uncomfortable, Bond felt a hundred percent better. The mysterious concoction of herbs and ointments which Li's Chinese doctor had used had been remarkably effective, although Bond had been extremely skeptical at first. He thought that when he returned to London he might seek out a doctor who practiced Chinese herbal medicine.

Hertz provided Bond with a 1995 Suzuki Vitara wagon. It wouldn't have been his first choice, but it would do. It was a red hardtop, two-door, short-wheel-base affair with a part-time four-wheel drive and a 5m/4a transmission. Bond didn't plan on going "off-road," as they called it in Australia, as there was a paved highway all the way to Kalgoorlie.

It was lovely country for the first half of the trip, as the land around the vicinity of Perth was rich and fertile. Once they were past Northam, things began to dry out. Even in June, a winter month in Australia, it was quite warm. The scenery turned to golden brown, and Bond felt they had entered an entirely different country. This was the desert, and it wouldn't do to be stranded on the highway. They had bought a supply of drinking water, and he personally checked out the tires and running condition of the Vitara before starting out.

As the land grew flat and expansive, traffic thinned out. They felt totally alone.

"This is beautiful," Sunni said. "I remember going to Las Vegas when I was a child. It was a lot like this."

Bond nodded. "I've been to Vegas myself a few times. I've never been here, though."

A large rabbit scampered across the road.

"There's something about the desert that is so mysterious," she said. "It looks like nothing could live here, yet it is full of life. I wonder if we'll see any kangaroos."

They drove in silence for a while. Finally, Sunni asked, "All right. You haven't said a word about all of this, and we were on that damn airplane for ten hours. When are you going to let me in on what's going on? I know you're some kind of cop for the British government. What are you doing in Hong Kong? Why are we in Australia now?"

Bond had wondered when she would start asking questions. He didn't see any reason to keep her in the dark. "You know about the terrorist acts that have been committed in Hong Kong over the last month?"

"Who doesn't?"

"I'm investigating them. At first I thought your Triad was involved, but it wasn't true. There was a rather impetuous Chinese general up in Guangzhou who is no longer with us—he may have been responsible. I'm checking out one more lead in Kalgoorlie. A major British company has a gold mine there. I have a hunch I'm going to find some things there that will shed more light on the whole situation."

"Will we be back for the handover?"

"Yes. We have to be. I have an appointment with the Royal Navy on the thirtieth."

"And when will we leave Hong Kong? On the first of July?"

Bond hesitated. He remembered what M had said.

"I'm not sure yet, Sunni," he said. "I'm working on that."

"I can't wait to get out. England sounds nice, but I will probably go back to America. I'd like to go back to school and study medicine. I think I know enough about the human anatomy to have a head start. What do you think?" She laughed, rubbing her hand along Bond's leg.

"You'd make a wonderful doctor," Bond said, smiling. "Your bedside manner is particularly inviting."

She laughed, then became silent. After a moment, she said, "I'm not ashamed of what I've been doing. I had to do it. There are many girls who find themselves in the same situation. It supported me and my mother. I had a nice home. I had money . . ." Her voice choked as she attempted to hold back tears. Bond put his arm around her and kept one hand on the wheel.

"Sunni, you're right," he said. "You don't have to justify anything to me. Or to yourself. You did what you had to do."

"I was exploited," she said. "I'm damaged goods."

"No, you're not," he said. "You have a strong heart and a good head on your shoulders. You can leave all that behind you."

"I *am* anxious to go," she said. "I have no family ties in Hong Kong anymore." She was quiet for a few minutes, then wiped away a tear. Bond knew the poor girl hadn't been able to grieve properly since her mother's death. Finally, she said, "You're right. I can start over. Will you help me, James?"

"I'll do my best, Sunni," he said truthfully.

By late afternoon they had entered Australia's gold fields, and they drove through the ghost town of Coolgardie, at one time the gold-rush capital of Australia. Half an hour later they finally entered the frontier town of Kalgoorlie and its sister suburb, Boulder. Kalgoorlie was a semithriving hub and was dubbed the "Queen" of the "Golden Mile," reputedly the world's richest square mile of gold-bearing earth. The surrounding land was hot, flat, and terribly arid. If it hadn't been for the gold rush of the 1890s, the town wouldn't exist. At one time, there were more than one hundred working mines in the Golden Mile. Kalgoorlie's gold fields continued to produce during the 1920s but faltered after the war. A big nickel boom in the 1960s brought renewed prosperity and tourism to the town.

The streets were very wide. If it were not for the modern streetlights and the cars, the place might be mistaken for the set of a Hollywood western. The historic main street, Hannan, was lined with antiques shops, pubs, hotels, and large buildings that displayed the long-gone wealth and opulence associated with gold frenzy. The side streets were home to all manner of industrial service facilities such as gas and electric providers, bitumen and bobcat services, machinery-repair shops, and drilling-equipment sales. It was clearly a roughneck, hard-hatted man's world. Bond now understood why the local law-enforcement agencies quietly allowed brothels to prosper along notorious Hay Street, which ran parallel to Hannan Street.

They stopped at the Star and Garter, a motel on Hannan and Nethercott streets. Bond got a room that was overpriced, considering the rustic "quaintness" of the place. Sunni appeared to be extremely happy with it, though.

It had been a long drive, and they were hungry. They walked along Hannan Street toward the downtown area until they found a noisy pub. Bond thought he had stepped back in time when he entered the place. It was more like a Wild West saloon than any sort of English pub. The place was full of men, the hard-drinking type, and they all looked like extras from a Crocodile Dundee movie. All conversation halted when they got a look at Sunni and her long legs. Then there was a long, loud whistle, followed by raucous laughter. A barmaid yelled, "That's enough!"

Bond led Sunni to a table away from the bar and whispered, "Are you all right in here?"

She nodded confidently. "After what I've done for a living, nothing can faze me."

The men at the bar started talking to each other again. Bond overheard the words "Sheila," "bird," "skirt," and "beaut," all "Strine" words, or Australian slang, meaning an attractive woman or a tart, depending on the context.

The barmaid, who looked as if she had been born during the gold rush, took their order. She was smiling, but her manner was such that she might have thought they were aliens from Mars.

"She'll be right," the woman said. Bond took this to mean they needn't worry. "They've been on the piss for a while," she went on. "Where you from?"

"England," Bond said.

"You too?" the woman asked Sunni.

"I'm from America," Sunni replied.

The woman sniffed, then said, "Whadallibe?" Bond, amused, translated this as "What will it be?"

"If you're hungry, all we got is counter lunch."

A man at the bar called out a little too loudly, "It's your shout, Skip!" The man he addressed groaned and ordered a round of drinks for his buddies.

"What's counter lunch?" Sunni asked.

The woman looked at her. "Steak and chips."

"That's fine," Bond said.

The woman scribbled on a notepad. "You get a salad, too."

"We'll have a couple of pints of beer. I understand you brew your own here."

"Goodonyamate. Hannan's—best beer in Western Australia. Two pots, then?"

"Hold it, Mary," one of the men said. The one who had been

addressed as Skip brought over two large mugs of beer. "It was my shout, so our two guests here are included." He plopped the two mugs down on the table and held out his hand to Bond. "I'm Skip Stewart. Welcome, mate."

Bond shook his hand. "Thank you. I'm James, and this is Sunni."

"Sun-*ni!*" he said, making a slight bow to her.

Skip Stewart was dressed for the bush, in sturdy boots, blue jeans, and a grimy cotton shirt with the sleeves rolled up. He also had on an Akubra, a hat sitting high on his head so that a forelock could be seen. Strapped to his right calf was a large knife in a sheath. "What brings you to our fair city?"

"Just passing through," Bond said.

"Ya know, I can tell you a thing or two about this town," Stewart said. "My great-granddaddy on my mother's side was an engineer who first brought water to Kalgoorlie."

"Is that so?"

"That's right. C. Y. O'Connor was his name. It was at the turn of the century, during the gold rush." Stewart took a chair at the table and proceeded to tell his story. Bond didn't mind, and Sunni was grinning at the man. He was overflowing with local color.

"Ya see, the miners were dropping like flies, what for the lack of water. Drinking water, that is. My great-granddaddy came up with an invention—a wood and pitch water pipe that stretched from Kalgoorlie all the way to Mundaring Weir, near Perth. Nobody thought he would succeed. They all called him a strop, but he kept going. Well, the pipeline was finished and turned on, and after three days—there weren't no water yet! My poor great-granddaddy shot himself 'cause he thought he'd failed, eh? But you know what?"

"What?" Sunni asked.

"He didn't realize that the water would take *two weeks* to travel that distance, eh? He *had* solved the problem. A week and a half after he killed himself, water poured out of the pipeline and began to fill up the town's new reservoir!"

"That's quite a story," Bond said.

"It's true, mate."

The men at the bar called to Stewart and held up their empty mugs.

"Oh, um, it's your shout, mate," Stewart said to Bond.

That meant it was Bond's turn to buy everyone in the bar a round of drinks. "Sure," he said and nodded to the bartender.

Skip Stewart stood up, obviously pleased with Bond's response at the men's request. "Goodonyamate. I can tell you're no two-pot screamer. Hey, if you need anything while you're here, you don't hesitate to call on me. I run guided-tour packages into the outback. I have four-by-fours, utes, campers, and dirt bikes. If you need to get somewhere in a hurry, I've got a little plane at the airstrip for hire. Rent the plane, you get the pilot for free."

"Who's the pilot?" Bond asked.

"You're lookin' at him," Stewart said. He reached into his back pocket, pulled out a business card, and handed it to Bond. It was a little limp and damp from the man's sweat. "That's my card, mate. Like I said, call if you need anything. I'll leave you two to your dinner now." He took the opportunity to get another eyeful of Sunni, then sauntered back to the bar and rejoined his friends.

Bond stuck the man's card in his pocket and smiled at Sunni. She was enjoying this. The barmaid brought the counter lunch, which consisted of greasy, tough, overcooked steak and thick, oily french fries. The salad was a couple of lettuce leaves, one piece of sliced tomato, and a slice of canned beetroot. Bond ate it anyway. Sunni picked at hers.

"We'll go to a proper restaurant next time," he promised.

"It's all right," she said. "I'm not that hungry. When are we going back to the motel?"

When they got back to the Star and Garter, Sunni bolted the door, turned, and leaned back against it. She held her arms out to Bond. Still dressed, he went to her and they embraced. He pressed her against the door with his own hard body. "Oh, darling James," she moaned as she wrapped her long legs around his waist. He held her, suspended between the door and his torso, thrusting his pelvis between her legs and grinding into her slowly with force. They kissed deeply, forgetting their surroundings and losing themselves in each other.

She unwrapped her legs and moved him toward the bed. They removed their clothes. Because the wounds on his backside and legs were still sensitive, she pulled him on top of her smooth, soft body. She undulated beneath him, rocking against his flesh with a rhythm not unlike the waves in Victoria Harbour. They continued to kiss, all the while exploring each other's skin with their hands. Eventually she grasped him firmly and guided him inside. Locked together, they moved with passion and anticipation, urging each other on toward the moment of climax that they finally experienced together.

They continued to make love for what seemed like hours. The bed squeaked and the air conditioner rumbled, but at least the room was cool.

Zero Minus Three: June 28, 1997, 5:00 A.M.

"I'm coming with you," Sunni said, slipping on her shorts and blouse. Bond had already showered and was dressed.

They had got a few hours of sleep after a blissful night. Bond thought he should go to the facility alone, and he had hoped he could slip away without waking her.

"Sunni, I don't know what I'm going to find there. There could be trouble."

"Oh, stop treating me like a helpless bimbo. I could watch your back. You've seen me in action. I'm a Hong Kong girl, remember?"

"All right, but put on something to cover up your legs. We're going down a mine."

The sun was just beginning to rise as they drove away from the motel and out of town, heading north toward more remote mining towns such as Broad Arrow, Comet Vale, and Leonora. The EurAsia Enterprises facility was about an hour's drive away.

Many of the mines in Kalgoorlie-Boulder were open-pit mines. This meant that the ore was mined and hauled from what was basically a large hole in the ground. The maximum amount of payable ore was moved by the shortest route to the processing plant with the minimum amount of waste. The aptly named "Super Pit" was the largest of this kind in the area, and the city's gold-mining industry was now primarily centered around it. The Super Pit would eventually swallow the last of the traditional underground mine shafts that could be found in the Golden Mile.

EurAsia's mining operation was of the old-fashioned underground type. The ore was drilled and blasted by conventional means, leaving a cavern that was partially filled with barren rock from the same mine. The broken ore produced by the blast was carried by haul trucks or rail cars to a primary crusher underground, before being winched to the surface via a shaft. Trucks, loaders, and other vehicles and equipment used underground were dismantled on the surface and lowered in pieces down the shaft. They were then reassembled in workshops cut from the rock beneath the surface. Large headframes, prominent features in the Kalgoorlie-Boulder skyline, were used for hauling ore to the surface or raising and lowering miners and equipment.

The entrance to the facility was just off the highway. A faded sign read "EurAsia Enterprises Australia Pty—Private Property—No Trespassing." A dirt road led from the paved highway off into the distance. Bond turned into the drive, then moved off the dirt road and traveled along the side of it over the rough terrain.

"What are you doing?" Sunni asked.

"I don't want to leave fresh tire treads in the dirt road. No one will notice the tracks out here."

After ten minutes, the adjacent dirt road opened up into a large gravel-topped area surrounded by a barbed-wire fence. A closed gate barred entrance to the compound. There was a two-story, white wooden building just inside the fence. Several 4 × 4 vehicles and a couple of other standard cars were parked in front. Most notable was the private airstrip alongside the building. A Cessna Grand Caravan single turboprop sat on the runway. Bond thought it was probably used by company executives to get to and from Perth in a hurry. It was the type of plane that was utilized by corporations and even private individuals in an area as large as Western Australia.

Bond parked the Vitara behind a clump of eucalyptus trees that he hoped would shield it from sight. He and Sunni got out and moved closer to the fence. Some distance away, on the other side of the white building, was the entrance to the mine. A head-frame, fifty meters high, marked the spot. Two trucks sat on the "decline," the dirt road that led into the big dark hole. Another small structure was next to it, most likely a miners' barracks or storehouse. Two men wearing coveralls were walking toward the main building. Bond wondered how many more employees would be present.

From this vantage point, he could see inside the loading dock of the building. Sitting on a flatbed lorry was the dark brown sampan with the red hood that he had seen at the EurAsia warehouse at Kwai Chung. What the hell was it doing here? Hadn't the *Taitai* shipped it to Singapore? That ship couldn't have traveled as far as Perth in four days. It was quite curious—there was not a body of water for miles, and these people had a Chinese boat sitting in the loading dock of a mining operation.

He held the barbed wire open for them to slip through. They both ran for cover behind a pile of boulders near the mine entrance. When the coast was clear, Bond slipped over to the small structure and listened at the door. There was silence. He gestured for Sunni, and together they entered the small building.

He had been right. It was full of mining tools, hard hats, lockers, and a shower. Bond tossed a pair of coveralls to Sunni and put some on himself. They found hard hats that fit (Sunni tucked her long hair underneath the hat), took a couple of torches and pickaxes, then proceeded out the door. There was no one in sight. It was probably too early for the miners. If they hurried, they could be in and out before anyone arrived for the beginning of the working day.

Bond and Sunni entered the mine and made their way down the decline into darkness. They switched on the flashlights, revealing a colorless shaft of stone not much higher than Bond's head. Pillars were constructed every few yards to support the ceiling. He consulted the map he had found at Kwai Chung.

"We have to travel quite a way to this point here," he said, referring to a junction some distance away. The decline curved to the left there, while the map showed another passage leading right toward the "Off Limits Area."

It was about fifteen degrees cooler in the mine, which felt wonderful, but the air was stale and smelled of minerals. They soon came to an area that had recently been excavated. A couple of pickaxes were on the ground, and the wall to their left had been chipped away. Bond pointed his flashlight at the wall. Streaks of dull brown-yellow spread through the rock.

"See that?" Bond gestured. "That's gold."

Sunni was amazed. "Really? It doesn't look like gold."

"That's because gold is never bright and shiny when you first find it. It's actually quite dull. It's very soft and malleable, too. The stuff that sparkles is really 'fool's gold.'"

They moved on farther into the mine and finally came to the junction. The passage to the right was so narrow that they had to squeeze through single file. They moved down the tunnel for several minutes until it opened up into a large, dug-out cavern. Bond consulted the map.

"We're nearly beneath the main building. They've excavated back under the compound. I wonder if they have lifts or something going up to the surface."

He shone the torch around the room and saw that work lights had been installed in the ceiling. Bond found the switch and turned them on. The room was furnished with tables, lockers, chairs, and a vending machine for soft drinks. A large steel door was built into the far wall, with a sign reading "Off Limits Area. Danger: Radiation." There was a small porthole window in the door. Bond walked over to it and looked inside. It was some kind of air lock, for another steel door was just a few feet away.

Radiation? What was behind that steel door? Bond's heart suddenly started to race. What had he stumbled on? Had he found the source of the Australian nuclear explosion? Could this possibly be the answer?

He quickly turned and searched the lockers. They were full of radiation-resistant body suits. He took one and put it on.

"Wait here," he told Sunni. "I'm going inside."

"Be careful," was all she said. She was getting a little nervous now.

Bond found the air-lock controls easily enough and opened the outer door. He stepped inside and closed it behind him. He then opened the inner door and stepped into another mine shaft. He flicked on an electric generator, which powered up some work lights. Bond studied the rock walls and found no traces of gold. Instead, he saw netlike veins of a dull, black, sooty material that was neither smooth nor craggy. He didn't need a Geiger counter to identify the oxide. EurAsia Enterprises was mining uranium!

He followed the passage into another large work area, this one set up more like a laboratory. A lift had been installed here, and Bond presumed it went up into the main building on the surface. There were also other large machines in the room, and Bond thought they might be reactors that converted the nonfissionable uranium 238, or natural uranium, into uranium 235, which was the material used in atomic bombs. He knew that natural Uranium contained both isotopes, but usually only 0.6% of the material was the fissionable U-235.

A U-235 atom was so unstable that a blow from a single neutron was enough to split it and bring on a chain reaction. When a U-235 atom was split, it would give off energy in the form of heat and gamma radiation, which was the most dynamic form of radioactivity and the most lethal. The split atom would also emit two or three spare neutrons that would fly out with sufficient force to split other atoms they came in contact with. In theory, it was necessary to split only one U-235 atom, and the neutrons from this one would split other atoms, which would split more . . . and so on. All of this happened within a millionth of a second. Bond knew that the minimum amount to start a chain reaction was known as super critical mass.

It took only the materials, the recipe, and a certain amount of expertise to make a bomb. Bond saw that the first two of these elements were in this room, and someone obviously had the necessary skill.

The big question in Bond's mind was whether Guy Thackeray himself had been involved at all. The man was dead, but this facility was obviously still operating. Who was behind it?

In the center of the room, on a steel table, was a metal object that resembled a large bowling pin. After closer examination, Bond knew it was a bomb that was almost complete. The top of the device had been removed. It was the section of the bomb that held the detonator and fuse that were used to set off the chain reaction. A hollow cylinder of U-235 was inside the device. The missing section would contain another phallic-shaped portion of U-235, which would be injected by a plunger into the cylinder, thereby causing super critical mass. The detonator that fired the plunger was activated by a fuse set to a timer, not an altimeter. This bomb was going to be placed somewhere, not dropped from an airplane.

He had to get out of there and contact London immediately. Bond could handle M's displeasure that he had disobeyed orders and left Hong Kong. If she suspended him, so be it. At least he had found the source of the nuclear "accident." Now, if he only knew who was behind it and what their motives were.

Bond switched off the lights, went back through the passage, and opened the door to the air lock. He closed the door behind him, then opened the outer door.

He stepped into the room where he had left Sunni and got the shock of his life.

The three albino Chinese thugs, the ones he had dubbed Tom, Dick, and Harry, were armed with pistols, facing him. Harry had Sunni, with his hand over her mouth.

It was the fourth man in the room who took Bond completely by surprise.

"Did you find what you were looking for, Mr. Bond?" asked Guy Thackeray, alive and well and looking very fit.

19

Farewell to Hong Kong

The albino Tom immediately moved forward and disarmed Bond. He tucked the Walther PPK in his belt, then moved back into position. Harry slowly released Sunni, and she moved to join Bond.

"How touching," Thackeray said. "It looks as if you two have some sort of affection for each other. Surprised to see me, Mr. Bond?"

Bond was speechless.

"No, I'm not a ghost," Thackeray said. "Still alive. I haven't felt better in years!"

"What's going on, Thackeray?" Bond spit. "Let us go."

"But you two are my guests!" the man said with mock sincerity. "I was about to have breakfast. Won't you join me? I promise to tell all." He gestured to the albinos. Bond and Sunni were shoved roughly toward the passageway. Bond removed his radioactive-resistant suit, then the entire party made their way out of the mine. They walked across the gravel toward the main building. The temperature had risen considerably in the hour Bond and Sunni had been underground.

They were led into a comfortable private dining area on the second floor. Tom shoved Bond toward a chair. Angered, 007 turned and swung at the albino. Tom was unbelievably quick for his size—he blocked the blow effortlessly, grabbed Bond's arm, and twisted it sharply. Bond winced in agony.

"Enough of that!" Thackeray commanded. Tom released Bond, who jerked his arm away from the albino and stared at him with menace.

"Who are the three stooges, Thackeray? I should have known they worked for you when I first saw them in Macau."

"Oh, these are the Chang brothers. All three of them were born albino. Their parents were my grandfather's servants. My own father saw to it that they were raised in a safe environment, and they have been loyal to my family ever since," Thackeray said. "Sit down, Mr. Bond. Sit down, miss . . . um, what shall I call your lovely companion?"

Before Sunni could answer, Bond replied, "Her name is no concern of yours. She's completely innocent. You should let her go. She won't go to the police."

"I cannot believe she is *completely* innocent, Bond," Thackeray said.

"For that matter," Bond said, "you have no right to keep me either. I promise you my newspaper won't publish anything about you."

"Your newspaper?" Thackeray laughed loudly. "Come, come, Bond. Cut the crap, *please*. I know all about you. You're no reporter. I knew you weren't a reporter before we parted company in Macau. You work for the British Secret Service. You see, my albino friends here kept tabs on Mr. Woo after he had played *mahjong* with me a couple of times. I wanted to know more about him. It wasn't difficult to ascertain that he worked for your government. You people are really becoming careless, you know. I was about to do something about him, but General Wong in China beat me to it. Woo knew too much. It wasn't a huge leap of logic to see through you, Mr. Bond."

A Chinese servant brought in a tray of food—scrambled eggs, bacon, toast, orange juice, and coffee.

"Ah, breakfast," Thackeray said. "Eat up, please. It may be the last good breakfast you'll ever have!" He sat down and started piling food on his plate.

Bond looked at Sunni. She was terribly frightened. He took her hand. It was trembling. He wished she had stayed at the motel and was angry with himself for allowing her to come. He had once again put a girl he cared about in jeopardy. Bond gave her hand a squeeze as if to say, "Don't worry." Then he put on his best facade of nonchalance.

"I'll bet you say that to all your guests, Thackeray," he said, sitting down. "This looks good. We're quite hungry, aren't we, Sunni?"

She looked at him as if he were crazy. Bond gestured with his head for her to sit. Sunni sat down and played with her food.

"So tell me," Bond said, "how did you manage to survive that car bomb?"

"Oh, that," Thackeray said. "Simple stage illusion. I once made a paltry living doing magic, but you probably already know that. I used to perform the same trick on stage with a cabinet and a drape. I'd step into the cabinet, and my assistants would hold a large drape in front of it. The top of the cabinet could be seen behind the drape, but it shielded my escape through the bottom of it. The cabinet was set on fire, and then I miraculously appeared at the back of the house and walked down the aisle to the thunderous applause of the audience. It was a nice illusion. On the day of my 'disappearance,' I simply got out of the limo when the vehicle was shielded by a large truck that pulled up beside it. I jumped onto the side of the truck and rode with it up the street. A man I hired then threw the bomb into the car. It was quite spectacular, if I do say so myself. I understand you had something to do with the man's demise?"

Of course, Bond thought. He should have known it had been a magician's illusion. It just proved the old adage that the hand really was quicker than the eye.

"Very clever, Thackeray," Bond said. "But why? I know all about the contract between your great-great-grandfather and Li Xu Nan's great-great-grandfather. But why disappear? Unless it was simply to escape being arrested as a drug smuggler . . ."

"Yes, well, the contract . . ." Thackeray suddenly seemed lost in thought. "It's extraordinary, isn't it? My father had told me about the agreement, and I thought it had been lost forever. Li Xu Nan hated me on principle. He thought my family had cheated his family. But *we* didn't lose the contract. The Thackerays had nothing to do with his family's exile from China. Yet he blamed me for some reason." Thackeray chuckled. "It didn't stop him from doing business with me."

"And then General Wong came to see you . . ."

Thackeray nodded. "Yes. A black day, to be sure. General Wong came to see me in . . . what year was it? 1985. At first I couldn't believe he could get away with what he told me. I was determined to find a legal defense against him. At the same time, though, I had to keep silent. I couldn't put the company's market value in jeopardy. If the news that EurAsia Enterprises was going to change 'management' in 1997 had been made public then, I could not have conducted business. There are plenty of big corporations that have pulled out of Hong Kong in the last ten years. I was stuck, so I had to make it work until that fateful day."

Thackeray stood and began to walk around the room as he spoke. He took a bottle of vodka, poured some into a glass, and drank it quickly. For the next half hour, he continued to refill the glass. His address slowly became a rant, as if he was justifying himself to the gods rather than talking to people in the same room with him.

"I had to live with it for ten years!" he said. "Ten . . . bloody . . . years. Imagine it! Imagine knowing that everything your family had built was going to vanish in one swift blow, and there wasn't a goddamned thing you could do about it! I alone carried that weight on my shoulders. Donaldson, my solicitor, knew, of course, but he was helpless as well. So, about a year ago, I finally knew what I had to do. I would get everything I could out of the company, escape, and then wreak havoc on the society that had destroyed five generations of wealth and success."

He sat down again and faced Bond and the girl. His face was flushed and he was now beginning to lose his composure. "I *hate* the Chinese. I hate the two-faced bastards. They smile to your face, eager to please, but behind your back they have nothing but contempt for you. And you know something? The British are no better! I hate them as well! What idiots! They agreed to hand over the wealthiest city-state in Asia to the yellow bastards, and it was rightfully theirs!"

So, Bond thought, not only was Thackeray a raving madman, but he was a racist as well. "There are many who would argue with you, Thackeray," he said. "It was the Chinese who got the unfair deals back in the nineteenth century. The land was originally theirs. Hong Kong was won only because of the greed and fortitude of opium traders. That was the reasoning behind the treaty Britain signed with China in 1984. China has lived with what they felt was shame and humiliation that England has nurtured one of her children. Hong Kong is a part of China, Thackeray. You cannot refute that."

"Balls!" Thackeray shouted. "Don't speak to me about opium traders! My great-great-grandfather was a pioneer, and if it weren't for men like him, there wouldn't *be* a Hong Kong! Do you think the territory would have flourished the way it did if it had been under Chinese rule all this time? It might never have been developed at all! No, Bond, I don't buy that argument. You think Britain is selling out because she feels *guilty*? If that is the truth, then it's a stupid, unfathomable reason to hand over a gold mine to a country full of ignorant people who will most likely run it into the ground!"

"Mr. Thackeray," Bond said evenly, "China is full of people

who have worked and sweated all their lives just to have a piece of land on which to build a home. They have a heritage of defending themselves against all manner of threats. Their country has been conquered and restructured countless times over the centuries. They have learned that not everything in life is about wealth. You know as well as anyone how important *maijiang* is in the East. If Britain decided to hand over Hong Kong, it was because she felt it was the honorable thing to do. She had to save face."

"Don't talk to me of honor, Bond. It was a business transaction. Nothing more."

"I'm afraid there are a lot of people who don't see it that way."

"And after the first of July, will those people still see it as an act of honor? When six million people suddenly find themselves living under communist rule, they will come to the realization that they were the pawns in a business transaction gone wrong. They were betrayed. I think they'd rather be dead."

"What are you saying, Thackeray?" Bond was now beginning to lose his temper too. "What is it you're planning to do? I know you have a bomb down there in your mine. It was you who tested a device in the outback a few weeks ago, wasn't it?"

"Yes, that was me. I had to make sure my little homemade toy worked before I exacted my revenge against those who have done me wrong."

"And who might that be?"

"Don't you see?" Thackeray pounded the table. "If I can't have my company, no one is going to have it! If Britain can't have Hong Kong, then no one is going to inhabit it! The world has to be taught a lesson."

The magnitude of what Thackeray was implying hit Bond with great force. "You were responsible for all those terrorist acts, weren't you! You've been intentionally trying to start a conflict between Britain and China!"

"Bravo, Mr. Bond, bravo!" he said with sarcasm. "Yes, I was behind it all. I decided that if my plan was going to be a success, then I had to build up to it. I had to plant the seeds in everyone's minds that China and Britain were at each other's throats."

"What the hell is your plan?"

"Why, it is the culmination of a hundred and fifty years of lies, betrayals, and pretention," Thackeray said. "No more kowtowing on either side. No more speculation about what will happen in Hong Kong's future. At exactly one minute after midnight on the first of July, that bomb will detonate somewhere in the Hong Kong territory—successfully wiping away the entire legacy."

This time it was Sunni who cried out. "No! You're a madman! Why do you want to kill six million innocent people? You're a child having a tantrum! Someone's taken away your toy and now you want to get even! You're pathetic!"

There was silence for a moment as Thackeray stared at her. Bond finally said, "I couldn't have said it better."

Thackeray stood again and began to pace the room. He was trembling with rage. The alcohol was starting to get to him, too. He was displaying the same signs of recklessness he had shown in Macau. It was not even midmorning, and already the man was drunk on his feet. "You don't know the half of it. Starting about a month ago, I slowly began to transfer EurAsia holdings into a private Swiss bank account. A little at a time. I had to be careful, for there were many people in the organization who could have found me out. First I had to get rid of my solicitor, Gregory Donaldson. He knew too much. At the same time, I could get at that bastard General Wong. I was going to make sure *he* wouldn't get EurAsia! I made Donaldson's death look like Wong was responsible. Once that was done, I thought that Britain should reciprocate. When nothing happened, I had my aide Simon Sinclair assassinate the two officials from Beijing. I later got rid of *him* for that very reason. You were present at his demise, Bond."

"The massacre in Macau? *You* staged that?"

"Of course I staged it! I wanted it to look like a Triad hit. The Chang brothers here hired some men to do the dirty work. You and your friend Woo should have been killed that night, too, but it didn't work out that way."

"What about the floating restaurant? You killed your entire board of directors?"

Thackeray nodded, his eyes wide. As he stared into space, he involuntarily brought his hand up and pulled on the left side of his face. Bond thought he resembled the famous detail in Michelangelo's Sistine Chapel painting in which a condemned sinner suddenly realizes that his soul is damned forever.

"Yes, I did that," he whispered, almost to himself. "They all had to go. They would have found out what I was doing." Thackeray was talking to himself like a child, as if he were defending his actions to an adult who had caught him doing something wrong.

For a moment he seemed lost, his mind in a faraway place. Then he quickly snapped out of it and turned to Bond. He became his vindictive, angry old self once again.

"I blamed that on General Wong, too, of course. For a while, it was working," he said. "Britain sent a Royal Navy fleet to southeast Asia. Chinese troops lined the border. The fuse had been lit. You, Mr. Bond, helped it along without any prompting on my part. You assassinated General Wong, didn't you? I have my sources. I know all about it. It *was* you, was it not? You did it for that gangster Li, right? Tell me I'm right."

Bond lied. "It wasn't me."

"I don't believe you, but it doesn't matter. Wong is dead, and I can't tell you how happy that makes me. I suppose Li has that document now. Well, if he thinks *he's* going to take over EurAsia Enterprises, then he needs to throw the *chim* again. He's not going to be so lucky. Anyway, Wong's murder only made China that much more suspicious and confrontational. My little surprise the other night was the penultimate move."

"What was that?" Bond asked.

"Oh, you probably haven't heard. One of the Star Ferries sank. Someone put a bomb on board."

"You bastard," Sunni whispered.

"And now the stage is set for the big transition," Thackeray said. "Just as Hong Kong changes hands, my bomb will explode. No one will know who to blame. China will blame Britain. Britain will blame China. There are sure to be some . . . misunderstandings." He laughed. "It will be *wonderful!*"

"You're going to start what might be World War Three!" Bond said. "Why? What do you get out of it? Just revenge? You think that by destroying one of the wonders of modern civilization, it will make you happy? I don't think so, Thackeray. I think you're going to remain the miserable drunken wretch you are for the rest of your life, no matter what you do."

"Oh, I intend to be perfectly happy, Mr. Bond. As I said, I've been slowly transferring my assets to a Swiss bank account. The company's coffers are almost dry. I liquidated my entire stock the morning of my press conference, the day of my 'death.' It's a good thing I died when I did, too! I probably would be under arrest for drug smuggling, wouldn't I? I heard about the warehouse. You were probably responsible for that, too, weren't you, Bond? Never mind. To answer your question, I think I will be very happy to see Hong Kong go up in flames. I plan to live anonymously here in Australia for the rest of my life. The Chang brothers will look after me. They are very loyal. I pay them well, too."

Bond knew he had to stop the man. He needed to find out more about the bomb, so that in case he got away he could alert SIS. "How did you make an atomic bomb, Thackeray? It's not something you learn out of a textbook."

Thackeray laughed. "No, not a textbook. It was the Internet, actually. I found a most peculiar website called 'How to Make an Atomic Bomb.' That gave me the idea, and I hired the right people to help me. I had discovered uranium in my gold mine several years ago, but I never reported it. I hired a nuclear physicist named VanBlaricum to work on it and design the machines you saw down below to extract U-235 from the U-238. That's the difficult part.

It's not a sophisticated bomb. It's really quite crude. But it's big enough to do the trick. It will be the best trick I've ever performed!"

"Where will you plant it? How will it be detonated?"

"You ask too many questions, Bond. I'm certainly not going to tell you where it's going to be, even though you won't be alive to witness it. Detonating it is easy. A small digital clock will be inside the cone. You know, it runs off of one of those small round batteries you find in wristwatches. It will be set as a timer to explode at twelve-oh-one on the first of July. When the time comes, the detonator will set off some conventional explosive inside the cone, thrusting a small portion of U-235 into the main chamber, thereby achieving super critical mass. In an instant . . . farewell to Hong Kong! It will destroy forever China's hopes of regaining the colony, and it will teach Queen and Country a lesson she will never forget. I have nothing for which to thank England. I have lived in Hong Kong and Australia all my life. England can go hang, for all I care."

Thackeray seemed to be in a better mood now. He was quite drunk, but he was no longer in a rage. He moved behind Sunni and put his hand on her long, soft hair. She recoiled, but he grasped her neck and held her firmly. "You're full of fight, you know that, my dear? I think you'll make a nice figurehead for my little firecracker. I'll see to it that you make it back to Hong Kong safely, and you can witness the event from a front-row seat! My ship is docked in Singapore, and it's got a lot of nooks and crannies where we can hide you. I have a cargo seaplane in Perth waiting to take us to meet her. It's a rather long voyage, so we must get started."

He released her, then nodded to Tom and Dick. The two albinos grabbed Sunni and pulled her from the table. She screamed, "No!" and started to struggle. Bond rose to come to her aid, but Harry aimed an AK-47 at him and gestured for him to be still. Sunni attempted to use karate, but the two men held her fast, and they removed her from the room. The sound of her struggles became fainter as they took her to another part of the building.

Thackeray produced a pistol from thin air—another sleight-of-hand trick. It was Bond's own Walther PPK. "Now, what shall we do with you, Mr. Bond? I can't let you live, that much is certain. I should probably just shoot you here and now and get it over with. I've always wondered why the bad guys never do that to the heroes in action movies. Instead, they have to use some elaborate method of torture or execution. The hero ultimately uses the delay to his advantage and escapes. So I should just shoot you now, right?"

For a second Bond thought the sight of the madman pointing his own gun at him would be the last thing he would ever see. Thackeray only smiled.

"No," he said. "Not yet. I don't want anyone from your service coming to look for you. The Australian police and INTERPOL have already done a thorough search of our facility here a couple of weeks ago. As you can imagine, every mining company in Kalgoorlie was investigated over my little nuclear test in the outback. One of the area's many side industries is explosives. Luckily, my uranium lode was adequately hidden, and EurAsia Enterprises Australia was given an all clear. But one can't be too careful. I don't want anyone finding your body, or any remains of it."

He gestured to Harry. "My friend Mr. Chang will take you for a ride in my private airplane. We'll take you to a part of the country you've probably never seen. For that matter, it's a part of the country you'd probably never want to see. We'll shoot you there and dump your body. If anyone other than an Aborigine ever does find it, it will have been completely eaten by predators. I think that is best." He then nodded to Harry, giving him a signal.

Harry slammed the butt of the AK-47 into the back of Bond's head. Bond saw a flash of light, felt a moment of extreme pain, and then was plunged into total darkness.

Walkabout

June 28, 1997, 6:00 P.M.

The white and red Cessna Grand Caravan was the largest single-engine utility multi-use turboprop, and was widely used by mail carriers and cargo-delivering companies. Its overall length was 41.6 feet, with a wingspan of 52.1 feet. Its engine was a PT6A-114A with 675 SHP, and could take the plane on a cruising speed of 341 kilometers per hour. The Grand Caravan was exceptional because up to five distinctive interiors could be customized. At the moment, it was fitted out with a ten-seat commuter interior—ideal for carrying passengers in first-class comfort.

Cruising at 182 knots at an altitude of 20,000 feet, James Bond was anything but comfortable. He awoke from a deep sleep, strapped into the last seat on the right side of the cabin. His head was pounding, and he felt drugged. They must have given him some kind of sedative after the head injury. The unmistakable hum told him where he was and what was happening. The plane's cabin had two rows of five seats each, the front two in the cockpit. One man he hadn't seen before was piloting the aircraft, while Harry, the smallest but wiriest of the three albinos, was sitting two seats up from Bond in the opposite row. They were the only passengers in the plane.

Bond squinted out of the window. The sun was setting, and the ground below looked golden brown. They were flying over what seemed to be an infinite desert.

He tried to move, but he was strapped in tightly with duct tape wrapped around his body and the chair. They were probably going to land somewhere very soon, kill him, dump his body, then take off back to Kalgoorlie. Guy Thackeray and his bomb were most likely already on their way back to Hong Kong—with Sunni in tow.

Bond groaned, indicating to his captor that he was just waking up. Harry turned around to look at him. The man got out of his seat and moved back to Bond. He was carrying the AK-47. There seemed to be an awful lot of AK-47s in this part of the world!

Harry grunted at Bond as if to say, "Oh, you're awake. Having fun?"

"Untie me, you bastard," Bond moaned. "This is uncomfortable."

Harry said something in Cantonese that Bond couldn't understand. He caught only the words "almost there."

"Come on," Bond said in Cantonese. "I have to stand up and stretch. My head is killing me."

The albino thought about it. Finally, he said in English, "No tricks."

"You're the one with the gun, my friend," Bond said.

Harry produced a pocketknife with his left hand, and sliced through the duct tape. Bond pulled his hands free and ripped the tape away from his body. Harry resumed pointing the gun at his prisoner. Bond stood up and held his hands high. The cabin's ceiling was low, so he couldn't stand up perfectly straight. In fact, he had to lean over to stretch.

"I'm unarmed, see?" he said. "No need to point that at me yet." He squatted on his haunches and twisted his body back and forth, working out the kinks.

"What did you shoot me up with?" he asked. "I feel as if I'm in a recovery room. Where are we, anyway?"

He started to move into the aisle and toward the cockpit, but Harry stopped him. He gestured toward the chair. "Down" was all he said.

"Oh come on, now," Bond said. "You just let me up. Can't I move around a bit?" Harry fired a single shot from the AK-47 at the seat next to Bond, blowing a hole right through it. "All right, all right, you made your point," Bond said. "Does your boss always allow you to shoot up his plane like that? You know, it's not a smart thing to do, firing guns in a pressurized cabin. There was a Korean fellow I knew once . . ."

Then Bond used the oldest trick in the book, and it actually worked. He looked toward the cockpit and feigned an expression of alarm. "Christ, what the hell is your pilot *doing*?" he said.

Harry turned toward the cockpit, and Bond jumped at him. It was vital to get the machine gun away from the man, so he used both hands to grab it and Harry's right arm. He threw the weight of his body into Harry's smaller frame, knocking them both to the cabin floor in the middle of the aisle. Harry was on his back, and Bond was on top of him, and they both struggled for control of the gun. A blast of gunfire ripped across the ceiling of the plane, and all hell broke loose inside the cabin. Every unsecured object flew toward the holes, disorienting the two fighting men. The noise of the escaping pressure was deafening. The pilot shouted something, but no one could hear him.

Harry was firing the gun wildly. Bond could barely hold on to the man's arm, for the recoil was intense and Harry was quite agile. He didn't want any of the windows blown, or they all might be sucked out into the sky. The pilot reached for a pistol hidden in a compartment by his side, but the plane lurched and forced the pilot to stay with the controls of the aircraft.

Bond repeatedly slammed his elbow into Harry's face, but the man still clutched the AK-47. Finally, in an attempt to pull the gun up and away from Bond, the albino swung his arms above his head. Unfortunately, this action aimed the gun toward the cockpit. Another blast of gunfire riddled the control panel and the pilot, who slumped forward in his chair.

The plane immediately swerved and started to dive. Bond and Harry were slammed against a right row seat, and Harry dropped the gun. They continued to roll as the plane spun upside down. The cabin's ceiling was now the floor as they rolled over the seats. The little man suddenly delivered severely painful karate blows to Bond's sides, then squirmed away from him. He was trying to find the gun again, but it had fallen out of sight.

The plane rotated again so that everything was right side up, but it was dangerously out of control. Both of them were tossed against the seats. Harry leaped toward Bond and began to pummel him. Stiff and in pain, Bond did his best to ward off the blows and protect himself. If only he could get a good punch in . . . But all he was able to do was to push the man's face back with his right hand. It was enough to cause the albino to fall back. Bond jack-knifed up, held on to a seat, and kicked Harry hard in the head. It didn't seem to disable him, for he grabbed Bond's foot and twisted it sharply, nearly spraining his ankle. Bond cried out in pain, then used his other foot to kick Harry, who let go and scrambled into the aisle. He had seen the machine gun and was going for it.

Bond jumped onto the albino's back as he crawled toward the AK-47, which was not quite within his reach, but he was so wiry that he slipped through Bond's arms and managed to get hold of the gun. He then attempted to get himself off the floor and onto his knees, but the plane lurched again, knocking both of them against the exit panel on the left side of the craft. Bond went for the gun, which Harry held across his chest. The albino's back was pressed against the door, and the men were face-to-face.

By now all of the pressure had escaped from the cabin. It was difficult to breathe, but Bond could now use this to his advantage. Using all the strength he could muster, he kept his right hand on the gun to keep Harry from pointing it at him, and used his left hand to reach behind the albino to get at the door's emergency lock. He found it and released it.

The door swung open and Harry fell out, the gun still in hand. He screamed, a look of horror on his face as he flew away from the craft to his death. Bond managed to brace himself against the opening, then slowly climbed back through the aisle toward the cockpit.

He threw the dead pilot out of his seat and quickly buckled himself in behind the controls of the aircraft. Christ, they were only a mile from the ground! Could he land the plane without smashing it to pieces? Bond leveled the aircraft as best he could, slowing it to a safer speed. There was a patch of flat, sandy ground below. It would have to do. Thank God there were no cliffs or canyons in the area.

Bond took her down, but it was going to be a crash landing no matter what he did. He braced himself, attempting to keep the plane straight so that the wheels would touch the ground before the nose did. Bond covered his face and hands and bent forward.

As it happened, the plane landed square on the front and left wheels. The front wheel broke away and the nose slammed into the ground. Miraculously, it wasn't crushed, but the propeller snapped off and the windshield shattered into a hundred pieces. The entire aircraft skidded across the sand and finally came to a halt. It was broken and useless, but still in one piece. It was a testament to Cessna's reputation and the durability of the Grand Caravan.

Bond released several deep breaths and took stock of his body. He hadn't been hurt. He slowly got out of the seat. The enormity of what he had just been through paled when he suddenly realized where he was. He looked out of the broken windshield at his surroundings. Outside the sun was setting on a vast horizon of nothingness. He was quite literally in the middle of nowhere.

The first thing he did was try the plane's radio, but it was inoperable. The burst of gunfire from the AK-47 had blown a hole through it. Next he searched the cockpit for anything that might be useful—maps, canisters of water, and the like. There were some navigational maps of Western Australia and the Northern Territory, but they didn't tell Bond where the plane had actually crashed. He folded the maps and put them in his pocket. The pilot had reached for a gun in a compartment. It happened to be Bond's own Walther PPK, but there were only a few bullets left in the magazine. Unfortunately, there was not a single bottle of water. The only other possibly useful items in the plane were a couple of life jackets, a fire extinguisher, a blanket, a pillow, and a torch. He tried the torch, but the batteries were dead. Wonderful.

Bond climbed out of the plane and looked around. The horizon was a simple straight line, circling him 360 degrees. The sun was setting quickly to his left, so it was fairly easy to ascertain the cardinal directions. However, knowing where north and south was didn't answer the big questions—where in God's name was he, and how far was he from civilization?

Fear gripped Bond's heart. He could withstand many tortures, but if he was stranded many miles into the outback he would never be able to stop Guy Thackeray from destroying Hong Kong. He couldn't even send a message to someone. He was totally alone.

It was dusk, the sun casting a breathtaking orange splash across the sky. Bond noted its relation to the plane so that he could at least remember which way was west. How cold would it get at night? Bond tried to remember all of the esoteric details of the Special Forces desert-survival training course he took many, many years ago. He had not once been called to practice any of the things he had learned when he was much younger and very green.

Bond sat down on a rocky patch of brown dirt and removed his left shoe. He used the prying tool to open it, then took out the miniature microfilm reader and a thin packet of microfiche he had checked out of the Q Branch library before departing from London. He had known he was going to Hong Kong, so he picked up as many maps of the surrounding area as he could. Australia had been an afterthought, as the nuclear testing in the outback was on his mind at the time. It was a damned good thing he had done so, he thought.

Although he would have to wait until the stars were out before he could make a reliable estimatation of his location, Bond could study the maps and compare them to the navigational charts he had taken from the cockpit. He started with the Kalgoorlie-Boulder area. He examined the maps and determined that the plane must have flown north over the desert. Exactly how far it had flown he didn't know.

How long had the plane been in the air before Bond awoke? He had been unconscious for at least six hours, as the last thing he remembered was an unpleasant breakfast. The navigational chart showed previously marked flight paths to and from Perth, Alice Springs, and Uluru. Alice Springs, or "Alice," was the legendary town in the heart of Australia famous for the red-baked ground and its status as a popular tourist station for exploring the outback. Uluru was also known as Ayers Rock, one of the natural wonders of the world. It was billed as the largest monolith on the globe, and some people believe that it might be the crest of a mountain buried beneath the ground. The Aborigines regard it as a sacred site, and recently the Australian government gave Ayers Rock and the surrounding land back to them. They renamed it Uluru, the proper Aboriginal name for the rock. They have retained and managed the tourist business at the site, operating the attraction as a national park.

Bond guessed he was somewhere along the route to Alice Springs or the route to Uluru. They weren't that dissimilar. Alice Springs was a little northeast of Ayers Rock. The plane would have eventually flown over Aboriginal reserve land.

It was starting to get chilly. The desert could become frighteningly cold at night. It was a good thing he had the blanket.

In an hour, the sun had completely disappeared. He had never seen a night sky so clear and so abundantly filled with stars. He spent a half hour studying the constellations and compared them to Southern Hemisphere winter sky charts that came with the microfiche. The microfilm reader conveniently provided its own illumination. The bisecting lines of the Southern Cross was the celestial south pole. It was sharp and bright in the sky. Using simple geometry, Bond compared the south pole star to the spot on the horizon where the sun had set. The angle was less than ninety degrees, indicating that the plane had indeed flown northeast. He had two choices—walk back southwest toward Kalgoorlie, or continue northeast. The other small mining towns like Leonora were very far away.

The Aborigines are known for practicing something called a "walkabout," a rite of passage for young and old people alike. They go out into the bush and stay there for days, weeks, or even months, living off the land, becoming one with the spirits who they believe live there, and then return. Some say that the spirits act as guides and protect the humans. Bond wasn't a religious man, but he stood there under the stars and closed his eyes. He breathed deeply several times, concentrating on the silence of the desert.

Following the instincts that had brought him luck and fortune in some of the world's elite casinos, Bond started walking northeast. He was gambling that the plane had been flying at least two hours, maybe more. He believed he was closer to Uluru than to any other inhabited place.

With the blanket wrapped around him, Bond walked across the flat land. He kept the south pole star in sight, checking his route every half hour. He tried to remember what types of plants indigenous to Australia the Aborigines used for water and food. He knew that the mulga tree had moist roots and seeds and the Bottle tree contained water in its trunk, but he was damned if he could remember what they looked like. There were others, he knew, but most of them grew in other parts of the continent. Central Australia and most of the Northern Territory were the most barren and arid sections of the country. Some bushes and plants held fruit, but he wasn't sure which were poisonous and which were safe to eat. There was something called a yellow bush tomato, which he thought he might recognize, and another called the ruby saltbush. He might find a desert fig bush if he was lucky. It was difficult at night, so he would just have to wait until the sun came up before he could seriously examine the flora. He was already hungry, but he could wait. The important thing was to travel as far as possible while it was cool.

The minutes turned into hours, and Bond kept walking on course. At one point, he heard the howls of wolves. No, they weren't wolves—they were dingoes, the wild dogs of Australia. He saw them, a pack of eight, some twenty meters behind him. They were curious, following him. Were wild dingoes dangerous? He couldn't remember. There was one famous case in which a woman claimed they stole her baby from a camping area, but would they attack a full-grown man? He was certainly in danger if they were rabid.

The dingoes moved closer, surrounding him. They resembled small wolves in the moonlight. He didn't want to waste the few bullets he had in his pistol, but he would if he had to. Perhaps there was another way to get rid of them.

Bond sat down and removed his left shoe. He extracted one of the inflammable shoelaces and two pieces of flint. Then he broke off a three-foot branch from a dried bush nearby. The dingoes growled when he did that. Bond rubbed the flint against the steel. A couple of sparks flew, then the shoelace caught fire. He quickly wrapped it around the branch, and eventually he had a torch.

007 jumped up abruptly, shouting at the dingoes and waving the torch. A few of them yelped and immediately ran away, but three of the larger dogs stubbornly held their ground. They growled and bared their teeth, then barked fiercely. Bond ran at them, swinging the torch and yelling. Two dingoes backed off, but the third, the leader, attacked. Bond swung the torch at the animal, hitting it on the head. It yelped and retreated, having got the mes-

sage that the human was indeed too much for them to handle. Once the leader moved away, the others followed. In minutes they were gone.

Bond carried the torch until it was extinguished. Then he walked on.

Zero Minus Two: June 29, 1997, 6:00 A.M.

The sun rose over the land, bringing warmth and life to the desolation around him. He folded the blanket and tucked it into his trousers. He sat down to rest awhile and removed his right shoe. He took out the tube of sunblock ointment that Major Boothroyd had thoughtfully included in the field shoe and applied some of it to his face, neck, and arms.

He was very hungry and thirsty now. If he was to keep up the same pace in the hot sun, Bond desperately needed water. He looked around him. There was some vegetation here and there, but he didn't know what it was. It all appeared to be dead. He stopped and dug up one to examine its roots. They were black, dry, and totally useless.

At midmorning, he saw three kangaroos in the distance. They were feeding off some kind of bush. When they heard him, they scampered away. Bond examined the bushes and found that there were several specimens of yellow tomatolike fruit still attached. If the kangaroos were eating these things, then the fruit couldn't possibly be poisonous. He recalled his desert-survival instructor's words—be sure to take notice of the wildlife, for animals were usually good judges of what was nutritious and what was deadly. Bond plucked one of the small yellow tomatoes and bit into it. It was sour, but it was fresh and full of liquid. He ate two of them, then picked the remaining five and put them in his pockets.

By midday, Bond was sweating profusely and was dehydrated. The sun seemed to fill the entire sky. He wished he had a hat, but the blanket became an asset once again. The fruits provided nourishment and some liquid, but he needed water badly. He kept going, pausing to rest for five minutes every hour. Sometimes he would see an animal. There was an anteater frantically searching the ground for an ant bed. A perentie lizard scampered over some rocks. Bond would have liked to catch it, for he had heard that such lizards were edible. The most incongruous sight he saw was a herd of wild camels galloping across the desert. He had no idea where they had come from or where they were going—it was just another surreal occurrence in a land where anything, or nothing, could happen.

He came upon a large graceful tree, probably a she-oak, standing alone on the barren ground. The roots were thick and hard, but probably contained some kind of moisture. Bond removed the file from his shoe and started to dig around the base of the trunk, when he saw something that made his heart jump. There, in a patch of soft dirt, was a human footprint. It was probably a fresh one, for it was perfectly formed and showed no signs of erosion. It was a small bare print, probably belonging to a child. Were there Aborigines nearby? Bond knew he was on their land. Aborigines were traditionally a peaceful group—they could very well offer him assistance.

He stood up and looked around. There was nothing but the horizon. He put his hands to his mouth and called out, "Hello!" He did it three times in every direction. If there was anyone within a mile, they might have heard him.

Bond knelt back down and continued digging around the base of the tree. After a while, one of the roots was exposed. He wasn't sure what to do next. It was too large and thick to break with his bare hands, and he had no appropriate tool for cutting it. He tugged on it and squeezed it, but quickly found he was wasting energy.

Damn! There were other plants that contained water, he was sure of it. As he pondered the problem, he ate one of the yellow fruits from his pocket. It went a long way toward quenching his thirst. Perhaps he could make it through the rest of the day without water, but what about tomorrow? And the next day? Of course, by then it would be too late. In fact, if he didn't reach civilization by midnight, he doubted that he would make it back to Hong Kong before the July 1 deadline. Maybe he could alert the proper authorities in time. Then the problem would be finding the bomb. They surely wouldn't have much time to search an entire territory. The situation seemed quite hopeless.

Bond sighed, then stood up. He glanced at the sun to get his bearings, then turned to continue walking. What he saw stopped him dead in his tracks.

A black girl stood twenty feet away from him. She was an Aborigine, probably in her late teens or early twenties, and was wearing a dirty white T-shirt and dusty khaki shorts. Her legs and feet were bare. The girl was thin but looked healthy. It had most likely been her footprint that Bond had seen. She was carrying a long, thin, sharpened wooden stick in one hand, and also had a netted bag slung over one shoulder. The bag was full of tubers of some kind.

She looked at Bond with a mixture of curiosity and fear. Her brow was creased, as if she were questioning her own eyes.

Slowly, Bond raised his hand in the universal gesture. "Hello," he said pleasantly.

The girl tensed and looked as if she might run.

"Wait," Bond said. "Don't be afraid." He dropped the file he was holding and held out both hands. "Can you help me?" He gestured toward the tree. "I was trying to find water. You know . . . water?" He mimed drinking with cupped hands. Did Aborigines speak English? He thought they did; but now, out here, he wasn't sure. . . .

She just stood there, staring at him. Bond tried to review what he knew about Aboriginal people during the few seconds of silence. He knew that many were nomadic, were family-oriented, and were probably the most neglected and poorly treated races in history. He knew that the women were usually the food gatherers, while men hunted and performed spiritual rites. This woman was probably out gathering food for her family.

"Can you speak?" Bond asked. He pointed to himself. "James." She didn't respond.

He reached into his pocket and pulled out one of the yellow fruits. "Oh, I have some of these. You want one?" He showed it to her and offered it. She eyed it, then looked back at him. Her large brown eyes were full of wonder. She did not fear him anymore. She was wondering what the hell he was doing there.

Bond tossed the fruit to her, underhanded. She caught it with her free hand. Bond said, "Good catch." He smiled at her.

Her eyes never left his as she brought the fruit up to her mouth and bit into it. The juice ran down over her chin and dripped onto her shirt. The moisture spread until the erect nipples of her firm breasts clearly protruded through the fabric. Bond watched her eat the entire thing. Despite the heat, his thirst, and the awkwardness of the situation, he found the sight incredibly erotic.

When the fruit was gone, she did nothing to wipe the juice off her chin and neck. Then, suddenly, she laughed. Bond laughed with her, and nodded.

"Water?" he asked again. "Can you help me get water?" Once more he cupped his hands to his mouth.

The girl nodded. She confidently squatted on the ground by the tree and began to dig with her hands. Her hands were tough and coarse, virtual tools with which to dig into hard dirt. In less than five minutes, she had dug deeper than Bond had done with the file. She pulled on some smaller roots, breaking them off of the larger vein Bond had found earlier. She stood up and showed them to him. She snapped one in half, then sucked on the broken end of one part. The girl made a loud slurping noise, indicating that there was indeed moisture within the root. She handed the other end to Bond. He placed the broken root in his own mouth and sucked. There was water inside! It wasn't much, only three or four small swallows. He smiled at her and nodded. The girl squatted again and broke off more roots, then handed them to him. He sucked on a couple more, then stored the remainder in his pockets.

"Thank you," he said.

She nodded and smiled, although it looked a little like a smirk. "Uluru," he said. "I'm going to Uluru."

She nodded her head and pointed in the northeasterly direction Bond was traveling. He had been right.

They heard an animal cry in the distance. She turned around, waved, and made a similar shrill call. It hadn't been an animal cry at all. Off in the distance, Bond could see two other human figures. They were part of her family or tribe.

The girl turned back to Bond and did something very strange. She reached up and placed her hand on Bond's face. She felt his features, tracing his eyebrows and the bridge of his nose. She ran a finger along the faint scar on his right cheek. Then she felt his mouth, pinching his lips slightly. She inserted her index finger into his mouth and touched his teeth, as if she was amazed he still had a full set. Bond ran his tongue lightly across the tip of her finger. It tasted salty. She didn't remove her finger; instead, she giggled.

Then she spoke! "If you keep walking, mate, you'll reach Uluru by sundown."

"Christ, you speak English!" Bond exclaimed. "Why didn't you say so?"

The girl laughed, then abruptly turned and ran toward her companions.

Bond watched her go. The girl turned and waved at him, and soon she had disappeared beyond the horizon. She had made him feel foolish, but she was one of the most sensual creatures he had ever encountered.

Bond continued his walkabout. The sun's heat became worse as the day moved into afternoon. He applied more sunblock and used some more of the water-saturated roots. Around three P.M. he came upon a dirt road. It seemed to head in the same direction as his destination, so he followed it. At four o'clock he saw signs of civilization. An old tire had been discarded on the road. There were telephone poles in the distance.

Finally, he saw it. At the edge of the horizon was a red bump. From this distance, it was a mere pimple where the earth met the sky. As he walked closer, the bump grew in size until it was a mountain. Uluru . . . Ayers Rock, the big red heart of Australia. It was a sacred shrine to the Aborigines, and the one reason why tourists ventured to the desolation of central Australia. The 348-meter-high monolith was indeed a breathtaking sight. Its ecstatic glow and haunting colors were at a peak, ignited by the setting sun.

It was six P.M. Bond had spent nearly twenty-four hours in the Australian outback, and he had made it to civilization. He nearly wept with awe, joy, and relief.

21

Countdown

James Bond stumbled into the Uluru National Park Ranger Station and nearly collapsed on the floor. An Aborigine dressed in a park ranger uniform stood up in surprise.

"You all right, mate?" he asked.

"Water . . . phone . . ." Bond whispered.

An hour later, Bond had showered, eaten a meal, and spent fifteen minutes with his eyes closed. He was dead tired and probably had a mild case of heat exhaustion. He would liked to have crawled into a hole for a week, but there was just a little more than twenty-four hours left. It was precious little time, and he had to find the quickest way back to Hong Kong. The rangers had provided him with a clean uniform, as his clothes were soiled and torn. When he went through his pockets, Bond found the business card that Skip Stewart had given him in the pub in Kalgoorlie. Perhaps the man's tour guide service would come in handy after all. Bond placed a phone call to Stewart and luckily found him in.

Stewart agreed to fly to the Ayers Rock airport and pick up Bond for a small fee. He would arrive in about three hours.

Now it was time to call London. He dreaded M's wrath, but it had to be done. He went through the usual security measures, was connected to Bill Tanner, and finally spoke to M herself.

"007? Where the hell are you?"

"Australia, ma'am. I've found the source of the nuclear explosion, and it's directly related to our man Thackeray and EurAsia Enterprises," he said quickly.

There was silence at the other end. He expected her to say something about orders to remain in Hong Kong.

"Tell me more," she finally said.

Bond gave a capsulized version of everything that had happened in the last forty-eight hours and how he had got to be where he was.

"You're lucky to be alive," she said. "I'll put out an all-alert to our fleet in Hong Kong. Any idea where Thackeray is going to put this bomb?"

"No idea. Could be anywhere. We haven't much time."

"Precisely. How fast can you get back to Hong Kong?"

"I expect a ride back to Perth in a little while. I'm afraid the only transportation I can get back to Hong Kong is a commercial airline. Leaves tomorrow morning and doesn't get in until the evening."

"That's cutting it much too fine," she said. "All right, do what you can. When you get back to Hong Kong, contact Captain Plante aboard the *Peacock*. She's one of our Peacock-class patrol craft, and she'll be in Victoria Harbour. Got it?"

"Yes, ma'am, but I request permission to contact Li Xu Nan again. He may be able to help with this."

"007, this department does not sanction you dealing with Triad members or any other criminal organization. We'll deal with your insubordination and leaving Hong Kong against my orders when you're back in London. Mind you, if you hadn't discovered what you did, I'd have had your hide."

Countdown

She rang off. Without a second thought, Bond dialed Li Xu Nan's private number in Kowloon.

Skip Stewart arrived at 9:30 P.M. He flew a Piper Navajo PA-310, an American-manufactured plane that had an all-weather and night capacity performance.

"Howzitgoin', mate?" he asked when he jumped out of the cockpit to greet Bond. "When did you become a park ranger? Never mind. How do you like her? I bought her from the Royal Flying Doctors a couple of years ago when their Alice Springs headquarters upgraded."

"Just get me to Perth before morning, Skip," Bond said. "I have a Qantas flight to Hong Kong that leaves at eight-thirty."

"No worries, mate. My little Airy-Jane will get you there. We'll have to stop in Kalgoorlie for a refill, ya know," he said. "Wish I could help you out and take you all the way to Hong Kong, but my little bird, there's only so far she can go. Say, did I tell you about my auntie who struck gold in Coolgardie when she was twelve years old?"

By ten P.M., James Bond was in the air over the outback once again. The only problem this time was that he had to listen to three hours' worth of bush stories.

Zero Minus One: June 30, 1997, 9:30 P.M., Hong Kong

The news had hit the morning papers of June 29. The *South China Morning Post* front-page headline declared, "Chinese General in Drug-Smuggling Scheme." The *Hong Kong Standard* carried the photographs Li's men had taken, accompanied by the headline "Murdered Chinese General in Drug Plot." The story detailed how Wong was involved with "Triad societies" in a worldwide drug-smuggling plot that also involved EurAsia Enterprises. The general was also implicated in the several terrorist acts that had occurred in the territory over the past few weeks, including the car-bomb murder of Guy Thackeray. Wong's own assassination was being attributed to a disgruntled EurAsia employee. According to the article, the assassin had been caught and killed at the border. Even the official Chinese news agency, Xinhua, issued a statement denouncing General Wong's involvement with a criminal organization. Although Beijing stopped short of an apology for accusing Britain of Wong's murder, the official word was that the general deserved what he had got.

The news literally saved Hong Kong from an early Chinese takeover. The troops had been prepared to march south across the border on the morning of June 29. The Royal Navy fleet of the three Peacock-class patrol craft had been joined by the destroyer and two frigates that had arrived on June 28, and had combined forces with the Hong Kong naval fleet. Royal Marines had moved on to the peninsula and were now stationed in the New Territories, anticipating the crisis that ultimately never happened. The Hong Kong government breathed a sigh of relief at the news, for it meant that perhaps the handover, scheduled for midnight on the thirtieth, would be a peaceful one after all. Despite the aversion of the immediate crisis, tensions were still very high and mistrust of China was rampant.

Festivities began early on the morning of the thirtieth. The Chinese New Year was a secondary holiday compared to the importance placed on the coming event. Shops closed and the population took to the streets. There were celebrations at every corner. Hong Kong Park was full of both pro-democracy and pro-China groups. The Royal Hong Kong Police had to provide a heavy presence to ensure that peace was maintained. Statue Square was blocked off from traffic in preparation for the night's event, and visiting officials from around the world had flown in for the occasion. Every hotel was totally booked.

Once again James Bond disobeyed his superior's orders and went straight to Li Xu Nan's office building when he got to Kowloon that evening. The Dragon Head had assembled ten men, all outfitted with miscellaneous automatic weapons. They were ready to move at a moment's notice.

Bond made contact with Captain Plante aboard the *Peacock*. Although Plante was perturbed that 007 was in Kowloon, he was willing to cooperate and do whatever he could to find Thackeray and the bomb. The Royal Hong Kong Police had been put on alert as well, and they were working double time searching the Central District.

"Where could Thackeray place that bomb for maximum effect?" Bond asked Li.

"I have been thinking about that. I would suspect that it would be Central. That is where EurAsia's headquarters is, and where all the important bank buildings and businesses are. It is the financial center of Hong Kong. The police are already searching the area."

"That's what I thought, too. Somehow, though, I feel it's wrong," Bond said. "It's too obvious."

"Yes, I know what you mean."

Something was nagging at Bond's memory, and he knew that it was a clue to the bomb's whereabouts.

"Think, Mr. Bond," said Li. "Did Thackeray say anything about where he might put it? Did its shape or size indicate where it might be placed?"

Bond went over everything he could recall about his fateful meeting in Australia. Mostly he remembered an alcoholic madman with a childish scheme for revenge.

"He's also got Sunni," Bond said. "He said that . . ."

And then he remembered. "My God," he said. "Do you have a boat? It's going to be in the harbor on a boat."

"How do you know?"

"Thackeray said that Sunni would make a 'nice figurehead' for the bomb. There was a sampan at the Kwai Chung warehouse, and I saw it again in Australia. They're going to put the bomb inside the sampan and casually float it out into the harbor!"

Li nodded. "I have a boat. Let's go!"

Li's Sealine Statesman 420 was a high-quality British import, equipped with twin 370-hp Volvo diesels, that had a cruising speed of 27.7 knots and a top end of 33.5. A large yacht, the Statesman 420 was nevertheless sleek and sporty. She had sped out into the harbor precisely at 11:00, but quickly had to reduce her speed because of the congestion in the water. Bond and Li were on the upper deck, looking through binoculars at the hundreds of vessels crowding the relatively small body of water.

The Marine Police had given up directing the traffic on this particular night. Too many seagoing individuals wanted a good view of the fireworks display scheduled for midnight. A free-for-all was finally allowed, as long as everyone kept their speed down and didn't crash into each other. Along with the numerous police and Royal Navy vessels, there were sampans, junks, tugboats, cargo ships, ferries, sailboats, yachts, motorboats, and rowboats—all jamming what was at that moment the world's busiest harbor.

Bond was looking for a dark brown sampan with a red hood. Unfortunately, most sampans were dark brown. He prayed that the red hood would give it away.

There was no sign of the *Taitai*, and Bond wondered where she could possibly be. Keeping close contact with Captain Plante, Bond had made inquiries about the ship's movements. Records showed that the *Taitai* had indeed left Singapore two days before and was headed for Hong Kong, but no one had seen her since. Bond could only speculate that Thackeray was lying low, probably lurking near one of the outlying islands. The sampan was probably flown to Singapore in the same cargo seaplane that Thackeray and Sunni took from Perth. It made sense—cargo seaplanes had long been used to rendezvous with and smuggle drugs onto oceangoing vessels. The *Taitai* had sailed to the waters near Singapore, where the sampan was loaded onto the seaplane and then flown to Australia. The trip was made in reverse to get it back to Hong Kong. The sampan would probably be sent in by itself, piloted by an unsuspecting minion.

"Can't we get this thing going any faster?" Bond snapped.

"I am sorry," Li said. "You can see the harbor is crowded. This is as fast as we can go."

"We'll never make it across to the other side at this rate," Bond said. He felt utterly helpless.

A call came in on the radio for Bond. It was Captain Plante.

"Um, Commander Bond?"

"Yes, Captain?"

"You say you're looking for a sampan with a red roof?"

"Yes!"

"Well, there's an odd thing over here by us. There's a cargo ship, a British one, I think. Called the *Glory*. They have a sampan fitting that description tied to the side like a lifeboat."

Captain Plante was calling from the *Peacock*, which was directly in the center of the harbor, facing Central. Bond turned and scanned the area with his binoculars.

"Where's the *Glory* in relation to you, Captain?" he asked.

"Due north, about a mile."

Bond found the ship. The *Glory* looked exactly like the *Taitai*, except that it had red stripes painted across the hull. The *Taitai* had been entirely white.

"The bastard painted his ship," Bond said. "He's disguised the *Taitai* and renamed her. That's it there!"

Li barked an order to the man at the helm of the Statesman, and they turned toward the *Glory/Taitai*. They had about forty-five minutes to find the bomb and disarm it.

22

No Tears for Hong Kong

The Statesman approached the *Glory* and stopped thirty meters away. The sampan was tied and hung over the starboard side of the ship like a lifeboat, ready to be lowered into the water. Bond wasn't sure, but he thought he could see the outline of a figure inside the small boat. Was it Sunni?

The *Peacock* had pulled away from its position as well, and was heading toward the *Glory*. The Royal Navy ship's movement must have alerted the crew of the *Glory*, for Bond and Li saw men appear on its deck. A tarpaulin covered a large object amidships. The men pulled off the tarpaulin to reveal a 76mm OTO Melara gun. They began to swing it toward the *Peacock*.

"Captain Plante," Bond said into the radio. "The *Glory* has a gun aiming at you. Take defensive action immediately. We're preparing to assault the ship."

Plante acknowledged the call and wished Bond good luck. He was going to radio the other ships for backup. Unfortunately, they were all deployed evenly across the harbor. Due to the congestion, it might take a half hour for the ships to work their way through to the site. If Thackeray was going to be stopped before midnight, it would be up to the teams aboard the Statesman and the *Peacock*.

"Li, give the order to begin the assault," Bond said.

Li shouted in Cantonese to his small band of dedicated gangsters-turned-patriots. He then gave an order to the man at the helm. The Statesman was brought as close as possible alongside the *Glory*. Then three men aimed M-16 .233 semiautomatic gunlines and fired grappling hooks, attached to long ropes, at the deck of the big ship. The hooks stuck, and the men, dressed in black, immediately used harness-and-pulley systems to pull themselves over and board the enemy vessel.

Bond followed behind the first wave of men. He heard a siren wailing on the deck of the *Glory*, alerting her entire crew that they were under attack. Then the gunfire started.

Thackeray's men were leaning over the side of the ship and firing machine guns at the Statesman. Two of the men on the ropes were hit and fell into the harbor. Bond clenched his teeth and kept climbing. He felt the hot air of a few rounds whiz past his head, but he kept moving. He reached the rail on the side of the *Glory* and hauled himself up. He was met head-on by a man who attempted to push him back overboard. Bond swiftly dispatched him by punching him hard in the stomach, then slinging him over his shoulder and into the water. He moved to a metal ladder and climbed it to a higher vantage point and crouched behind a smokestack. Armed only with his Walther PPK, Bond began to pick off Thackeray's force one by one.

Li held what looked like an M-16 and was firing from the deck of the Statesman. It was difficult to tell how many of the Triads were left to fight. The first barrage of gunfire had knocked off several of them. Bond could see at least four bodies lying on the deck, and he knew at least two had fallen into the water. The *Peacock* was still some distance away.

Suddenly, the *Glory*'s big gun went off. It scored a minor hit on the *Peacock*, setting the bow on fire. Damn! Bond moved forward from his position until he was above the Melara gun. Bond shot the two men manning the weapon, then jumped down and ran for the sampan.

Thackeray's voice boomed out over a loudspeaker, "Get them all, damn you! Take out that yacht! I'm lowering the sampan now!"

The man was probably at the helm or somewhere nearby. Bond would deal with him later. He had to reach Sunni first. The girl's figure could be seen huddled just inside the sampan. She was tied up, unable to move. Another object was built into the sampan's deck, beneath the hood. It was the bomb.

Before he could reach the hoist, however, Bond was confronted by one of the albinos, the big one he called Tom. 007 raised his gun to fire, but the albino adeptly kicked the Walther out of his hand. The man was big, but he had amazing agility. Bond attempted to return a blow with a back kick, but Tom grabbed his leg, twisted it, and effortlessly slammed Bond hard against the side of a cabin wall. He fell to the deck, only to be on the receiving end of three vicious kicks in the ribs.

Li Xu Nan was having troubles of his own. He had climbed one of the ropes onto the *Glory* and was struggling with the other albino henchman, Dick. They were of equal height and weight, and both of them were skilled martial arts practitioners. If their fight hadn't been a life-or-death struggle, it would have been one of the most impressive displays of Eastern fighting techniques imaginable. Each blow delivered by one man was calculated to kill or maim, but it was met by an equally considered counterblow from the other. They moved with great speed, forcing each other to think split seconds ahead of their actions.

Bond managed to get to his feet. He leaped for Tom and grabbed hold of the man's head. The large albino simply locked Bond in a bear hug and picked him up off the deck. Bond used his free arms to deliver sword-hand blows to his opponent's neck and shoulders, but they seemed to have little effect. Tom was squeezing him hard, and Bond began to feel the strain against his rib cage. My God, he thought, the man was strong enough to crush him with his bare arms!

If that wasn't enough for him to worry about, Bond heard the hoist rumble into life. The sampan was being lowered into the water.

The fight was interrupted by a huge, deafening explosion that rocked the *Glory*. It caused Tom to release his grip on Bond and the two men fell to the deck. At first Bond thought the bomb had detonated, but he soon realized that the *Peacock* had returned fire with its own Melara gun. The *Glory* had taken a critical hit broadside. At least the Royal Navy were better marksmen than Thackeray's crew!

Bond jumped up and leaned over the rail. The sampan, with Sunni and the bomb, was floating away from the ship. Large hands grabbed his shoulders and pulled him away, and he was thrown back against the cabin wall. Tom was on him again. Bond gave the henchman everything he had. He knew a few tricks of his own, and delivered them with skill and determination. Bond struck the man's abdomen with a *Nidan-geri* double kick, chopped him on the throat with vicious one-two spear-handed blows, then swung his body around, leaped, and kicked the man full in the face. Tom staggered back against the ship's rail, broke it, and fell overboard.

Bond caught his breath and surveyed the situation. The *Glory* was on fire. Several of Thackeray's men had given up the fight and were running to lifeboats. The *Peacock* was close. The Navy forces had extinguished their own fire and Bond could see three RIBs— Rigid Inflatable Boats—manned with several men and heading toward the *Glory*. Turning toward the Statesman, he could see that Li's yacht was on fire and was sinking. He peered through the smoke on the deck of the *Glory* to try to find Li. Then he saw them. Li and the other albino, Dick, were fighting dangerously close to the flames. Bond tried to run toward them, but a burst of machine-gun fire stopped him in his tracks. He leaped to the side of the cabin wall for cover.

"I'll get you, you bloody bastard!" It was Thackeray's voice, coming from a deck above him. Bond had to snake along the wall to avoid being hit. A companionway was twenty yards away from him. If he could make it there before Thackeray did . . .

Li and Dick continued their assault on each other. Dick executed two brutal kicks at Li. The Dragon Head retaliated by jumping up, grabbing a low-hanging pipe, and swinging out toward his opponent. Li's feet caught Dick in the head, knocking him backward into the flames. Li jumped down to the deck and bulldozed the albino headfirst. He hit the man in the stomach, successfully pushing him farther into the fire. The albino fell to the burning deck. His clothes were on fire, and he was screaming. Suddenly, the wooden planks beneath him gave way, and he fell into the inferno below.

Li moved back away from the fire and saw Bond. 007 pointed above his head and shouted, "Look out!" Li looked up and saw Thackeray on the upper deck, aiming the machine gun at him. Bond couldn't see the Englishman—he saw only Li's expression change from shock to resignation.

The Cho Kun of the Dragon Wing Society looked death in the face and accepted it with honor. The machine-gun blast caught him in the chest. Li Xu Nan was propelled back into the flames, where five generations of secret society leadership finally ended.

Bond reached the companionway and climbed to the upper deck. He caught a glimpse of Thackeray running to the other side of the ship. The *Glory* was going down fast. There were no signs of any of Thackeray's men left aboard.

He took off after Thackeray and chased him down a ladder into the depths of the ship. At one point, Thackeray turned to fire the machine gun at Bond, but he leaped out of the way, successfully dodging the bullets. Thackeray moved on. Bond followed him through a smoky passageway that was filling with water. It was difficult to breathe, and Bond knew it was extremely dangerous to continue. He could die of smoke inhalation before he got to the man. He pressed on, though, determined to stop Thackeray from reaching wherever he might be headed.

The answer to that question became obvious when Bond saw an open hatch at the end of the passageway through which Thackeray had jumped. Bond looked out of the hatch and saw that Thackeray had dropped into a speedboat, large enough to carry four people, that had been hoisted on the port side of the *Glory*, just as the sampan had been tied on the opposite side. It was about eight feet below the hatch. Thackeray was preparing to release the cables securing it to the *Glory*. This had been Thackeray's planned escape mechanism. He had intended to set the sampan and bomb afloat, then speed away in this boat, probably with his albino henchmen, and easily maneuver through the crowded harbor to a safe distance. He would have fled to one of the outlying islands, then flown to safety in a hidden airplane.

Thackeray was fiddling with the controls of the hoist that would drop the speedboat thirty feet down to the water. His attention was not on Bond for a few precious seconds. 007 leaped out of the hatch just as the cables released the boat. As the speedboat dropped, Bond was falling just a few feet above it.

The boat hit the water hard, knocking Thackeray to its deck. A second later, Bond landed in the boat with force. He might have broken his legs if the recoil from the boat hitting the water hadn't caused it to bounce and somewhat cushion Bond's fall. Even so, his right leg was injured badly. His knee hurt like hell.

"You!" Thackeray shouted. He leaped on top of Bond, and the two men locked their hands around each other's throats. Temporarily dazed by the fall into the boat, Bond was at a disadvantage. Thackeray squeezed hard, attempting to crush Bond's windpipe. 007 almost passed out, but managed to bring his knee up hard into Thackeray's side. The man's years of alcohol abuse probably saved Bond, for the blow hit Thackeray hard in the liver. Thackeray jerked in pain, then released his grip on Bond's neck. He rolled off, clutching his side.

Bond sat up to catch his breath. Thackeray was doubled up in pain.

"All right, Thackeray, let's go and disarm that bomb," Bond said.

Thackeray, with a grimace on his face, simply nodded. Bond turned the ignition and got the outboard engine started, then something hard hit him in the head. The next thing he knew, half of his body was hanging over the side of the motorboat.

Thackeray had taken an oar from the bottom of the boat. He had hit Bond with it, attempting to knock him overboard. Thackeray hit him again across the back, sending a jolt of pain up Bond's spine. 007 willed himself to turn the pain into energy. He swung around and rolled just in time to avoid another direct hit from the oar. Now it was his turn. He lunged for Thackeray's legs and tackled him. They both fell overboard into the harbor.

It was murky, smelly water, but at least it wasn't freezing. In fact, it was rather warm. The bodies clung to each other and thrashed around. Thackeray was struggling to get to the surface. Now Bond had the advantage, for he was an excellent swimmer. Despite his injuries and the pain in his knee, he was able to turn the harbor into his element.

Their heads broke the surface. Thackeray had a look of rage and terror on his face. He tried to reach for the motorboat, but Bond swam and latched on to his adversary's waist. Thackeray clutched Bond's hair and pulled it as hard as he could. He squirmed and kicked, hoping Bond would loosen his grip. Bond swam away from the motorboat with Thackeray, lifeguard-style. Thackeray was yelling something, but Bond paid no attention. They submerged again, and this time Thackeray broke away from Bond. He reached for 007's neck and locked his fingers around it. Bond tried to pry the man's fingers away, but Thackeray's adrenaline was pumping hard. If it was going to be a test of stamina, Bond thought, then so be it. He locked his own fingers around Thackeray's neck and started to squeeze. It was now a matter of who would give out first.

The bodies rolled and twirled in the dark water, performing a grotesque underwater ballet as they tried to choke the life out of each other. For nearly a full minute, which to Bond seemed like an hour, they were locked together, somersaulting like a single jellyfish. Finally, Thackeray's face changed. His eyes bulged, and bubbles began to escape from his mouth. The eyes rolled up into his head, and his grip on Bond's neck relaxed. Because of his years of training and experience, Bond was able to hold his own breath for an uncanny amount of time. He kept his grip tight on Thackeray's neck until he was sure that the man was unconscious. The *taipan* of EurAsia Enterprises, heir to a fortune won and then lost, drowned in Victoria Harbour at the hands of James Bond.

Bond let Thackeray's body drift away, then he swam to the motorboat and climbed aboard. He looked at his watch. It was 11:45. Bond quickly got the boat going and sped around the sinking *Glory* to the other side.

The *Peacock* was broadside of the damaged cargo ship, and the RIBs were busy overtaking the enemy lifeboats and arresting Thackeray's remaining men. Bond guessed that none of the Triads survived. With their leader dead as well, he thought that the Dragon Wing Society would most likely fade into obscurity, or be absorbed by some other secret criminal society.

The sampan had not drifted far. Bond reached it in minutes, cut the motor, and leaped aboard. Sunni was tied and gagged, her eyes wide with fear and surprise. Bond removed the gag.

"James! Oh God, James!" she cried.

"It's all right! Hold on," he said, untying her. Once she was free, he gave her a quick hug and kiss. She didn't want to let him go, but he broke away.

"Sunni, the bomb!" he said, then turned his attention to the large metal bowling pin fastened to the deck of the sampan.

The cone was screwed to the main casing. Bond removed his left shoe and opened it up. He took out the metal file, which was just the appropriate size to use on the screws. He removed the cone, revealing a digital clock face, its mechanism, and wires connecting it to the main casing and the conventional explosives surrounding the U-235 within. The clock read 11:55.

Before Bond could progress any further, the sampan lurched hard to one side. Someone was pulling himself onto the boat! Sunni screamed. It was Tom, the largest and strongest of the albino henchmen! Bond had forgotten about him after the man had fallen off the *Glory*.

"Stay with the bomb, James. I'll take care of this creep!" Sunni shouted.

Fine, Bond thought. Do it, girl. He had to concentrate. What would be the quickest way to disarm the damned thing? Maybe he could simply stop the clock.

Sunni, who once displayed a knack for street fighting, used the frustration and pent-up energy from being tied up to attack the big man like a dynamo. She hit him hard in the face with a *Mae-geri* front kick, swung around and kicked him again, then leaned in and struck him hard in the solar plexus with a stiff spear-hand. Surprised by the girl's ability, Tom was momentarily stunned. He swung at her, but she deftly dodged the blow, ducked, then brought herself up with a leap nearly as high as his head. In midair, Sunni kicked out hard at the man, knocking him on his back.

Bond remembered what Thackeray had said about the clock. It was run by a small battery—"the kind used in wristwatches." Bond used the file to pry off the clock face, revealing the circuitry. A small, round lithium battery was encased in metal connectors. The file was too large a tool to pop it out. Bond tried using his fingers, but that was too awkward.

Sunni continued attacking the albino henchman as if she was making up for years of abuse, exploitation, and pain. She wouldn't let up. The big man couldn't get a maneuver in to save his life. With one great lurch, though, he managed to get to his feet. He was standing with his back to the side of the sampan, dazed and confused. Sunni, with one final dynamic leap in the air, double-kicked the man hard on the breastplate. It was enough to force him overboard and into the water. By that time, a Royal Navy RIB had

269

arrived. A naval officer trained his gun on the albino and was prepared to arrest him, but it wasn't necessary. Sunni had broken the man's sternum and stopped his heart.

The digital numbers read 11:58. Once again, Bond looked at the contents of the shoe that Major Boothroyd had given him. Was there another tool? Of course! The tweezers! Bond plucked them from their position in the shoe and used them to carefully and neatly extract the lithium battery. The digital clock blinked out at 11:59. The crisis was over. Thackeray's bomb was a dud.

Bond and Sunni climbed into the RIB, which took them over to the *Peacock*. Captain Plante met them on deck.

"Commander Bond?"

Bond nodded. "The bomb's defused. Your men can salvage it off that sampan."

"Excellent, Commander. Your chief is on the line there on the bridge," he said. "Just up those steps. I've got orders to deliver you back to England."

What about Sunni? Bond thought. What were they going to do with her?

Bond got on the line, and after a few pips, heard M's strained voice.

"Well, 007, I see that you persist in disobeying my orders," she said.

"I'm sorry, ma'am. I assure you it won't be a habit. It's just that—"

"Never mind, 007. I understand you stopped that man Thackeray from doing whatever it was he was planning."

"Yes, ma'am."

"I imagine the handover ceremony is in progress as we speak."

"It's midnight here, ma'am," Bond said. "I suppose so."

"Good. You're to accompany Captain Plante back to England. I'm putting you on three months' suspension for insubordination."

Bond closed his eyes. Fine, if that's the way she wants to play it.

Then M added, "With pay."

"Ma'am?" He wasn't sure he heard her correctly.

"As for the girl, I've arranged for a passport in her name. Just give the details to the chief of staff. We'll need to know what country she prefers. She can choose between England, America, and Canada."

Bond couldn't believe it. "Thank you, ma'am. I'll ask her. I'm sure she'll be very appreciative."

They rang off, and Bond joined Sunni on the deck of the ship. It began to pull away, heading east out of the harbor.

He put his arm around her. "England, America, or Canada?" he asked.

"What?"

"You have your foreign passport."

"Oh, James!" She kissed him. "Do I have to decide this second?"

"No."

They looked out at the magnificent skyline of Hong Kong Island. At that moment, its sovereignty was changing. The future of the fabled city-state was now in the hands of the People's Republic of China.

Bond thought about T. Y. Woo and his brother, and the lives they gave for the colony that was now lost. He made a mental note to contact Woo's son in England and offer to provide any assistance that Chen Chen might need. As for himself, he would have to live with the guilt he felt for being forced to turn his back on T.Y. that fateful day in Guangzhou. He knew he could eventually bury it, for it was no different from what he felt when his friend Felix Leiter lost a leg at the hands of Mr. Big's men in Florida, or when his colleague Darko Kerim was killed by Russian agents on the Orient Express, or when his companion Quarrel was burned alive on that island in the Caribbean. James Bond had lost many friends during his career with the Secret Service. He had learned long ago how to deal with it and turn the pain into an asset that contributed to his self-made shell—the hardened, tough armor that protected him from the inevitably maddening, and conceivably fatal, aspects of consciousness called human emotions.

He looked over at Sunni and saw that tears were streaming down her cheeks. Bond gently used his finger to wipe them away.

"You miss your mother, don't you," he said tenderly.

She nodded. "That's not why I'm crying, though," she said. "I'm crying for Hong Kong. I fear for the people."

"No," Bond said, kissing her softly. "The people will manage. Don't worry about them. They are strong, and they are determined. So don't cry."

"All right." Sunni smiled and wiped her face. "No tears for Hong Kong."

She allowed him to encircle her with his arms as they looked toward the skyline to watch the fireworks.

Zero: July 1, 1997, 12:01 A.M.

At Statue Square, the handover of the British Crown Colony known as Hong Kong was executed peacefully and smoothly. Formal statements were read by both sides, and the representatives from China shook hands with the representatives from Great Britain. As soon as the transition was declared official, there were tumultuous cries from the people who were standing in the congested streets. Some were cries of joy, and others were cries of sadness. The fireworks began, filling the sky with colors, noise, and celebration.

Over at Government House, a few blocks away, the Union Jack was lowered for the last time, and the red and yellow Chinese flag was raised in its place. A new chapter in the history of Asia, and mankind, had begun.

ABOUT THE AUTHOR

Raymond Benson is the author of *The James Bond Bedside Companion*, which was nominated for an Edgar Allan Poe Award for Best Biographical/Critical work and is considered by 007 fans to be a definitive work on the world of James Bond. He is a Director of The Ian Fleming Foundation and served as Vice President of the American James Bond 007 Fan Club for several years. Mr. Benson is also the Designer and Writer of several award-winning interactive software products, and spent over a decade in New York City directing stage productions and composing music. He has taught film-theory classes at The New School for Social Research in New York and a course called "Interactive Screenwriting" at Columbia College Chicago. Mr. Benson is married, has one son, and lives in the Chicago area. *Zero Minus Ten* is his first novel.